Aiden Shepherd

and the Terosian Academy

First Edition

I0652733

Book One of the Aiden Shepherd Series

A novel by Dillon J. Hammon

Acknowledgements

This story is dedicated to my loving fiancée, Christine. She has been my faithful partner for over ten years and without her support I never could have become a writer.

I would also like to dedicate this work to my friends and family who have continuously encouraged me to pursue my dreams, no matter how difficult of a challenge they may be.

Preface

This story is very dear to me. I began writing this series at a time in my life when I had found a passion within myself to try to further my own walk with God and discover the things He, and The Holy Spirit were waiting to teach me. I had been contemplating many of the lessons this story tried to teach for years and had often thought that I should try to write a non-fiction book that would offer people a "Young Man's Daily Wisdom". But when I sat down to begin writing that book I learned that the lessons I grew up with were best learned through the fantastic stories I enjoyed hearing.

I starting typing and the characters just began flowing from a place within me I couldn't quite explain. I would write everyday for almost six months until I was finished with my first draft and first revision. At this point my father gifted me with a professional grade critique from renowned New York Times Best Selling Author: Michael Levin. This man I came to learn was not only an author, but also taught writing in college, and was a professional writing coach and ghost-writer.

He sent me a very detailed breakdown of my novel and I anxiously began to read the first page of his assessment. Mind you, I have never taken any special classes in writing other than the required English courses in college and high school. His reaction genuinely warmed my heart. He said that it is his job to tell writers if they can make it or not and though he was unable to determine how I had intuitively learned to write – I could make it.

I truly hope whoever reads this book is somehow inspired to take a look at their own spiritual lives and dreams and know that it doesn't require any more special training to be able to do something unknown to you than your will to see it through.

"Fifty thousand light years I traveled, just to learn that God was right beside me from the beginning..."

-Captain Aiden J. Shepherd

Prologue

"Take cover!" Aiden could barely hear the voice to his left call out, as the sounds of gunfire rang throughout the city of Edath. Aiden took a moment to catch his breath and then, heeding the voice's advice, took cover behind a crumbled wall. The gunfire ceased momentarily as another great flash illuminated the blood-red skies. The silhouettes of buildings shook violently for what seemed like forever, before calming once again. One or two isolated rifles gave defiant pops and the battle resumed with more ferocious intensity. Aiden's lungs were on fire; his hands trembled uncontrollably and he felt the amount of adrenaline in his body would surely kill him as his heart hammered from within his chest, begging to break free.   The reality of what he had just done was sinking deep within his soul and numbness emanated throughout his body. His hands began to calm but now he fought desperately against the urge to be sick. He searched the depths of his mind for an "off button" but it was no use.

"Lord just make me forget it, just help me get out of this and I'll never do anything to offend you ever again..." He thought as the scene replayed itself over and over.

He had kicked open the door, pointed his weapon, and prepared to fire but something strange had happened. As the memory slowed down Aiden remembered that split second before he fired when the soldier had looked up from the woman he was so frantically trying to force and his eyes had connected with Aiden's. They were lustful eyes, full of hatred and rage. Beads of sweat crawled down the man's face as he let go of the woman and slowly reached for his rifle. Aiden held his pistol with an unnatural steadiness and though everything within him was screaming for his finger to let go of the trigger, he ignored the impulse and squeezed off two shots.

The blinding blue bolts of plasma sprang forth from the end of the barrel like miniature comets, flying straight for the soldier's chest. The soldier tried to summon every ounce of agility he had to evade the attack but the shots from Aiden's pistol were already boring two perfect tunnels through his heart and lung. The man froze as the shots breached the wall behind him and looked down at the damage he had just received. A curious sensation trickled through him as he reached up and felt the holes; they were cauterized and did not bleed. The sensation intensified and a chill pulsated from his heart as he fell to his knees and drew his last breath.

An explosion across the street shook Aiden out of the memory and he refocused his attention to the task at hand – they had to escape the city before it was too late. The woman he had just rescued lay beside him, hidden by a thick fold in the wall. She looked sallow skinned and panted heavily with a nervous, almost uncontrollable shaking of her arms and legs. On the other side of her crouched Aiden's friend Kyon. Kyon's eyes looked cold and focused as he continued to put down suppressive fire in one of the adjacent buildings. Although Aiden was not able to see from his angle where Kyon's bombardment was landing, the screams and moans of dying men confirmed that he was hitting his targets. Every now and then Kyon would pause just long enough to throw an insult at the opposing forces, provoking them to give away their positions once more.

Aiden did not want to move; he wanted to sit there, close his eyes, and wake up from this nightmare. How did he get here, and how could this be happening? He almost welcomed the prospect of being back home on Earth; living a normal life. Kyon turned and looked back at Aiden.

"Alright!" Kyon shouted, "On the count of three we're going to make a break for those motorcycles near the entrance." He grasped the girl's quivering hand and looked her dead in the eyes, "You run with me, okay?" She gave a nod and Kyon began the countdown. "One….Two….THREE!" Kyon led the way, firing wildly at the last men remaining within the shattered building. Aiden did the same and followed closely behind. The whines of bullets enveloped the three of them like a pack of angry wasps. They were only a few strides from the bikes when a sudden rush of air blew Aiden off his feet; the deafening sound of the mortar clogged his eardrums as shrapnel peppered his left arm.

Aiden landed with a sickening crunch and felt unable to move. His head rang and the dim red of the sky began to fade from view.

"Is this what it feels like to die?" This didn't seem like the way it should end. He closed his eyes and let the sounds of the battle slip away from his mind; all that was left was silence and darkness.

Chapter 1 - June 12th

As a stack of papers landed on his desk, Aiden jolted upright in his seat and realized that class was nearly over and the teacher had finished grading their essays. He stared at the first page, but saw no evil red pen marks. He flipped the page, but again saw nothing wrong. After scanning the last two pages and finding nothing he looked around in a confused way and saw his peers' papers; each covered in the red ink. He finally checked the very back side of his essay and his eyes met the single worst phrase a student could get, *"Please see me after class."* Aiden felt his heart stop and his stomach lurch in horror. What had he done wrong? He had spent a good week on the essay, proof-read it, revised, and proof-read again. He knew he met the prompt requested - *"Write about something interesting to you."* Aiden wrote about everything he loved: the wonders of the world; the weird, the paranormal, the impossible, everything that dazzled his thoughts and kept him from falling asleep at night or focusing in class.

"How could I have possibly screwed up on a prompt like that!?" He drew a deep breath and glanced at the clock- Ten minutes left. He rubbed small circles around his temples and closed his eyes, praying for the strength to stay calm.

"The clock must be broken!" Aiden thought as he checked it for the twentieth time. Five minutes left. Four. Three. Two. One. *RING!* A swarm of high school students sprang for the door, their cell phones jumping out of their pockets as if the small electronic creatures had been holding their breath for the past fifty minutes. Aiden finished packing his bag and slowly walked up to the front of the class as the last of the students exited. His teacher was making a cup of coffee.

"You wanted to see me?" Aiden said sternly.

"Ah, Aiden! Yes I did." Mr. Johnston replied. "Firstly can I ask you what inspired you to choose your topic?"

"Umm," Aiden said, wondering why it mattered. "I just went with what I spend most of my time thinking about, you know, things I find interesting."

"Well I must say I have never been as pleased with a student's final paper as yours," Continued Mr. Johnston. "I have been teaching for ten years and I often receive the usual baloney that seniors love to toss at me as the year starts winding down. But I was pleasantly surprised with your honesty and courage in writing about what is so often overlooked."

Aiden could hardly believe his ears, "Wait, so, I didn't fail the assignment?" He asked, feeling confused again.

"Fail!?" Mr. Johnston began to laugh, "No no, you didn't fail, I'll give you an "A". I was so intrigued with the subject matter that I daresay I must have forgotten to provide feedback about the minor stuff like commas and such, but I'm confident you are a fine writer. I'm sorry if I gave you a bit of a scare."

"Oh, well thanks!" Aiden responded with a smile as well. He grabbed his essay and walked to his next class: Psychology.

Euphoria emanated from him as his anxiousness subsided. *"What did Mr. Johnston mean about my paper? Why did he find it so intriguing? It's not like people haven't heard about those topics before. I'll just think about it later."* Aiden decided as he entered his Psychology class. This was one of his favorite classes and he always looked forward to listening to his eccentric teacher, Ms. Paterson. She always fascinated the class with some quirky story or news that kept the atmosphere in her room very fun. Today she discussed a study she had been conducting for the past three weeks.

"I have been reading up on how people have learned to control some of their autonomic body functions...." She began. When most of the class showed little understanding of this phrase, she quickly explained. "It's stuff like your heart beat, blood pressure, brain waves, you know...things your body just does without you having to think about it. So anyway this one guy was able to raise and lower different levels within his body at the same time! I was just blown away! I mean, I've heard of people being able to block out pain but I never knew there was such a wide range of study done on the subject."

After she finished telling them more she informed them that today they were going to be doing personality and brain analysis tests. The personality test didn't reveal to Aiden anything new. *"Introverted, logical, creative, blah blah blah..."* He didn't need a test to remind him for the millionth time that he had almost no friends. He never really concerned himself with this though, as he was perfectly happy with his social life the way it was.

The second test captured his interest much more. It consisted of a series of questions that would analyze if a person was left or right brained. The left brain is the more logical; a person who is better with words, numbers, and facts. The right brain is the creative, artistic, "feeling" side of the brain. Ms. Paterson lectured for about twenty minutes on the test and its origins, then put on some music and let everyone begin. The questions were very simple and Aiden finished in five minutes, as did most of the rest of the class. After a few more moments of waiting, she finally announced,

"Now tally up the points for each question, some will give more for left brain, others for the right brain. Then we'll compare and see if you agree with what the test says."

Aiden began to add up his scores, he quickly noticed the pattern the test was looking for and began to wonder which side he would be. A moment later he finished and saw his scores: thirty points left, thirty points right. "*Huh?*" He asked himself as he started redoing his calculations – but once again he got the same scores.

"Okay, now everyone with left brain dominate stand over here, and right brain dominate stand over there." Ms. Paterson commanded. Aiden watched everyone in the class divide and he stood looking from one side to the other. "Aiden is there a problem?" His teacher asked warmly.

"Oh, no I just got an even score on both so I'm standing in the middle," he answered. A number of people giggled and snickered as he stood there, feeling very uncomfortable. The teacher pondered for a moment and instructed everyone to compare scores in their respective groups.

"Can I see your test, Aiden?" She asked, and he walked over to her. She studied it for a few minutes and checked the scores twice. "Well, this is the first time I've had a student get a totally equal score on this test, quite unusual I must say. You didn't cheat did you?" Aiden shook his head and she shrugged. "A majority of people fall into one or the other as you can see from your classmates, but you obviously have a very balanced outlook on things." She concluded. Aiden shrugged too and sat back down as she consulted other students. He stared at the paper and a thought kept revolving in his head,

"This was just one more thing that makes you different from everyone else." Ever since middle school he had been thinking he was different than his peers. Not better or worse, but he just never fit properly into the common groups of people he observed around him. If a group was considered smart, maybe they weren't interested

in sports so Aiden didn't really mesh as he was very athletic; But then his teammates never seemed to talk about anything that really captured his interest either. This trend seemed to correlate to everything he did, which eventually led him to stop wondering about it and accept it.

The bell rang and the students exited, everyone looking forward to lunch. Aiden did not have to stay for his last class, volleyball, since the game didn't start for a few hours. He left class and took a short cut through the staff parking lot and headed for the path along the creek behind the school. He halted just shy of the fence and sat at one of the picnic tables, waiting for his best friend, Jeri Spencer, to meet him. He observed a pair of military choppers fly overhead and closed his eyes, letting the warm, Southern California sunlight wrap around his face for a few moments. He tuned in to the subtle noises around him – a crow flapping its wings, a lizard darting back into the bushes, and a fresh breeze rustling the trees overhead. He loved days like this, when he could lose himself in something as simple as taking a few minutes to observe the world he lived in.

"Hello there!" Jeri greeted. Aiden turned and greeted his friend and they began walking towards the IHOP restaurant across the street. As they neared the parking lot,

Jeri stubbed his toe on a harmless looking root. Clearly irritated he asked, "When the hell are we going to actually park *on* campus!?"

"How many times do I have to tell you?!" Aiden exclaimed. "I don't trust the idiots driving at school. I've witnessed about three or four people bump or scrape into other's cars while trying to park and then drive off as if nothing happened!"

"I Know," Jeri grinned. "I just like giving you a hard time about our lovely hike we have to endure every day."

"Yeah, well, a little exercise never hurt anyone," Aiden chuckled, they climbed into Aiden's 1988 BMW 535 and drove towards Jeri's house.

"So, what are you doing later?" Aiden asked.

"Oh not much," Jeri remarked, playing with the piece of leather upholstery that had begun to hang carelessly from its panel. "Probably going to neglect my chores and play some games on my computer. Why, you have something in mind?"

"Yeah I have a volleyball game at four if you want to come," Aiden said and gave Jeri a moment to answer, then added, "It's the last one of my high school career."

"I don't know man," began Jeri, "It's kind of hard for me to tell you this, but after all these years I just can't get over how boring it is to watch a ball go back and forth over a net. Just give me a call after you get home, maybe we can go out and do something later."

"Nice, Thanks a lot." Aiden replied as he saw Jeri's menacing smile.

"It's what I'm here for buddy!" Laughed Jeri, the small leather piece had finally endured enough stress and tore away from the door panel. He gave Aiden a quick glance to check if he noticed then slipped the leather scrap under the seat. "Life is tough, good luck though!"

Aiden dropped Jeri off a few minutes later and headed for home. He arrived to his three highly energized dogs rushing in from the backyard to greet him. Apparently they had been enjoying a carefree day of sunbathing.

"Hey pups! How you guys doin?" Aiden said playfully. "Huh? You guys doin good? Those are my good dogs, sit, no......sit....good dogs!"

Aiden passed treats out and went upstairs into his room. Nearly three hours of free time until his game, what would he do? He turned on his computer and checked his email, browsed a few sites he usually checked for daily news, and listened to some of his favorite songs. He then put his headphones on and prepared himself for one of his favorite hobbies: online gaming. He loved to be a paladin fighting the forces of darkness one minute, and a sniper on a battlefield the next. The added bonus of being able to play with other people around the world just made it even more enjoyable. Of course there was the occasional gamer whose sole mission was to cause other players grief but even those made for some interesting experiences in the online world. Aiden could be whoever he wanted here; he could act without fear of the consequences. He could show kindness and generosity when in reality he may feel strange to do so. The main draw of such an interactive world was that *anything was possible* here.

The smallest of the three dogs, a Maltese, trotted into Aiden's room and stood on her hind legs beside his desk. He smiled and scratched her behind the ears. "Be nice if the real world were like this, huh girl?" He said. Meanwhile his virtual character was shot by a friendly player for standing around.

In the middle of a raid on a goblin colony, he felt one of the larger dogs clumsily bump in to his chair, which caused him to pull his eyes from the computer screen. He glanced at the clock on his shelf, then back at the screen, and then as if he had been mentally pinched, threw off his headset, jumped out the chair and, almost stumbling over the dog that now lay on his floor, hurried to his closet. *"Where had the time gone*!?" He only had forty minutes until game time. He flung on his uniform and squeezed on his untied sneakers, deciding he would lace them up when he got there. Then not wanting to show up with obvious "headset" hair, he ran to the bathroom on his way out of the garage door.

He fixed his dirty-blond hair in the mirror, and momentarily caught his glimpse. He sometimes stared at the bright emerald eyes looking back at him and there were times when he felt there was something strange about the person standing before him. He did his best to get his hair into a suitable state then arrived at the main gym ten minutes later.

"Aiden, we're missing one today so we'll need you to play all-around," said Coach Phelps.

"Okay! Awesome!" Aiden responded. He rarely got to play back row since they had enough people to rotate, and players usually had specific skill sets. Coach Phelps seemed to think Aiden was best in the front row, although Aiden himself liked to think he was pretty decent all-around. A few minutes later the opposing team showed up and they all began to do some hitting warm-ups. Playing volleyball was invigorating; Aiden loved the anticipation of where an opponent would hit next, or coordinating a complex play using his teammates. Diving on the floor, sustaining cuts and bruises, and getting back up always made him feel like he was giving a worthy sacrifice for the game, like making a payment for the incredible experience he had while on the court. Although not as popular as football or baseball, Aiden felt the skills required for volleyball were just as important as other sports.

Since today was the final match of the year, the walls and bleachers in the gym were decorated with posters cheering on the senior members of the team; there were five seniors graduating this year, Aiden included. The announcer gave a small comment on each of the seniors and the crowd applauded each. Aiden scanned the stands to find his family. His parents and step-parents sat beside his youngest brother on the top row of the bleachers under a large mural of a growling Wolverine, his team's mascot. They exchanged waves and Aiden took to the court. His teammates each wished the opposing players "good luck" and then they huddled in a circle on their respective sides.

Aiden's team captain, Patrick, looked each of his teammates in the eyes and spoke, "For most of us this is our last game so make it count guys." Patrick placed his hand in the center of the circle and the rest followed. "TEAM ON THREE, ONE, TWO, THREE!" he shouted. Aiden and rest yelled "Team!" in unison and they moved to their places on the court. Aiden ran his hand over the bottom of his sneakers to clear away some of the dust sticking and add more traction.

He never really felt nervous during his games and today was no different; he wouldn't hold anything back. The players readied themselves and waited for the referee to blow his whistle, signaling the start of the first serve.

The referee gave a loud *Toot* of his whistle and Patrick jump served the ball perfectly over the net; the back row player on the opposing team made a fair pass and Aiden positioned himself to block the first attack made by the opponents' left-side player, he crouched and sprang with all his might, extending his arms, and spreading his fingers wide!

BANG!!

The ball ricocheted off his hands and landed back on the opponents' side. The crowd erupted with praise for the play and Aiden exchanged high-fives with his teammates. The first game yielded a few more dazzling blocks and hits by both teams. Aiden had scored a number of points with well placed shots, but was disappointed at the lack of action he was receiving in the back row. Halfway through the second game his attention was diverted by a group of rude fans cheering the opposing team. They were heckling the weakest player on Aiden's team and caused him to miss his serve. The moment of anger forced Aiden to miss two perfect opportunities to pass a ball in his area. He gave the ground a light punch and reignited his focus. He made the next few "digs" and set himself up for a perfect chance to crush a ball, he sprang off the floor, arched his arm back and hit the ball with such force it ricocheted off the face of a player on the other team. The cheers from the fans supporting Aiden's team drowned the "boo's" of the group of boys.

The second game ended and his team was winning two games to none. One more victory would give Aiden a great end to his high school volleyball career. The third game seemed to spark some fury in the opposing team; they were making incredible saves and easily keeping up with Aiden's team. Only a few more points left and both teams were tied. One of Aiden's teammates aced a serve and now one point stoop between him and victory. The ball was served, the set was made, and *Wham!* The ball had been partially blocked and was quickly soaring out-of-bounds! Aiden planted his foot and dove with all his strength to position his hands between the ground and the spiraling ball.

Thump!

Aiden had landed hard on the ground and hadn't noticed the remainder of the play. Certainly the sight of his team running towards him smiling and cheering wildly must mean that something good had happened. His team helped him to his feet and Aiden discovered what happened as the announcer retold the play, adding the details that the ball had landed on the back line, barely inbounds for the game-winning point. The two teams shook hands and Aiden's team posed for a few pictures. Aiden was soon greeted by his family.

"Great job sweetie!" His mother leaned in and kissed him on the cheek.

"That was awesome Bro!" Tyler began. "You kicked some serious...."

"Tyler....careful with that language" His mother interjected.

"Mom I was just going to say 'butt' jeeze...." Tyler lied.

"Thanks for coming guys," Aiden said and gave each a hug. "I'll see you later little bro, I'm gonna try to get Jeri to come hang out so we'll probably spend the night over there."

"Alright, cool!" His brother responded. Aiden said his goodbyes and drove back home. After a quick shower he redressed and gave Jeri a call.

"What's up man," Jeri answered.

"Just got back from my volleyball match," Aiden replied.

"Nice, so did you own some noobs?" Jeri joked.

"Yeah…I owned them…." Aiden said with a laugh. Like many other tech-savvy people, He and Jeri often implemented gamer language into everyday conversation. "So, Jeri, I'm going to hang out at my mom's house later. Since you ditched me earlier you want to come hang out now?"

"I don't know man, got a lot of homework to get done…….." Jeri said. Aiden gave a few seconds pause trying to tell if Jeri was breaking into a smile on the other end of the phone.

"You ass! There's literally no possible way you have *any* homework! Class grades are done! We basically get to watch movies for the next week of school, I'm coming over in five minutes, be outside!" Aiden laughed. He hopped in his car and sped off towards Jeri's house.

Aiden and Jeri arrived a short time later at Aiden's mother's house. It was a beautiful home with a vast assortment of customized yards wrapping around the exterior. Aiden's step-father, Tristan, owned a remodeling business that not only offered work on the inside of the house, but the outside as well. It was not uncommon for Aiden to see his step-father in the backyard until past midnight, cleaning the various koi ponds, replanting flowers, or planning his next big idea to improve it overall. Aiden would normally have thought this to be an obsession, but it was different; Tristan took great pride in his hobbies and poured that passion into a daily routine of working with his hands.

Aiden found his mother, Eve, in the kitchen seasoning a dish full of mouth-watering steaks for dinner. On the stove was a crackling mixture of onions and mushrooms. The house was always filled with the most awesome aromas.

"Hey honey, Hi Jeri, hope you two are hungry." His mother greeted.

"Oh I'm always hungry when you cook, Mrs. Stuart!" Jeri said, eyeing one of the steaks. Dinner was, as always, very delicious. After stuffing themselves silly, Aiden and Jeri accompanied Tyler back upstairs into his room.

"I swear kid, you are spoiled." Aiden said looking around his old room now belonging to his younger brother. A queen-sized bed now occupied the space where his twin bed used to be (which had been too small since his feet hung off the end). New couches sat before an enormous flat-screen plasma television, and Aiden also caught sight of Tyler's brand-new computer with a high-definition 24-inch screen.

"Yeah, I guess mom just loves me more," Tyler said jokingly.

"Oh ha-ha, they probably just feel bad for you 'cause I got all the brains in the family." Aiden retorted.

"Naw man....I'm pretty sure your parents like Tyler better." Jeri interjected, seating himself in front of the TV and scanning through the channels. "I mean look at this, he's even got all the movie channels." Aiden rolled his eyes and sat down next to Jeri.

After a few competitive video game matches between the three of them, Aiden and Jeri left Tyler and went outside near the fire-pit to enjoy the warm breeze that indicated Summer would soon be upon them.

"So did you talk with your dad yet?" Jeri asked.

"About what?" Aiden answered. Throwing a dead leaf in the pit and watching the ashes dance upwards.

"College. Last week you said you'd consider talking to your parents about possibly going to video-game design school with me." Jeri reminded him.

"Oh yeah, I don't know," Aiden said and rubbed the back of his neck. "I didn't really get a chance, plus I don't think I want to anymore..."

"Why not?" Jeri persisted.

"I just don't feel like it's what I'm supposed to do." Aiden replied, tossing another dead leaf in the flames.

"Well no one *knows* what they're supposed to do right after high school, that's why you go, to find out." Jeri clarified.

"No I know, I just don't know if that's what I want to do as a career," Said Aiden.

"Yeah, well if you're not careful you will end up not doing anything." Jeri concluded. Aiden tried to forget the conversation; he hated thinking about being tied down to only one job in the future - even if he could change careers later on.

"So, how'd you end up doing on Mr. Johnston's essay?" Jeri asked a minute later. Aiden retold his version of the odd conversation he had earlier that day.

"Hmm, what exactly did you write about?" Jeri asked with increasing curiosity.

"Let me grab my essay, you can skim through it." Aiden said and retrieved his backpack. Jeri scanned the page and read the first paragraph aloud:

"The first topic I'd like to mention is the current subject of my ongoing research into unusual happenings. I've been reading about lucid dreaming-The ability of a person dreaming to suddenly become aware they are in a dream, and they can make conscious decisions in regards to their dream world. Personally I have only experienced a few of these types of dreams, but a chance

discovery recently gave me more information on the subject. I read that one can learn to have lucid dreams whenever they desire and can learn to better control the activity and setting of the dream. The benefits of being able to do this have ranged from better mental health to people being able to solve real-life problems they would otherwise suffer with....."

Jeri stopped there and looked up. "Yeah, that's cool, so let's see what else is in here."

He flipped the page and began on the next topic:

"For centuries people have been writing about gods and people with abilities that allowed them to do extraordinary things. Paintings show humans performing impossible feats such as being able to fly like a bird; even modern-day mythology has story tellers writing comics about super heroes dressed in fashionable costumes and rushing in to save the day using their powers. But then I began to think about my religious beliefs - as a Christian I believe in God and Jesus being God's son, but when I read about the wondrous miracles he and his followers displayed, I always find myself unable to get past a barrier of disbelief. Even more difficult to believe is that people who follow in his footsteps will be able to do the same....."

Jeri stopped again and looked up, this time looking slightly more interested. He flipped to the next page and read the topic printed:

"I have grown up watching movies such as Star Wars and Star Trek, and I have personally spent countless hours staring up at the heavens, wondering what is out there. And I have concluded that Space is simply too big for humans to be here all alone. How many worlds out there have someone like me staring out into the night sky right now? These questions led me to do some research into the field of UFOlogy. Some people like to divide belief of UFOs into groups: there is the group of "crazy" people who report every bright light they see in the sky; and those 'normal' people who maintain the healthy view that aliens do not exist. Again I do not feel I fit into either group so I made my category; a person who believes that we are not alone but not exactly obsessed or fanatical...."

For the third time Jeri looked up and had a big smile on his face. "Dude, for the last seven years we've been best friends, and we have had some laughs about our constant pondering about random stuff..." he said, and the smile began to become more serious. "But are you like, serious about all this stuff?"

"Yeah, I guess......" Aiden admitted.

"Well, I can maybe believe a little about your ideas on dreaming, but you're talking about fantasy and aliens man!" Jeri sighed. "I just don't know."

"Think about it," said Aiden. "If you look at the evidence, it actually seems sort of stupid *not* to believe in this. I mean take religion for example, we both have Christian views, yes?"

"Sure," Agreed Jeri.

"Ok, so we believe that God sent his son, Jesus, to save all of humanity from their sins. While on Earth, Jesus performed many extraordinary miracles, which included raising people from the dead! He healed any illness or ailment, walked on water, and changed water into wine....." Jeri nodded in agreement. "So the point I'm trying to make is that by saying we are Christians we should *believe* in supernatural things. The Bible even says that people who follow Christ would be able to do the same miracles and even greater acts." Aiden said excitedly.

"Ok, then why don't we see them today?" Jeri rebutted.

"Exactly! *Why* don't we?" said Aiden with more conviction. "That is what I want to know! It's maddening! The lack of miracles today has had a huge effect on not only my faith but perhaps many others around the world too!"

Jeri scratched his chin and stared up. "Whew, pretty crazy stuff man. I think I'd have to see it to believe it..." he said and rose to his feet. "Getting kinda late, I should be getting home soon."

"Alright," Aiden sighed. "I'll grab my keys." He knew Jeri didn't quite share his passion for the topic but there was no use trying to force the conversation.

After driving his friend home, Aiden returned to his father's house, and crept silently into his room. He put his keys and wallet on his dresser and rolled onto his bed with a deep sigh. He closed his eyes and prayed the prayer he had been reciting for several years, "*Lord, help me to maintain the strength and courage to continue pursuing the passions you have blessed me with. In a world that is in such desperate need of healing I cannot believe that you wouldn't want us to use the very tools you allowed your Son to use. I pray with all my heart that you help me to understand this all better. In your names- Amen.*"

"Where am I?" Aiden spoke, as he looked around. He was standing in a forest surrounded by the most beautiful mountains he had ever seen. The sun was crawling up from behind the highest peak. In an instant he was standing at the edge of a lake. He could see a figure in his peripheral vision but wasn't sure he recognized him. It was a man who looked like he was in his thirties, and he was staring towards the lake. *"What the-!"* Aiden gasped. *"This is…. I know what this is! I'm dreaming!"* He tried to turn his head to see the man better, but his vision faded as a loud screech ripped him back to reality.

Aiden's alarm blared with malice; he quickly turned it off and looked for his pen and journal. When he began his lucid dreaming research, he made it a habit to record as many vivid dreams as possible, and as a bonus he noted that he achieved lucidity this morning. He dressed and looked at his calendar; just two more days before he would be saying good-bye to his high school days. Many people might have felt fear about going to college but Aiden welcomed the change. Normally he would be on his way to school at this time, but one tradition at Aliso Niguel High School was that seniors never show up the last few days of class. He instead drove to his mother's house. Today he was going shopping with his mom to pick up a few things he needed for his upcoming camping trip. Aiden and Jeri had been invited by a few of his volleyball teammates to take a road trip up north to go camping for a week. It had taken the better part of five days of pleading to convince Jeri to join them. Aiden parked his car on the street at his mother's house and hopped into her car.

After a minute she hung up her cell phone and addressed him,

"Hey sweetie, I figure we'll just head to the mall. I have a few things I gotta return anyway," his mother said as they pulled onto the main highway.

"Sounds good!" Aiden replied.

They arrived nearly ten minutes later at Mission Viejo Mall. Aiden was not used to seeing the mall so under-populated; he usually went late in the afternoon when everyone was shopping. Deciding to get lunch while his mother made a few exchanges for recently purchased items, Aiden bought an oversized slice of New York Upper Crust Pizza and sat at an empty table in the food court. He cherished these times – "people-watching" had been a fun hobby of his for years, yet he rarely exercised his observation skills these days.

To his left he saw a younger couple that was locked at the lips and clearly must have forgotten that they were in a public place. To his right was a group of elder ladies that were scowling the couple kissing and making hushed remarks regarding their disapproval. Aiden sipped his lemonade gently and continued to scan the scene until he noticed that just ahead of him was a pair of eyes, apparently also engaged in "people-watching."

A few tables away a girl no older than two or three sat backwards in her chair and stared brightly at him as though she completely understood what he was doing and wanted to be a part of this game. He smiled, so did she; he waved, she waved; "*What a cute little girl...*" he thought as he took a bite of his pizza. "*Mmmm.*" He felt the steaming bite send ripples of warmth throughout his body. He took a few more bites and looked back up towards where the little girl had been sitting. She was now crying and Aiden could have sworn he heard the girl's mother say something along the lines of "How many times do I have to tell you to sit properly in your seat!"

Aiden sighed and shook his head. *"What the hell lady, she's only a kid!"* he wished he could say. Telling people off was definitely something Aiden didn't do if he could help it; he always thought it brought more conflict than solutions, but trying to understand why people choose to do certain things was beyond him. A moment later his *I-phone* buzzed. His mother had texted him.

"Hey hon, if ur all done head on ovr to the sprting goods store on 1ˢᵗ flor." Aiden finished his crust and set off for the sporting goods store. Just before leaving the food court he walked behind the mother that he wished he could reprimand and caught the young girl's attention just long enough to make a funny face and cause her to laugh once more. Once at the Sporting Goods store, he found his mother browsing the women's athletic-wear section.

"Hey babe," she greeted. "Just throw what you need in the cart. I'm going to try to find some outfits for yoga."

"Okay," he replied. First he tried on a pair of hiking boots. After trying three more pairs, he found some he liked and tossed them into the cart. Next, he stopped by the knives counter and surveyed the rows of glimmering blades. He chose a Swiss Army Knife and put it in his cart. A shout from a nearby rack of clothes caught his attention and he turned to see a young boy throw a tantrum by knocking over as many piles of clothes as possible. The reason for this outrage, Aiden quickly observed, was the refusal of the boy's mother to buy him a new pair of shoes, which he clearly needed. She instead smacked his bottom and dragged him across the store to finish *her* shopping.

Just then he received a call. "Aiden? Hey it's Patrick. So there's a little change in plans. Instead of camping at Coral Beach, we were thinking of going up to Yosemite. You still in?"

"Uh, yeah, I'll just have to ask Jeri. " Aiden answered.

"Ok, sweet. Just be at my house on Friday morning, eight o'clock. Oh and make sure you bring a coat or something; we might get some rain up there. See ya!"

Aiden hung up and looked around the store. He found a comfortable jacket and looked around for his mother. They went for the check out and for the second time Aiden's ears met the distressful cry of someone throwing a tantrum. The twist this time though, was the very mother who refused her son was now yelling at a cashier.

"What do you mean my card's declined!?" She screeched. "You wait 'til my husband hears about this! I'll make sure you're fired!" As she marched away Aiden could not help but laugh, but he was more upset than happy for the "justice" of what had just happened. Every time he looked at someone he could see how desperately screwed up they were. He found himself wishing the children of these parents had different circumstances because the cycle will continue for years to come. Of course Aiden understood the need for discipline in young children but there's a fine line between discipline and abuse. People always think that abused children are those beaten by alcoholic fathers, but the real abuse is the lack of moral education they supply their children, and by the time the kids grow up it is usually too late – at least too late to stop them from making a mess of their lives. Aiden's mother purchased their items and Aiden continued to distract himself on the car-ride home.

"You didn't get very much," she commented as they walked back to the car.

"Yeah," he replied. "Tristan has tents and sleeping bags for me so I don't need that much." Aiden's step-father had more than just tents and sleeping bags. He served in the United States Marine Corps for several years before starting his business, once discharged he began to feed a pretty serious taste for hunting. So he literally had more than the average person would ever need for a friendly camping trip. Aiden spent the rest of the afternoon packing, but took breaks to join Jeri online to play games.

The next day he went to the beach. Salt Creek was the same beach he had visited for years. It had a gorgeous view from the top of the hill leading down to the white sand. Aiden didn't really like to swim, or surf, or really do anything that was common for kids his age. He loved to just walk in the water that shot up the shoreline, and enjoy the strong salty winds. It was times like these that made Aiden reconsider if he was happier being more introverted than others. He would watch the families and groups of friends enjoying their day, but would always wonder, *"At the end of the day, are all these people happy with their lives? Does how they look match how they feel?"*

After the beach Aiden met up with Jeri to grab a bite. "How was the beach?" Jeri asked.

"I don't know, it's nice, but today was a bit crowded."

"Yeah, that's why I don't ever go; that and the fact that my skin burns in about five minutes."

"Ha-ha, yeah." Aiden laughed, finishing his French-fries.

Aiden spent the rest of his evening watching movies. Tomorrow he would graduate and would be celebrating on his trip the day after. He lay down and drifted off to sleep. His dreams carried him back to the same mountains where he had been a few nights before. This time it seemed a bit more vivid. He again found himself standing before a lake. The surface was dark and smooth as glass. The man was also standing next to him again. Except this time, Aiden was able to turn and see him. He was tall with long, wavy, blond hair; his facial features depicted a warm but strict person. His eyes were the bluest Aiden had ever seen. He was holding out his hand as if he was trying to offer something to Aiden, but he wasn't holding anything. Then he smiled and turned back towards the lake, waiting with his hands behind his back. Aiden wanted to ask him something, but found himself being pulled back to reality.

Graduation day had finally arrived! Aiden instantly forgot about the strange dream, and hastily showered and got dressed. He made sure to grab his cap and gown and set off to pick up Jeri, who as usual, was running late. So they had to rush to get to the school on time. The parking lot was full so they parked on the street nearby. They couldn't have been any closer to missing the ceremony. They were just now arranging the students into lines based on their last names. Jeri and Aiden both jumped into the "S" line and began to march towards the football stadium. Everyone took their seats and listened to the band finish their tune.

"Ladies and gentlemen," announced the principal. "Before you sit, please join with me in applauding the seniors for their hard work over these past four years."The stands filled with cheers and applause. "Now, since I'm sure these fine young men and women would like to get out of here as quickly as possible, let's begin." The principal called each of the students up to shake hands with various members of the school board and faculty. Aiden spent the time looking in the stands for his family, but he couldn't find them in the thousands of faces staring back. After a while he heard "R," and regained his awareness that his row would come next. Then he heard "S" and stood with his row. He was just a few minutes away from receiving his little piece of useless paper, declaring him finished with high school. "Jordan Robert Shenders," said the principal. Aiden was next!

"Aiden James Shepherd!"

Aiden smiled wide and accepted his diploma; he shook hands with everyone, and relished in the spotlight. He felt great; it was finally over. A moment later he heard,

"Jeri Thomas Spencer!" He looked over his shoulder and saw Jeri also claim a diploma before performing a victory dance. They sat down again and watched the last few rows get called.

The valedictorian now addressed the students to present the closing speech, this young man had been the most ambitious student Aiden had ever known. He was class president for two years straight, got straight A's in all his advanced placement classes, and was even part of the worship team of Aiden's church. With all the time spent in pursuit of the highest achievements known to man, it's hard to imagine him ever enjoying a day as a normal kid. Aiden realized he was missing the speech and tuned in for the last part.

"....It feels like our high school journey just started; yet, so soon, it now comes to an end. Some of us will now go and do great things, and some will spend a ton of money and put ourselves in debt by going to college. Regardless of what we do from here on, remember this; whatever your dream is, it is never out of reach. If you want something badly enough, then strive for it, and never ever let anyone tell you what you dream can't be yours. Great job everyone; now let's get outta here!" A roar like thunder swept through the stadium as students and spectators cheered. Caps were flying skyward and people were searching for their families. Aiden saw his four parents, three brothers, and grandparents heading towards him, all looking very proud.

"Great job, son," Mr. Shepherd said, and offered a big hug.

"Thanks dad!" Aiden responded. "All of you, thanks for coming!" He gave each of them hugs as they congratulated him then he met up with Jeri so they could leave before traffic got too crazy. They walked towards Aiden's car and slipped away as a line of cars jammed the exit.

"Whew! It's done; we have been freed after years of incarceration!" Jeri joked, switching the channel on the radio.

"Yep, it was like torture," Aiden agreed.

"Just think about all those incoming freshmen and how much it must suck to be them! They have no idea what they're in for!" Jeri continued.

Aiden laughed and shook his head. That night they were having pizza at Aiden's mom's house. It was probably the first time the food was ready *before* Aiden had arrived.

"Yumm, looks delicious," he said as he greeted his family. Today, Aiden's two older brothers were visiting: Brenden was twenty-two, and Steven was twenty years old. Brenden lived across town and was getting ready to marry his fiancée, Tiffany. He recently finished college and was working for Aiden's father, who owned a retirement planning business. Steven was attending Azusa Pacific Christian College to study Communications. He had received a partial scholarship to play basketball, and from what Aiden had heard Steven greatly enjoyed studying there.

"Good job guys," they both said as Aiden and Jeri helped themselves to a few slices of pepperoni.

"Thanks," they answered.

The rest of the night they laughed and enjoyed a hot Jacuzzi while watching a movie on the outdoor television. They went to sleep around one o'clock, knowing they would regret only getting a few hours of sleep before leaving on their camping trip early the next morning.

Chapter 4 - Earth and Sky

Aiden was restless throughout the night, unable to sleep peacefully as the waves of images swept through his mind. He couldn't make out the images clearly. A thousand different pictures flashed before his eyes but he had no time to distinguish any of them. A moment later he awoke and checked the time. *"6:40."* He decided to get up. He threw a pillow at a very loudly snoring Jeri.

"Hey, we gotta get ready. We need to be at Patrick's in about an hour," said Aiden tiredly.

Jeri groaned and sat up, "Awww man, there was this amazingly hot chick…. She was right about to….." Jeri started.

"Yeah…yeah, I get the picture. You can shower in the upstairs bathroom. Just be ready to leave in forty-five minutes." Aiden cut in.

"Aye aye!" Jeri saluted with a tone of sarcasm before falling back asleep.

After a breakfast of waffles and sausages they packed the car and Mrs. Stuart drove them to Patrick's house. As they pulled up she helped them unload their bags.

"Alright boys, I graduated once too and I remember what kids do on these kinds of trips." She said. "So please try to stay out of trouble. I love you Aiden; see you in a week." She hugged them both and drove off.

Aiden and Jeri transferred their bags into the pickup truck in which they would be riding. Apparently, a few groups would be meeting up at a campsite in Yosemite. Luckily, the other passengers in the car were the two other teammates from Aiden's volleyball team: Josh and Brett. After a few minutes they waved goodbye to the remaining parents and set off on their graduation journey.

"Well boys, we have a ton of booze and a handful of lovely ladies meeting us just a short drive up the road-- so sit back and enjoy the scenery!" Patrick said as they entered the freeway. Jeri pulled up a pillow and slumped over, determined to return to sleep. Aiden stared out the window and watched the world fly by.

Nearly six hours later he was jumbled awake by the vibrations of a rocky dirt road. He had fallen asleep a few hours ago by mistake and pleasantly missed the rest of the road trip. The truck rolled up to a campsite containing three other cars. As he exited the truck, Aiden saw a group of four guys sitting with beers on a picnic table, and a group of six girls attempting to construct a tent, which was clearly giving them trouble. He walked over to them and asked,

"Would you like a hand putting up your tent?"

"Really? Awww, that's so sweet!" one of the girls replied and skipped off with the rest of them towards the group of guys. Aiden sighed and looked down at the pile of disorganized tent parts.

"Well buddy, sometimes being a nice guy just means you get to do everyone else's work." Jeri laughed and helped him start piecing the tent together.

It took almost an hour to construct both the girls' and their own tent, but as they finished they finally sat down and relaxed with the rest of the group.

Aiden's phone rang a few minutes later but the reception was too poor to hear anyone on the other line. He instead received a forwarded text from his mother a minute later and the news was shocking.

"Danny Edelman, 18, was killed last night in a car crash after he lost control of his truck and hit another car head on. Danny was valedictorian of his high school and graduated

yesterday. At 1:06 A.M. Danny swerved into oncoming traffic and hit a car carrying a family of four. The two children in the car were alive but in critical condition and the father driving was killed instantly. Danny's blood alcohol level was 1.2 – well above the legal limit of .08. We hope this serves as an example to teens everywhere that when you choose to make a choice to drink and drive you put yourself and others in unnecessary danger. "

Aiden read the text several more times and his eyes welled with angry tears. Here was a kid that had the entire world ahead of him and one simple decision to be an idiot not only ruined his life, but an innocent family's. Aiden took a few minutes to get a hold of himself before returning to the group. He didn't have the heart to share the news with the rest of them. But tonight he would not be participating in any drinking.

They played a few card games and the trash near their camp slowly grew taller with crushed beer cans and empty bottles. One of the girls saw that Aiden passed up offers for beer and asked,

"What's the matter Aiden? You don't drink?"

"Ah, no. Not tonight," He answered. She rolled her eyes and returned to her chat with her friend. Aiden had made up a code of ethics for drinking a few years ago when he was last put in this situation. Even though he always told himself that since he turned eighteen he was old enough to drink, even though the drinking age was twenty-one. He didn't understand how the law would allow people to be drafted to fight in a war at eighteen (which required the use of a firearm), yet not be able to drink for three more years. Those kinds of things drove him crazy. He also promised himself that based on the situation he would have to determine if it could lead to a potential for irresponsibility; this was one of those situations. He only wished Danny had applied the same sense last night.

A large winged creature circled the lantern and several of the girls let out shrieks of horror – one even fell backwards off the seat, pulling her friend along with her and landing in a pile of joyous giggles. Not sharing the mood that his comrades were, Aiden dismissed himself and took a seat by the fire pit to roast marshmallows.

Just after midnight things began to quiet down. Aiden and Jeri lay on a blanket and glanced upward. Aiden's mood had lightened considerably. He used a number of things to distract him from Danny's tragedy and tried to enjoy the trip. The sky was dark and filled with thousands of stars; many more than they could see back home.

"So, aliens huh?" Jeri asked.

"Yup, they're out there," Aiden responded. "Just look at each star. Let's just say hypothetically that there's an average of five planets around each. So if there were one-hundred billion stars in a galaxy that would be five-hundred billion planets. Then multiply that by the number of galaxies ever observed. *Then* take into account that the universe is infinite. Now you tell me if that doesn't make sense for other people to live somewhere out there."

"Dude I think if I thought that hard about anything my head would explode," Jeri laughed. "But I see your point. Just let me know if you meet any."

"Jeri just doesn't get it..." Aiden thought. *"Am I the only one on Earth who feels like there is a void that just can't be filled? What am I missing....?"*

They watched a few minutes longer, before retiring into their tent. Aiden woke every hour to bump Jeri in the attempt to stop his snoring, but every time he fell back to sleep, it started again. At eight o'clock he finally gave up trying to sleep, and got dressed in his hiking gear.

Today the group was going to explore some of the surrounding trails. He unzipped his tent and gazed upon the chaos from the previous night. Dozens of beer cans littered the ground and nobody had tied the trash shut, so rodents had done a great job of throwing their trash everywhere. Aiden gave a large sigh and grabbed a trash bag.

"Why does this stuff keep happening to me?! Does God have some a diabolical sense of humor, and I'm always going to be put in these situations?" he thought and finished stuffing the last of the rotting trash into a nearby dumpster.

Thirty minutes later the rest of the group awoke and met outside to get ready for a mid-day hike.

"Whoa, is it just me or is our camp a lot cleaner than it was last night?" Josh asked as he stretched his arms.

"Maybe the park rangers clean up for campers in Yosemite?" one of the girls suggested. Aiden shook his head and smiled. They had breakfast – which wasn't really a breakfast at all since everyone just ate crackers or leftovers from the night before – then they met near the edge of the camp.

"Alright everyone, make sure you have your water and snacks," Patrick directed. "Let's head out."

The views were some of the most surreal Aiden had ever witnessed. Shades of green he had never seen cascaded through the valley and a wall of mountains stood guard on either side, guiding a strong breeze over the towering trees above. The air here was pure and fresh. Within twenty minutes they had seen an eagle, a fox, and someone near the front of the group said they had seen a wolf but nobody believed him.

"Can we take a break?" one girl asked. "I'm getting some serious blisters on my feet!" The rest of the ladies nodded in agreement.

"Okay, but we've only gone about half a mile," Patrick remarked.

After a fifteen-minute break they started again. They walked a bit further down the hill and reached a creek that shimmered beautifully. Just beneath the surface they could see several fish dashing from under one algae-covered rock to the next. As Patrick began to cross one of them another of the girls cried out for a break. This time they stopped for almost thirty minutes. Aiden, filled with frustration, picked up his backpack and walked determinedly towards the front of the group.

"Hey, Aiden!" Patrick called from behind. "I think we're gonna turn back, there's a thunderstorm that's supposed to hit in a few hours."

"Okay, you guys can head back, but I came out here to go hiking," Aiden replied. "So I'll meet you all back at camp in a while."

"You sure about this, man?" Jeri interjected. "I've never heard any good stories about hikers going off alone."

"Yeah, Jeri, I'm sure. I'll just see you in a bit,"

"Okay, be careful out there," Patrick said and turned back up the trail.

"Yeah, don't go climbing any cliff-faces like a moron." Jeri added with his famous grin.

"Uh huh," Aiden nodded sarcastically and set off across the creek. This is what he had been waiting for-- just him against the elements. He walked for miles, stopping only when he needed to; all the while loving every moment of this experience. But he was enjoying it so much, he completely lost track of time. Sure enough, the dark clouds that had been hours away were now gathering overhead and a light sprinkle of rain enveloped the forest.

"Great..." he said as he pulled out his coat and started back along the path.

After nearly an hour of walking he began to wonder if he was still on the right trail. Nothing looked familiar and the clouds were now filling the valley so thickly that he couldn't tell what direction he was headed, with the added bonus of heavy rain he quickly recognized that this was a less than ideal situation. Aiden liked to think to himself that no matter what mess he found himself in, as long as he kept an optimistic outlook things would turn out fine. This feeling was thrown out the moment he rounded a corner and happened upon the rotting carcass of what looked like a mountain lion. Its entrails were spilled in several spots and the smell told Aiden it must have been dead for at least a few days. A number of large pieces had been picked at by other animals but Aiden did not want to be around if any of those predators returned for another meal. He jogged off and tried for the tenth time to call Jeri but there was just no signal in the valley. To make matters worse, Aiden had been suspecting he was going in circles but was not sure until he stepped out from a familiar corner and was met with the rotting mountain lion carcass, from an hour earlier. He swore loudly and decided to take a different route. He heard rushing water and jogged swiftly towards it,

"Finally! That must be the stream we stopped at earlier!" he thought. However as he approached the "stream" he soon realized this was a full sized river. There was no way of crossing here so he figured he would follow a path that ran along it to see if there was a more shallow clearing. He was imagining how unlucky he was and thought things couldn't possibly get any worse when bright flashes of lightning lit up the darkening valley. Each thunderclap seemed much louder as it bounced around the valley walls.

"Don't panic! If you have to find some shelter for the night and wait it out, you had better not waste more time here feeling stupid about wandering off alone," he thought. He started walking down the trail again, praying he would find somewhere to wait out the storm.

BOOM!!

A bolt of lightning cracked maliciously and hit a tree nearly a hundred yards ahead. The image burned into his eyes for a brief moment before Aiden felt the awesome blast knock him onto his back.

"YOU'VE GOT TO BE KIDDING ME!!" he shouted and climbed back to his feet, now not only wet, but covered in mud.

CRACK!!

Another bolt hit somewhere behind him, and the sound of splintering wood along with an actual sense of tingling in the air around him, like static electricity, forced him into a jog which turned into a run after a few more thunderclaps made his heart skip. His bag was heavy and rubbing his skin raw from the violent swishing from left to right as he ran. A few minutes later he stopped and looked around, panting. Across the river a faint light shun through the trees.

"Is that a lantern!? You made it, Aiden! You're back! Now all you have to do is cross this river..." He found a spot nearby that had some sizeable stones resting in the river, the water didn't seem to be moving that fast but Aiden felt it would be safer to jump across the stones rather than walk through. He leapt from stone to stone until he reached the middle of the river, for a moment his foot slipped but he caught his balance just before he fell in; unfortunately the time he spent regaining his balance distracted him from a large tree branch rocketing towards him from upstream. The

branch roared over the stone he stood on and kicked out his feet – causing him to knock his ribs against the stone. As he fell into the river the strength of the water instantly became must more apparent. He gasped for breath as the river winded down a few small rapids and flung icy froth into his lungs. He paddled with all his might but it was no use; he was at the mercy of the rapids.

Somewhere in the back of his mind he thought of the car crash with Danny. How devastated his family must be; how awful it must be for his friends right now, just days after graduation.

"No! That won't be me! I won't be another tragic story people look back on!" Aiden paddled with more vigor than before and reached for anything that he could grasp to pull himself ashore. To his relief his hand grasped a stone-solid grip and he felt himself pulled out of the water by a force that felt more powerful than that of the man that now stood over Aiden as he coughed the last of the water out and drew fresh oxygen.

"You know it's not the smartest thing to go hiking out in a thunderstorm," said the mysterious rescuer lightheartedly. "Or swimming for that matter." Aiden was too cold to say anything in return. The man helped him to his feet and threw his coat around Aiden before leading him to his tent nearby. Aiden was barely able to catch a glimpse of a square tent and cot before collapsing on the bed and falling quickly into a dreamless sleep.

He awoke to the smell of vanilla and cinnamon coffee and felt he must have imagined the whole trip, he would open his eyes and see the ceiling of his brother's room at his mother's house. But he was in a square tent – cold, soaked, and bruised.

"Why don't you sit up, Aiden?" suggested the man. "I was just making a pot of coffee; I daresay I didn't expect you here for a little while longer. Had I known I might have been able to prevent your little accident." Aiden remained speechless and glued to the spot. He watched the man exit for a moment and return with a pair of mugs. A minute later he poured the coffee into both and handed one to Aiden, then sat down on a cooler near the other side of the tent. Aiden's head was spinning, he felt nauseous and his body was shaking.

"Drink up, it'll help," the man said, and sipped from his own cup. Aiden did likewise and drank. Warmth he had never experienced flowed through every vein in his body. He felt his senses sharpen and felt full of energy. He continued to stare at the man and wracked his brain as he tried to find the right words.

"Thanks for your help." Aiden said, instantly feeling stupid that he had been so foolish to trek alone.

"It was my pleasure, Aiden." He answered. "I wish the circumstances of our meeting were a bit less dramatic but you're finally here nonetheless."

"Excuse me?" said Aiden as he realized he had been addressed by his name twice without properly introducing himself. "Do I know you?"

"Forgive me; my name is Zayn, Zayn Ka'tan." He replied and offered a hand-shake.

"Nice to meet you....Zayn," Aiden said and shook his hand. "Umm, I don't really know what to say. What do you mean I'm *finally* here?" Aiden surveyed the man for a moment and a faint feeling surfaced in his head. There was something familiar about this person, like he had seen him before.

"Let's just say for now that I'm here because of you," said Zayn. He sipped his coffee and continued, "You've always had dreams and fantasies about something like this happening, haven't you? A mysterious stranger showing up out the nowhere to tell you you're special, and different? Right?"

Aiden felt his cheeks go red and hastened to sip his coffee again to delay his uneasiness of a stranger knowing so much about him. "Yeah I suppose..."

"Well, that's why I'm here," Zayn said casually. "I know its torture to ask you to wait, but why don't you rest for a bit and then we'll talk."

As Zayn rose and left the tent Aiden drank more coffee and tried hard to think of where he had seen Zayn before. A lump on his head was throbbing and he laid back down to think. And then it hit him! The man he had seen for weeks in dreams was Zayn. But that couldn't be possible; did he know Zayn from somewhere? Was he a celebrity or someone from church? Zayn walked back in nearly fifteen minutes later.

"It's still coming down pretty good out there, but I'm afraid there's no more time to delay. Aiden would you like to take a walk? There's something I think you should see. If you would rather return to your camp; that can be arranged too."

Aiden stared deep into Zayn's blue eyes for a moment then answered, "Alright, let's walk."

"Excellent! Grab your coat and bag." Zayn said and hoisted his own backpack over his shoulder. "You may also help yourself to whatever is in the cooler as we have a bit of a journey ahead of us."

Aiden grabbed his things, and secretly pulled his pocket knife out of his bag and tucked it in his pocket. After all, he had no idea who Zayn was--- but *something* told him this man was sincere. He also took a few drinks and snacks out of the icebox, and followed Zayn into the dark night. The faint lantern Zayn held was the only thing that illuminated the darkness, and with each step Aiden felt as though the Earth itself would fall out from underneath him. Zayn said nothing as they hiked deeper into the forest. Aiden struggled silently as he followed behind this strange man; he knew he had seen Zayn somewhere before the dreams – he looked much too familiar but no matter how hard Aiden tried to picture where he had known Zayn, no answers came. A few hours had passed when they began to climb a steep hill.

"Are we almost there?" Aiden asked. His legs were burning and he had never felt so drenched.

"Patience, my friend, patience. We will be there at first light," said Zayn, who didn't seem to be the slightest bit tired.

"First light?! When would that be? Why couldn't he just say "an hour" or something? It's going to take a day to get back to my camp. I wonder if Jeri and the others notice I'm not back yet. Do I get cell phone reception out here, oh wait, my phone's broken...dammit!"

"You need to clear your head of all those questions or you're gonna get a headache." Zayn said.

"Wha-?" Aiden began, but then stopped as he saw the faint edge of a smile on Zayn's face.

"You see, time is not constant," Zayn continued. "It speeds up and slows down based on who's looking at it. Right now we have no time to lose. So by telling you "first light", you will not make time move slowly for us."

Aiden thought that strangely made sense but didn't reply. They walked for a few more minutes and Zayn spoke again,

"And to prove my point..." he pointed to their right. The faint hints of blue were growing lighter as the sun approached. The rain had stopped a while ago but everything was still saturated. They continued up the slope and Aiden could begin to make out the rest of the valley, but he could not recognize any of it. The sun was now hiding just behind a peak in the distance. Enormous cumulous clouds surrounded them, glowing orange in the morning sunlight. The wind at this altitude came in strong gusts, and threatened to dislodge Aiden's grasp on the final rocky mounds he was climbing.

At last they reached their destination. They walked around an oversized boulder and were met with a large lake; its surface looked like black glass. Aiden stared at it for a moment before he realized a lake should not be so calm with the amount of wind rushing around them. He reached down and touched the surface. It felt like normal water, but no ripples expanded when he pressed his hand into it.

"I've seen this before. This very spot--- in my dreams..." Aiden began.

"Tell me what you saw," Zayn commanded.

"I was standing here looking out at the lake." Aiden began. Then he stood and turned towards Zayn. "I turned and saw you-- you were holding out your hand towards me as if you were trying to give me something. Then you looked back towards the lake and waited. From then on, I always woke up," said Aiden, still surveying the lake.

"Not bad. You could say then that you already know what you're doing here." Zayn responded.

"But I don't. What does this all mean? --- Who are you?" Aiden said, locking Zayn's gaze with his own.

"First," Zayn said and cleared his throat. "You must understand that what I am about to tell you is neither a joke nor a lie. You have prayed for years that God would provide you with greater understanding of who you are, and why you are so passionate about seeking truth where many others fear answers. You have not been a perfect model for Christ-like living, but you have great potential to improve and a desire to know more. It is for those reasons that God has sent me."

"You're kidding right?" Aiden said with a fake laugh.

"No, like I said, I'm absolutely serious." Zayn answered, his expression unchanging.

"So you're supposed to be an angel or something?" Aiden questioned.

"Not exactly," Zayn laughed. "Let me simply say that I am a foreigner and I am going to offer you one chance to take an extraordinary step on behalf of your people. I am giving you the choice to follow me on a journey of great discovery and transformation. But, before you decide if you wish to accept, you must know that this decision does not come without sacrifice. The life you know will be gone. You will not be able to contact any loved ones for a time, and should you succeed in this quest you will face a difficult and dangerous life."

"I don't understand. What kind of journey is this?" Aiden asked, his curiosity now growing.

"Everything you have always wanted to know about will be answered. Whether or not you believe it and comprehend its full meaning is up to you. But again, time is short so I'm afraid you must choose now." Zayn proposed.

"This is ridiculous...I don't believe you. Stuff like this doesn't happen!" said Aiden, now becoming frustrated.

"Aren't you the one always trying to convince people these sorts of things *should* happen?" asked Zayn, still calm.

"Yeah, but this is just crazy. I'm outta here..." Aiden said and turned to leave.

"Aiden please, before you go..." Zayn stopped him then looked out at the lake, and closed his eyes for a moment.

Aiden glanced at Zayn then back at the lake. The smooth surface broke into a more natural ripple-filled state. From below the surface, a glimmer of metal appeared; then a moment later a triangular craft floated out of the lake and rested on top of the water. Its proportions were amazing! It had to have a diameter of nearly eight-hundred feet and stood about fifty feet tall. Aiden stood transfixed and instinctively took a few steps back, causing him to fall over; but the fall didn't seem to faze him.

"Pretty impressive, eh? Zayn said, and helped him to his feet.

"Th....th...this is impossible!" Aiden managed to utter.

"Psh! You ought to know that *anything is possible!*" Zayn exclaimed. "After all, didn't you do the research on similar craft?"

"Yeah, but hearing people talk about things and actually seeing it is a bit different." Aiden replied, eyes wide with a mixture of overwhelming fear and awe. "What are you saying? That you're an alien?!"

"Well, we don't call ourselves aliens." Zayn corrected him. "Like I said before, we're just foreigners. You live on Earth; we live on our planet. You are people, and so are we. Don't worry-- the shock will wear off-- happens to everyone. So what do you say? Shall we hop on board?"

This was it; his day had finally come. Aiden could never forgive himself if he passed up the opportunity to fulfill his dreams.

"What about my family?" Aiden asked. "And what about my friends back at camp? I can't just disappear and not expect them to be worried about me?

"I spoke with your family yesterday afternoon and explained the situation to them, I have known your father for many years now and he knows there is a great opportunity that awaits you." Zayn replied. "They don't know the details but I assured them that I would personally keep them informed of your well-being. As for your friends we had one of our crew pose as one of your family members and told them you had to return home for a family emergency.

Aiden hesitated for a minute then finally made his decision, " I...will go with you."

"Well done! That was the hard part," Zayn said and patted Aiden on the shoulder.

Aiden saw a small doorway appear on the exterior hull of the craft and lead to a dark interior. Zayn took a few steps toward the entrance and swept his arms in an "after you" gesture. Aiden swallowed hard and stepped into the spacecraft – his heart racing and hands trembling. Zayn followed behind him and the doorway closed. The darkness dissipated and light filled the large hall, illuminating nearly a hundred unfamiliar faces. Zayn walked out from around him and turned to face Aiden with the mass of people at his back.

"Aiden, we are proud to welcome you to a much larger world!" Zayn said loudly and they all broke into applause - Aiden forced a shy smile.

Chapter 5 - Light and Dark

Aiden stood in shock and awe of the extremely strange situation he was in. Just over a day ago he was your average young man getting ready for a hiking trip, now he was a guest on an actual spaceship; with a crew of very human-like people smiling back at him.

"Aiden if you would be so kind as to follow me," said Zayn and grabbed Aiden's bag. "I have prepared your room in our living quarters." Zayn led the way through the crowd to a very advanced –looking lift system in the middle of the room. Aiden wanted to look around but his head was spinning even worse than before so he kept his eyes on Zayn as best he could. He saw the lift doors open and emerged to a very beautiful hallway; it was as though every surface emitted its own unique form of light. They began to head down the hallway and Aiden could see what looked like small computer screens near each door they passed. All of them had writing that he couldn't understand. A moment later he saw a screen that he could read: "*Aiden James Shepherd, resident of Earth, Class: 1st*". The door opened and they both entered.

"Go ahead and make yourself at home," Zayn suggested, and placed Aiden's bag in a storage locker. "As I said we do have to get going soon so if you want to take a minute to gather yourself then meet me back on the main deck; the floor just below this one. I realize you are still a bit shaken but we will be leaving Earth behind us soon and I think you would love to see your planet as we depart."

Aiden did as he was told and returned back to the lift after he had taken a few minutes to calm himself. He shared the lift with another crewmember that greeted him with a very warm handshake.

"You are the new recruit?" asked the stranger.

"Excuse me? No, I'm just here with Zayn," denied Aiden.

"Yes, so you are a new recruit," the man persisted. "Don't worry he'll explain it. What's your name?"

"Aiden."

"Nice to meet you, Aiden. I'm Jaxcyn. First time leaving your planet?" Aiden gave a nod.

"Well congratulations, it's never easy for first-timers," Jaxcyn commented. "Most faint when they see the ship, let alone stay conscious to watch our departure. Enjoy it- it's a very magical experience." The lift doors opened to once again reveal the large hallway Aiden had entered when he first boarded. "It was a pleasure meeting you, Aiden; I hope to see you again sometime."

"Thanks, you too." Aiden shook his hand again and met up with Zayn, who was talking to a curiously familiar looking woman with unnatually dark, crimson hair. She was easily one of the most beautiful women Aiden had ever seen. In fact, now that he looked around, everyone looked similarly perfect. All the men were muscular and athletic, and the women were slim and fit. Zayn walked over to Aiden with a smile and Aiden pried his eyes away from the beautiful girl.

"I'm glad you made it back," said Zayn. "Now, if you'd like to head over to the Observation Room we'll be able to see a nice view from there." They walked to room across the hall and entered. This room was full of large fluffy chairs and couches. They all faced a large wall that was blank except for a small computer panel in the corner. Zayn walked over to the panel and pushed a few buttons. The wall instantly changed into a transparent window that showed the lake and surrounding mountains, right where they had been before Aiden had been brought on board.

"Alright Aiden, here we go." Zayn waved him over to the glass and looked back outside. After a few seconds the craft began to rise up and away from the lake. Aiden could see the immense forest beneath; they continued to ascend higher and higher. By now he was above the clouds and could see almost the whole state of California shrinking with every second. Now he could see the whole United States; they must be moving extremely fast. A few more seconds past and Aiden's eyes began to well-up with tears; he could see the entire Earth shrinking from the size of a basketball to a softball. A moment later it was the size of a marble, then, gone. He couldn't find anything to say due to the lump in his throat. He was staring out at the vast darkness of space. A mass of stars littered the heavens and he turned to Zayn, who also had tears in his eyes.

"Amazing isn't it?" Zayn offered, still gazing at the stars. "I've been living on that planet for eighteen years, and as much cruelty and tragedy as there is I can't help but feel like I'm going to miss being there."

"Where are we going?" Aiden asked and wiped his eyes.

"To my home planet, *Teros (Tair-ross)*," Zayn replied. "It is about fifteen-thousand light years away from Earth near the center of the Milky Way."

"So....I've got some time before we get there?" Aiden joked.

Zayn laughed, "Not too much time, we aren't actually traveling at the speed of light, we go much faster than that. At our current speed we would be there in about three hours. But we have a number of stops to pick up the rest of the recruits over the next few days."

"Recruits?" Aiden questioned.

"Yes, you and the thirty-nine other recruits we're picking up are going to the Terosian Science Academy," explained Zayn.

"An Academy?!" Aiden asked surprised. "And did you say thirty-nine *others*?"

"That's right, well that's not including the ones already there." Zayn answered with a nod. "We find that it is much better for everyone when people of similar circumstances are grouped. In the past we would train our members individually but our current system works much more efficiently. You may have noticed on your room panel it says *"Class: 1st"*, this means you are to be grouped with other First-Class recruits. This is our class of people with the greatest potential for quick success in achieving a new, stable belief structure. Surely you have noticed yourself that as strange a situation as you're in compared to a short time ago on Earth, your mind hasn't lost its grip on reality. Many people would be terrified of so many new changes in their belief system they would literally lose themselves and go insane. It is for this reason that I have had to wait very patiently for you to live your life up to a point that you could adapt to the *truth."* He paused a moment and placed his hand on Aiden's shoulder, "And you, Aiden, have already begun your journey to discover that truth; as have many others at The Academy."

"Aren't academies used to train people for military careers?" asked Aiden.

"Not always, but in this case they are." Zayn replied.

"You never said anything about me signing up for a military..." Aiden burst out.

"We're at war Aiden, I think many people forget that. God calls each of us to take up arms and storm the front lines." Zayn said calmly.

Aiden thought about this for a few minutes then asked more questions, "When we were at the lake earlier you said God had sent you to help teach me, but does that mean that you and your people are Christians? How can that be if Christ was born on Earth?"

"Again, very good question. We aren't Christians," Zayn answered.

"Then what religion do you follow?" Aiden followed up.

"We do not have a *Religion* we are all simply *Children of God*," Zayn stated. "On Earth your people create these religious systems that are doomed to cause confusion based on the simple fact that mankind is flawed in nature, so accordingly, religion is flawed. People need to learn to go straight to the source instead of seeking all their answers through their churches. Now I'm not saying that church is a bad thing, but it should be a place where people come together in collective praise and worship of *The Creator*. Not just select people lecturing the rest. This is where the conflict begins because mankind also needs organization and leadership, thus current churches reflect that need with a pastor or priest."

"So….who exactly is Jesus to you?" Aiden continued.

"Jesus Christ was your Earth's personal savior sent by God," said Zayn. "But on our planet Jesus appeared as our savior – *Teros Ka'tan*."

"Wait isn't Teros the name of your planet?" Aiden asked with a puzzled expression. "And isn't Ka'tan *your* last name?"

"We adopted his name to describe our world since he is the one who God chose to rule it," Zayn explained. "We also use his surname in each of our names because we are all one people united through him, so there is no need to make any further separation between us."

"So wait, everyone's last name on Teros is *Ka'tan?*" Aiden asked, still trying to grasp this idea.

"Correct" Zayn nodded. "Now as I was saying…for each of the thousands of other civilizations throughout our galaxy, each has followed a similar path of chaos for years before they all received a savior. But not all worlds succeed.

The time it takes before they reach the point of a "Second Coming" of their savior varies based on the people. Since we're all given the gift of free will we have the right to continue to pour fear, anger, and darkness into our worlds." Zayn mentioned with a hint of sadness.

"So has your savior returned yet?" Aiden pressed.

"Not yet, I fear there are still obstacles we must face before he does." Zayn speculated.

"Wow….don't think I've ever heard anyone suggest that aliens believed in the same God many people worship on Earth," said Aiden with a wave of comprehension.

"Indeed. I will say this though; you Earthlings sure have made up some interesting ideas about off-worlders," Zayn laughed. "While I lived there I must have seen at least a few dozen horror movies based on evil aliens."

"So everyone out here is friendly? " Aiden asked and motioned towards the stars rushing by; Zayn's warm smile began to fade to a more serious expression.

"Well…no," he said with a sigh. "Basically you have three different types of groups. You have people like those on Earth; some people who have heard the call but most have not yet embraced the light. They still struggle in darkness, blinded from the truth. Then you have those like my world, beings in this plane of existence that have gone very far in their development and live in peace with the Holy Spirit guiding our actions but still very far from perfection." He waited for Aiden to absorb this and sighed. "Lastly you have the dark ones, the ones we call *Shadows*." Zayn said darkly.

"Demons?" Aiden asked with a rising curiousity.

"Oh yes, demons. Including Lucifer himself," Zayn answered. "These are incredibly complex beings that exist in multi-dimensions. I won't lie to you Aiden, there are very dangerous parts to your new life that we will do all we can to prepare you for, but until you experience it yourself I cannot describe it very well."

"So how am I supposed to fight them?" asked Aiden.

"How else does one banish darkness? With light!" Zayn exclaimed. The power of God's word will light even the darkest places of the universe."

Aiden paused for another few minutes and spoke again, "You know I've never understood Satan."

"What do you mean?" asked Zayn.

"I remember going to church once and they spoke of how evil he is….," Aiden commented. "Then I remember star-gazing one night and a thought came to me I'd never really understood before. I tried to picture exactly what Satan is thinking. What compelled him to rebel? And why does he continue to struggle against an opponent he knows he has no chance of defeating? I tried to imagine what it would be like to talk with him. After thinking about all of that I started to pity him a bit. It's almost as if he has no choice."

"It is really quite extraordinary to be able to come up with such deductions at your age," Zayn insisted. "That is a powerful tool that usually takes years to learn. It is a gift that allows someone to look outside of the box. And to take it a step further, think of how God feels about Lucifer. Many times people associate them on two opposite sides of a spectrum, one hating the other. But you must remember that God loves everything he created, and he is very fond of Lucifer. To put it in Earth terms they "liked to kick it and chill together"." They shared a brief laugh before Zayn continued, "However I think Lucifer was always destined to fall. All of creation needed that evil to demonstrate the separation that exists if we reject God."

"I suppose," Aiden shrugged.

"You'll understand it better when you begin to see the higher truth of things throughout your training," Zayn concluded. "Which reminds me you really should head back to your quarters and get some rest, you've had quite a day!" Aiden nodded and headed for the exit. Just before he left Zayn called out, " Oh also, you are free to use the equipment in your room as well, but be sure to use the computer inside to ask how everything works. A few recruits managed to break some of their things already!" Zayn laughed and escorted Aiden back into the hall of the Main Deck.

Aiden rode the lift back up to the living quarters and found his room. The tunnel vision he'd been suffering since he boarded was finally starting to wear off and he was seeing more detail of his surroundings. His room was a rectangle of about twenty by thirty feet with rounded corners. It had one other door leading to a strange-looking restroom and had a very comfortable bed in the corner. There was also a chair sitting next to a desk with a large computer screen on it. In another corner was a series of cabinets, drawers and an odd box about the size of an oven.

The box had a lighted panel with various buttons and what looked like a headset sitting on top of it.

"That's one hell of an MP3 player," Aiden said with a grin.

"A what sir?" came a voice from behind him.

Aiden jumped and looked around the room for the mysterious voice, "Hello? Who's here?"

"*I* am here, sir. Your computer," said a woman's voice again.

"Oh, wow you talk?" he asked.

"Indeed I do, I see you perform that function as well sir."

"They program you with sarcasm as well?" Aiden asked, raising an eyebrow.

"My apologies sir, I have been uploaded with the knowledge of your native languages on Earth. I also downloaded everything about you while we were departing your world. It taught me a great deal about your personality."

"Don't worry about it," said Aiden, amazed that he had just insulted a computer. "So what do I call you, not just "computer" I hope."

"You are free to call me whatever you like, although I will agree that name sounds a bit too generic."

"Haha, true..." Aiden laughed. "Hmm, do you have a model number or anything?"

"I am simply a Student Operations Personal Handheld Interactive Entity."

"S...O....P....H...I...E..." Aiden spelled out. "Sophie! That's what I'll call you!"

"Very good sir, very original."

"Come on now, is Sophie alright?" Aiden pressed.

"Yes sir, Sophie is a lovely name."

"Thank you, now back to the box in the corner, what exactly is it?" Aiden said and turned back around.

"That is your food processor device, sir." Sophie explained. "It is operated by equipping the headset and thinking about what food or beverage the wearer wants. You must also specify what temperature you would like."

"No way!" Aiden gasped.

"Way sir, way." Joked Sophie.

Aiden darted across the room and put the headset on. He concentrated on a large bowl of mint chocolate chip ice cream. The device began to glow and hum for a few seconds then a soft tone indicated the meal was ready. He opened the door and sure enough, a large bowl of mint ice cream sat inside. He took a bite and experienced a feeling similar to the coffee he drank in Zayn's tent. Chills shot to every part of his body and a feeling of great pleasure swept through his mind. *"This food is probably more addictive than anything I could imagine,"* he thought and helped himself to another large spoonful. "Sophie, how can this thing create anything?"

"Do you want the complex version or the *idiot's guide version* sir?" Sophie asked politely.

"Funny…" he scowled. "Let's try the complex first."

"Very well Sir," She responded. "The F.P.D. stores highly dense levels of atoms that it draws from to replicate the molecular structure of the substance being requested…."

"What about the idiot's version?" Aiden interjected.

"It creates food by putting the jigsaw of molecule pieces together," Sophie replied.

"I see," he said with a nod. "I think I'll use the shower - be back in a bit."

Aiden was still very dirty from the hike and walked to the small room in the corner and looked inside. He saw a toilet-like structure, and a shower but was unable to see any soap or towels

"Umm, Sophie?" he asked and popped his head back in the room.

"That was very fast sir!" she answered swiftly.

"I haven't gone yet, where are the shampoo and towels?" he inquired.

"Not to worry sir!" Sophie assured him. "Just step into the shower and say, "Clean.""

"Right....." He said and closed the door. He undressed and stepped inside, and commanded, "Clean". He felt a tingling sensation surround his entire body and nearly 30 seconds later a tone sounded. Aiden exited with a confused expression. "Sophie....what the hell just happened? There wasn't any water!"

"Oh that's right sir, you're used to a bit different bathing routine."

"I feel refreshed and admit I smell great but what's the deal?" Aiden demanded.

"Complex or *idiot's guide?*" Sophie replied with a cheek.

"Just gimme the short version this time."

"Very well. The bathroom's shower and toilet systems rely on a series of lasers to eradicate all foreign molecules from the surface of your skin."

"Did you say toilet too? No toilet paper?"

"That's right sir, no toilet paper."

"Alright I think I've had enough weirdness for now. I'm going to try to get some sleep."

"Sleep well, sir."

"Thanks." He said and laid his head down. Aiden speedily drifted off to sleep, his brain overflowing with far too much new information to even begin to process it all.

He awoke every few hours and paced his room, asking Sophie as many questions as he could before taking a break and relaxing with his favorite novel on his bed. Zayn popped in for very brief checkups to ensure that Aiden was acclimatizing to his new wealth of information without too much trouble.

Aiden spent the next few days in either in his room reading or in the observation room watching the stars go by. A thought continuously bounced around in his mind, "If all this had been real all along, I wonder what else out there is true as well."

Chapter 6 - The Academy

"Wake up, sir! We are approaching the Teros system," Sophie shouted. Aiden jumped up as if he'd been shot with a taser.

"Geez, Sophie. In the future, try to not give me a heart attack. I thought we were going to crash or something."

"Very sorry, Sir!" Sophie apologized. "I have been instructed to get you prepared for our arrival. Your uniform is hanging inside the first cabinet near your bed. Please take everything you brought aboard to your new residence."

Aiden opened the cabinet and pulled out a black t-shirt, a navy-blue uniform coat with buttons running down the right side, a pair of navy-blue pants, and a pair of all terrain, shin-high, black boots. Patched near the shoulders of the coat's sleeves was a beautiful gold symbol of a pair of wings stemming from a rectangle; between the wings sat a circle, and within the circle lay a down-facing triangle – each point containing another circle. A hollowed gold triangle was also pinned on either side of his collar. He put on the outfit and admired himself in the mirror of his bathroom.

"Well, at least I still look good," Aiden joked. "Sophie, do all the recruits have the same uniform?"

"No sir." She answered promptly. "The range of colors is based on what class they are: Navy Blue is for First-Class students, Second-Class wears green, and Third-Class wears red."

"I see." Aiden said and straightened his collar. "Zayn mentioned the type of people who are in First-Class; but what about the other two classes?"

"Third-Class recruits...." Sophie began. "Are those who are chosen to be trained despite the fact that they still hold onto the false reality that they are alone on life's journey with no hope of finding peace. They generally have a very hard time believing in *The Creator* and have a very difficult time adapting when their belief system is shattered. There have been some very disturbing emotional incidents due to their heavy attachment to that false world. The Second-Class consists of people who have heard of some truths but reject them out of fear, and they remain skeptical about just how deep those truths extend. Most recruits are Second-Class."

"Interesting," Aiden muttered. "I have another question: How can the Terosian crew members understand me and how do they all know English?"

"That will be covered in your orientation later," She answered plainly. "But on a similar topic, you will notice that you cannot communicate directly with most other recruits; to do this you will have to use your portable computer and earpiece."

"I have to carry around a laptop?"Complained Aiden.

"No sir!" Sophie reassured. "On the desk there is a Portable Computer Device, or PCD, that straps to your wrist; on Earth it would be like wearing a cell phone. The earpiece fits comfortably in your ear, and, when someone speaks, the PCD will send the appropriate translation so you can understand them. This wrist device also has a small display screen that will contain whatever information you require at the time. This device serves as my primary abode with you throughout the remainder of your life."

"Remainder of my life? I hope you don't suffer from claustrophobia," joked Aiden.

"Oh sir, your wit has no end," Sophie reciprocated.

"Thank you, Sophie." He concluded. "I think I have everything."

Aiden packed his things and strapped his PCD onto his wrist and put in his earpiece. As he exited his room, he looked down the hall and saw at least ten other recruits exiting their rooms. He noted that they all looked very similar to earthly humans. Some had distinctive features like being taller or shorter than Aiden, or having certain facial features that weren't quite normal for a human. One with a particularly large head passed by and Aiden heard, "Hi there, how are you?" as Sophie translated.

"Oh, good thanks." Aiden responded.

The rest of the people in the hall greeted Aiden in a similar fashion, although some appeared a bit pale and shy. Then they entered the lift.

"What was that about?" Aiden asked Sophie.

"Well sir..." she spoke directly in his ear. "You may have noticed that two of them were Third-Classes, and the rest Second-Class."

"And?" he acknowledged, "What about it?"

"Isn't it obvious, sir? They look up to you," Sophie explained. "I don't think you realize just how rare it is to see a First-Class. Last year's class had seven, and I believe you are among only four this term."

Aiden felt flushed and took a deep breath. "Wow, so how many new recruits are there?"

"I believe the current roster is six-hundred twenty-one." Sophie recited.

"Four out of six hundred twenty one!" Aiden mumbled to himself as he got off the lift.

"Don't let it go you your head, sir." Sophie warned. "While it is a great honor to be recognized for your potential, you must remember that potential remains wasted until achieved. I know of many recruits that were too full of themselves, and they ended up being returned to their planet."

"You can be expelled here?" asked Aiden, clearly surprised.

"Oh yes. There are rules, and one must do all they can to never hinder their fellow classmates' development."

"I understand." He nodded.

95

As he entered the main deck hallway, he noticed what he had overlooked before--- all of the Terosian crew members were wearing uniforms of white, similar to Aiden's.

"Sophie does Teros have only one form of fashion?" he whispered.

She laughed, "No sir! These are just the uniforms for people associated with The Academy. The staff wears white; students wear a uniform of their respective color. When one graduates, most alumni choose to wear a black uniform with their class color showing somewhere in it. For example, you could wear black and a navy blue undershirt. This way the current recruits can identify that you were once where they are now. As for the rest of Teros, they have a very colorful variety of fashion."

Thirty-nine recruits stood single-file before a bright opening that led to a world completely unknown to each of them. Zayn walked over and motioned Aiden to take his place at the end of the line. He leaned over and whispered, "I'll see you later. Just follow the instructions and remember that this is all supposed to be fun and exciting. So try to set a proper example for your peers." Zayn nodded his head in the direction of the young man standing in front of Aiden.

The Third-Class boy was shaking and could hardly stand still. He had very short black hair, stood equal to Aiden's height, was well-built, and wore what looked like a futuristic pair of sunglasses. Aiden could empathize with him-- his own stomach was growling with butterflies and he could only begin to imagine what awaited them.

"Hey there," he said to the boy, who jumped and turned toward Aiden.

"I...I'm sorry did I bump you!?" said the boy nervously.

"Oh, no. I just wanted to introduce myself." Aiden assured him. "What's your name?"

"Phew, m...my name is Kyon."

"Kyon? Nice to meet you; I'm Aiden." He put out his hand and waited for Kyon to do the same. But the boy stared at Aiden's hand in a confused way. "Sorry. It's how people greet each other where I'm from. Guess I'll have to remember where I am now."

A man to their left spoke so all could hear; it was surprisingly easy to understand despite hearing the gibberish of the foreign language in his other ear.

"Recruits--- Welcome to Teros! I'm sure your curiosity will cause you to want to explore all over, but please stay in line. We will allow you plenty of time to look around once you've settled in. If you will all follow me!"

The man led the line through the bright exit and onto a platform. Aiden caught sight of the most massive airport, or spaceport, he had ever seen; ships were arriving and departing in all shapes, sizes, and colors. He looked at the sky and noted how extremely blue it was, and that an enormous portion of the sky was filled with a large moon surrounded by three other smaller moons. To the right of the moons he saw a large white sun slightly bigger and brighter than the one back on Earth. Gasps and awes sounded throughout the ranks of the fascinated recruits. They continued down the ramp and began boarding a large bus-like craft that floated a few feet above the ground. An announcement sounded throughout the spaceport,

"Now boarding: Tram from Theron Spaceport to the Terosian Science Academy. Platform 17!"

The tram had an upper floor and many rows of seats, which began filling with students. He spotted Kyon next to an empty seat and walked down the row to join him. Several pairs of eyes met him and some recruits even pointed and whispered as he passed. A few even scooted closer to their neighbor, trying to make more room for Aiden to fit. As he sat beside Kyon, he noticed a few people give disappointing scowls.

"Y...You don't have to sit next to me...." Kyon began.

"I would be delighted to sit here, and anyone else should feel as lucky," Aiden said and took his seat.

"Thanks," Kyon blushed almost as red as his uniform.

They pulled away from the spaceport and began racing down a stretch of tall buildings. Aiden noticed they had a range of objects and structures similar to Earth, such as parking lots and signs. But one key difference was that the roads did not have concrete or asphalt laid on them; instead they had grass-like plants or dirt. In fact, he saw trees and plants everywhere.

"Kyon? I've been meaning to ask you--- what's with the glasses?" Aiden said, pointing towards his eyes.

"Oh," Kyon answered and felt the side of the visor. "My mentor said this planet is much brighter than mine, so he told me it would be best if I wore eye protection."

"I see." Aiden replied. "Tell me about your planet."

"It is called Phobon," Kyon began. "It's fairly dark there. Our two suns are very red super-massive stars in their last few million years of life. Because it's so cold in the equator regions, most of my people live in the upper hemisphere. We don't see many stars due to the pollution. We also had a global scale war just before I was born about twenty years ago. My parents died on the way to new cities being built in the radiation-free zones. My mentor, Jaxcyn, said he lived there for about ten years." Kyon paused for a moment then looked back towards Aiden. "A week ago he showed up and asked me if I'd like to do something about my world's situation. I said yes, and he led me to a canyon that had a ship much smaller than the one we just came on. He let me take a look inside, I got a bit light-headed – then he told me to pack and wait a few days before returning to the canyon. Then, I went back out there today and found him waiting with a huge ship parked nearby!"

"Hey, I know Jaxcyn!" Aiden remarked. "I met him on the ship earlier the other day, just before we left my planet. He seemed like a great guy."

"He is!" Kyon agreed. "I always felt he was a bit different than others in my town. He looked like everyone else, but he didn't carry the same sadness like the others."

"Wow," Aiden sighed. "Sounds like you've been through a lot."

"Yeah, I guess." Kyon shrugged and looked back out the window. Aiden did as well and saw they had traveled up a hill nearly a thousand feet high and parked.

"Alright, everyone! We have arrived!" said the man that led them off the ship, "When you exit the vehicle, please look for the banner carrying your class color--- the orientation staff will familiarize you with the facility that will serve as your new home."

Aiden saw Kyon begin to shake with a fresh wave of butterflies again as they picked up their bags and exited the tram. They all felt an entirely new sensation of awe sweep over them as they tried to take in the immensity of the structure towering above them. Aiden tried to compare the style it resembled, but couldn't remember ever seeing anything like it on Earth. The only way he could describe the architecture was that of a futuristic fortress—towers sprang up in parts-- some rounded, some squared, and some a mix. Altogether some of the structures rose to what he guessed must have been at least twelve-hundred feet high, the main building was at least thirty-five hundred feet wide and two-thousand feet long. The walls had a charcoal metallic coloring, with an opaque reflective surface. Hundreds of windows of every shape and size littered the many floors. The grounds surrounding the building were filled with the most beautiful gardens one could dream of, and on the opposite side of the Academy was a view off a steep cliff to a brilliant red-sand beach and deep blue ocean that seemed to reach off into infinity.

"If only I'd brought my camera....." Aiden said to himself.

"I can capture images and video whenever you want, sir," Sophie said as a small antenna containing a panoramic bulb camera extended vertically from his PCD and took a picture that was immediately displayed on Sophie's view screen.

"Thanks Sophie. I'm gonna have to sit down and look through your manual sometime soon." Aiden said gratefully.

"You are very welcome sir!" The antenna flipped back down.

"Aiden? Aiden James Shepherd?!" shouted a voice nearby.

Aiden turned and saw the beautiful girl with stunning crimson hair standing beneath a blue banner and looking right at him. Her eyes glowed deep indigo and she had tan skin that looked like it was made of silk. She wore a white uniform like all the other staff and carried a very slim computer clipboard.

"Uh...uh...oh, yeah! That's me! I'm Aiden," he said as he broke her spell and regained his composure.

"Outstanding! It's a pleasure to meet you at last!" she said, and gave him a big hug. "Zayn has told me so much about you. I will be your Orientation Supervisor--- my name is Vyleah." For a moment Aiden tried to understand why her name struck him so deeply, though he did not want to seem rude so he brushed it aside for now.

"I remember seeing you talking to Zayn on the ship. He didn't say anything bad about me I hope," Aiden joked.

"No! Not at all!" Vyleah smiled. "I have a lot to show you, so let's not waste any time!"

"Just me?" Asked Aiden. "You don't need to wait for anyone else?"

"As you may have already heard…" Vyleah explained as they walked. "We have a class of six-hundred and twenty-one new students this term--- of those we have four First-Class students. My sole priority at this time is to get the First-Classes acquainted with our Academy. I have already shown the others, so it's just you and me." She led him towards a large metallic square resting atop the grass field next to the right-edge of the main Academy building.

"Deck One, please." She said and the square lift descended promptly to a rocky hanger. As Aiden looked around, he saw dozens of craft scattered in every direction. The walls of the hanger were decorated with pictures and schematics for things he never knew existed.

"This is our Vehicle Housing Facility or VHF." She instructed. "We have a wide array of Terosian space and land craft. We also have a replicator device to recreate any type of vehicle you desire; our library contains a great number of models from hundreds of planets. You will become more familiar with the VHF when you have your first lessons."

Vyleah led him back to the surface level and around to the left side of the Academy where a vast number of tall rock formations and boulders were scattered for miles. The rocks varied greatly in textures and colors that led Aiden to believe it was artificial.

"This is the Stone Forest," She explained. "It is a collection of monuments representing each planet we have visited. If the planet has someone come to train at the Academy, it is tradition for those recruits to leave a decorative monument to commemorate their planet. A large piece of white marble was delivered from Earth many years ago, though you are the first student to arrive since we started The Academy. In a few weeks you should be familiar enough to take a flight-capable ship to visit the monument."

"Cool!" Aiden exclaimed. "There're so many!"

"Yeah, we've been collecting for quite a while," she said with a giggle. Aiden glanced over and admired her gorgeous smile, but almost at once she put her authoritative expression back on her face and motioned towards the cliffs at the rear of the Academy.

"Over there is the Cliff-Side Tram that leads down to the beach. Students are allowed to use it whenever they want."

Aiden stared down the thousand-foot drop and felt a strong gust of wind rush up into his face, bringing fresh salty air into his lungs. He took the view in for a few more moments before speaking,

"This is all just amazing; everything here seems so perfect."

"Yes, but you must remember that everyone shares a history not too dissimilar to Earth's." Vyleah clarified. "Some repeat the same mistakes for thousands of years before learning; and as far as being perfect, we aren't. You will discover soon enough that we're just like you. But I'll admit we do know how to correct ourselves a bit better when we get side-tracked from *The Creator's* plan," she added with another smile. They walked through the last of the remaining gardens back towards the front entrance.

"So," Aiden said. "Earlier I asked my computer, Sophie, why everyone from Teros can understand me and also speak English. She said it would be covered in my orientation."

"Of course!" Vyleah exclaimed. "I almost forgot; many students ask this. The reason is that we have all learned to reconnect with *The Keeper.*"

"The Keeper? " Aiden asked, wondering if The Keeper was some Terosian internet provider.

"On Earth it is called *The Holy Spirit,* I believe?" she asked.

"Oh, yeah!" Aiden confirmed. "Why do you guys call it *The Keeper*?"

"There are three parts to God or as we call him, *The Creator*." She said and drew a deep breath. "First is his existence as an individual being. Then he exists in the form of *The Keeper*. This manifestation consists of the entirety of all knowledge that is and that can ever be learned. It may be difficult to understand now, but this *Being of Great Wisdom* serves as the intermediary between our souls and God. Lastly, you also know *The Creator* as a mortal man on Earth called *Jesus Christ*. Those who are chosen to help us as saviors are, what we call, *The Beacons.* They are the life-line thrown to us to help us find our way back to the light."

Aiden's eyes grew larger and he took a moment to absorb this. "Okay, so how do you speak English again?"

Vyleah laughed and gently laid her hand on his arm. "I told you it's going to take some time to adjust, but trust me, you'll be fine. Basically, when the first people were created, they were in perfect harmony with *The Creator*. But in one way or another they are given free will to follow the

Creator's plan, or disobey and choose to try to create their own existence, or individual journey to enlightenment. To live with God is to be <u>One</u> with him. Because of our disobedience, we could not be with him anymore in our altered state. Our connection to *The Keeper* was severed, and we fell into the darkness of ignorance and misperception -- all of creation did in a sense. You must understand that what you see and feel through your body's senses don't actually exist..."

"Wait....what?" Aiden said as he was plunged back into the deep end of incomprehension.

"Don't worry about that right now - the point I'm making is that we can learn to repair the connection to *The Keeper* so that we can be with *The Creator* again. When you learn how to communicate with him, he will grant us access to many tools, or gifts associated with *The Keeper* about how to serve *The Creator's Will*. One such tool is the ability to understand all languages spoken."

"I think you may have lost me again...." Aiden said as more confusion set in.

She smiled again and continued: "I know it's difficult to understand this right now; it will take some getting used to. But when you begin to learn how to use these gifts you will know what I mean."

"When I learn how?" Aiden swallowed hard. "I don't even know where to start..."

"You've already begun, Aiden." Vyleah comforted. "Just learning the truth is the first step in being able to use *His* truth. The last thing I'll tell you before we meet up with the other First-Classes-- when dealing with *The Keeper*, you must believe that *anything is possible* and it will be."

Aiden and Vyleah approached the front entrance, which had a large circular opening with no physical doors attached. Aiden tried to clean off some of the mud that had stuck to his boots from the freshly watered gardens, then continued to walk through and felt his face crunch into an invisible wall. He bounced backward and fell with a thud. A group of students following behind erupted into laugher.

"Oh my gosh!" Vyleah gasped and threw her hands up to her face. "I'm so sorry I totally forgot about the force-field!"

"Yeah...I guess I should have known you guys would have something like that," he replied and climbed back to his feet. She brushed off the dust on his back and approached the computer terminal near the entrance.

"New Recruit: Aiden James Shepherd, confirm enlistment status: Active," she said and the computer gave a compliant tone. "We have to register everyone to be able to allow passage inside. Otherwise that would happen to all the doors you tried to walk through. You can enter now."

She waved him in and he cautiously stepped through. They walked into a lobby where the symbol of the

Academy was inscribed on the stunning stone flooring. The lobby was a circular building with many combinations of triangle and circular windows lighting the room. They passed through the next hall and into the Main Chamber of the Academy: an enormous room containing fifty-foot statues of people and symbols standing in fountains. They ranged from golds and silvers to materials that looked entirely unknown on Earth. People in uniforms were everywhere; some sitting near the fountains, some on their way to a class. The interior architecture looked completely different from the exterior; it was full of light and color. Just like the ship, everything seemed to radiate and glow. The ceiling was one of the most extraordinary pieces of artwork Aiden had ever witnessed - it was a spectacular galactic map of the Milky Way; at the center the ceiling spiraled into an opening leading to a shaft that rose to the very top of the Academy where a series of mirrors allowed sunlight to flow into the chamber. Pillars and columns were scattered everywhere and all were covered in odd-looking inscriptions.

"It's Terosian writing," Vyleah said before he could ask.

Just then a short and strange bipedal creature with a human-like face and a white metallic body walked up and said, "May I sir?" and motioned to Aiden's mud-covered boots.

"Oh, umm, sure thanks." Aiden answered. The creature's right hand transformed into a smaller version of the laser emitter from Aiden's shower and vaporized the dirt, leaving a perfect shine; he then lifted Aiden's boots and cleaned the bottoms as well.

"Thank you, sir! Have a great day!" spoke the creature.

"You.....too?" Aiden turned to Vyleah as it left and began to ask, but she was again ready and gave the answer before he could.

"Those are the Cybernetic Autonomous Service Entities, or CASEs. They basically do all the dirty work on Teros, keeping things clean, running errands, whatever we need them to do."

Aiden laughed, "They kinda look like these robots from this one video game I used to play."

"A game, huh?" She inquired. "We might be able to find you something to play in the recreation center later."

"Sounds good!" he remarked.

"This way next," Vyleah said as she led him towards the hallway on the right wall where they entered an enclosed circular lift similar to the one on the ship. The door wrapped shut and Vyleah commanded, "First Class Tower." The doors opened a moment later and they stepped into a small lobby decorated in stone and metal panels of black, white, and navy blue. In the center was a fountain with a silver statue of the Academy's symbol rising out of it.

"Vyleah, what does that symbol mean exactly?" Aiden asked and pointed at the fountain. "I've been seeing it everywhere since we arrived."

"The triangle and the circles at the tips represent *The Trinity*; The Creator, The Keeper, and The Beacon;" She began. "The arms of the triangle shows Their universal relationship to each other and the outer circle is representative of the infinite universe they govern. The wings that surround them are symbolic of The Great Terosian Phoenix – a bird that was only seen on rare occasions while Teros Ka'tan walked our world. Scripture says the return of The Phoenix will precede the return of The Beacon."

"Ahh, okay I get it now." Aiden nodded. "Thanks."

They walked through the lobby and up a small passage to the leisure room. The walls were covered in banners displaying a large bit of writing followed by small bullet points of smaller writing.

"These are banners created by students to show what planet they are from and their names and class listed." Vyleah explained.

"Is there one for Earth?" he asked.

"Not yet, you can create one when you have time." Vyleah informed him. Aiden reached out and touched one of the banners, but his hand pressed against a flat wall.

"These aren't real?" he asked.

"It's a display screen," she replied. "The walls in here can be used to display holographic information."

"Wow, it's so life-like." Aiden said, swashing his hand through the hologram again. The rest of the room had couches facing a large wall, (Aiden assumed this was like the ship's observation room) and a circular fire-pit with bench chairs around it. On one of the walls there were two more lifts like the one they'd just used, and two of the walls had giant oval windows stretching nearly twenty feet wide, giving a great panoramic view of the rest of the Academy on one side and the great city near the ocean on the other. Vyleah walked over to a panel near the lifts and pressed a button. A light tone sounded and she spoke,

"Hello First-Class students, I would like the new cadets to meet your fourth member, please assemble in the leisure room." One by one they popped out of the lifts, two of them wearing big smiles. One looked human but the other two were the strangest Aiden had seen so far. One of them, a girl, had a larger than normal bald head, a fragile frame, pale skin, and very big brown eyes. The other wore a helmet with a tube running to a backpack and wore gloves so no part of his body showed. Aiden broke the ice and spoke,

"Hi there, nice to meet you all. My name is Aiden."

The human-like being responded first. "Pleasure Aiden, I'm Qendrin."

Next the girl answered and gave a deep bow, "An honor Aiden, I'm Mariel."

Aiden returned the bow and the third spoke and gave a salute by placing his left fist over his chest and giving a slight bow, "Greetings, My name is Shendu." Aiden again returned the salute and bow.

"Excellent, I'm glad you four got a chance to meet before the welcoming ceremony." Vyleah said and boarded one of the lifts. "If you three will excuse us I need to show Aiden his living quarters."

"Of course!" Mariel stepped aside so Aiden could enter.

"Thanks, see you all later!" Aiden said and joined Vyleah.

"Level 49," she ordered and they zoomed upward in a few seconds. They exited and stood before a triangular door with a panel beside it. As Aiden approached the door rose upward and admitted them. To his right was another enormous oval window that spanned the length of the room. A variety of beautiful plants rested in pots on the windowsill. Under the window was a rounded desk with a large computer screen and a hovering chair.

To the left was a second triangular door. Straight ahead he saw a large capsule standing vertical. It reached six feet in either direction, and stood tall as high as the ceiling.

In the corner left of the capsule was an opened hatch and a FPD (Food Processor Device) sitting atop it.

Suddenly the second door flew open and a CASE robot walked out, greeted them, sat down in the space beneath the FPD, and closed the hatch door. Aiden walked in the opened door and saw a very Earth-like bathroom. The ground and walls had travertine and a marble counter with a mirror was on his left. In the left corner was a large shower with the standard laser cleaning system, but it also appeared to have several normal water nozzles. To the right of this was an oversized spa tub with jets and was surrounded with scented candles and bubble bath. And finally to the right was a large walk-in closet, containing more spare uniforms and what appeared to be cloaks for rainy/cold weather. Sophie spoke without warning,

"I hope you like it sir! I had your CASE prepare this based off of a file I downloaded from your computer back home entitled, "Dream Home", unfortunately the only thing you had written so far was some ideas for the bathroom."

"Thanks Sophie!" Aiden said gratefully. "This all looks wonderful!"

"The welcome ceremony will start at six o'clock in the Main Lecture Hall." Vyleah declared. "Please be there on time. I have a few things I need to do in the mean time."

"How will I know where it is?" He asked.

"I can help you find it sir!" Sophie interjected.

"Ok then," he shrugged. "Thank you so much Vyleah, don't forget you said we'd try out a game later in the recreation center." Aiden said with an arrogant grin.

"Oh I wouldn't miss it! See you at the ceremony!" She rebutted and gave him another warm hug before exiting on the lift.

"*I guess Terosians like to hug...*" He thought as he looked over the room again and admired the breath-taking view of the ocean and city in the distance. He looked over at the capsule and pondered its use for a minute.

"Sophie," he said at last. "I'm going to take a wild guess that this thing here is where I'm supposed to sleep."

"You are very correct sir! That is the Anti-Gravity Sensory-Deprivation Capsule, or ASDC."

He giggled for a moment, "You guys sure do love acronyms huh?"

"We do indeed sir!" she exclaimed.

"Okay now I get sensory deprivation, but anti-gravity?" he said and scratched his neck. "You can't be serious."

"Give it a try sir!" Sophie encouraged. Aiden walked over and hit the green button labeled *"Open"*. A set of twin doors drew outward, exposing a plain interior that emitted a blue light; he took off his boots and coat, then stepped in.

"Now using the panel on the inside, hit the red button," she commanded. He did so and as the doors closed; the inside was filled with blue light and a panel was lit to show the options. There was an *"AG"* button in yellow and an *"Audio"* button in blue. He tried the audio button and a voice sounded,

"Please specify what audio you would like."

"Sophie, did you download all the music from my computer as well?" he asked.

"Yes I did sir!" she responded. "I have that plus all music, movies, games, or media you would want."

"So much for copy write laws... give me something futuristic sounding, I feel it's only appropriate considering where I am." The capsule filled with a synthesized collage of light guitar, piano, and trance music.

"Yeah that's nice." He reached over and pressed the "*AG*" button and instantly felt his body become weightless as it floated off the ground.

"Woah!" he said with a large grin.

"Wait till you try the one in the recreation center sir! This is just to sleep in. When you activate sleep mode you will be in total darkness and the noise-canceling sensors will block almost all sound. The capsule will keep you perfectly aligned in the center so you don't bump all over."

Aiden's stomach gave a loud groan and he checked Sophie's display, "*5:02*".

"I think I'll get something to eat before we head down for the ceremony. Let's put this FPD to the test."

He opened the capsule and went over to the Food Processing Device and put the headset on. He closed his eyes and imagined a delicious piece of filet mignon with mashed potatoes and steamed vegetables. The device lit up and hummed for a moment then a tone sounded. He opened the door and saw an identical meal sitting right before his eyes; even the utensils were replicated. Aiden brought the plate to his desk and sat in the incredibly comfortable floating chair. He cut a piece from the filet and took a bite. It was easily the best steak he had ever tried. It was almost as if every food had its own unique taste signature that brought an ever-changing sense of satisfaction. The potatoes were also the best ever, and though he normally didn't like green vegetables he guessed if everything else tasted great they might too -- and they most certainly did. He sat and ate for a while, staring out at the city. With his mouth completely stuffed he laughed and addressed Sophie,

"Oh….mmm….I'll tell ya Sophie….. I'll never have a problem eating healthy again." and he stuffed in another forkful of veggies.

"I'm glad, sir!" She offered. "But unfortunately we should be going, it's five fifty-five."

Aiden dropped his fork and looked at his PCD on his wrist. "SH…!" He cursed, his mouth still full. He threw his boots on, grabbed his coat, and rushed out to the lift.

"Alright Sophie, where do I go."

Sophie displayed a map of the Academy and started sounding off directions, "Go to the Leisure Room, then take the lift in the lobby to Level One, go back through the Main Chamber and to the opposite hallway. Take your first right, then another right, and down the ramp and you'll be there. It's right underneath the Main Chamber. Then just find the blue banner with Vyleah and the others."

He ran at full sprint and got there just as the last students were entering the round doors. A miniature coliseum wrapped itself around a stage with thirteen Terosians sitting on it. About five-thousand people sat waiting. Down in the front Aiden saw a blue banner with a small collection of about fifty people; about thirty-five of them were alumni in a variety of black, white, and navy-blue uniforms.

He gazed around at the rest of the stadium that was mostly green, about a third of them were alumni. Then the red section had about nine hundred people in and just a few alumni. Aiden rushed down the stairs and took the vacant seat near Vyleah, Qendrin, Mariel, and Shendu. Vyleah raised an eyebrow and he could almost hear her demanding where he's been.

"People! Quiet down!" said a man standing on the center stage. After the room had become silent he continued. "For those of you who don't know me, my name is Tchyntar (Shin-tar). I am the Director of Academy Operations for this term. Let us take this opportunity to officially welcome our six hundred twenty-one new members! Will the Third-Classes please stand!"

Seventy-three new members stood and everyone applauded.

"Now the Second-Classes!"

Five hundred forty-four new Second-Classes rose and received even more applause.

"And lastly our First-Classes!"

Aiden and his three fellows stood and received the loudest welcome.

"First off, let me congratulate each of you on being selected. It is my great pleasure to promote each of you to the rank of *Cadet*." The crowd once again gave a loud round of applause and Tchyntar waited until it died down before continuing,

"You must remember that it is not what color uniform you wear, but how you apply yourself that makes all the difference in the world. As you can see we have former graduates here that will be resources for you in whatever you need. And now, let us go over a few ground rules. Your Personal Computer Devices on your wrist will notify you of any specific rules should you ask or be in violation of any. But in general I ask that you refrain from inappropriate behavior that may have been considered common on your worlds: This can range from the seemingly harmless prank to making unwanted advances on your fellow classmates or staff."

Aiden looked over at some Second-Classes that didn't seem to care much for the lecture about rules.

"Next, For all intents and purposes, this is a military organization and as such I must ask you obey any instructions given by either your Mentor, or Academy staff to the best of your ability. Failure to do so has had fatal results in the past." A clamor of whispers swept through at this news and Tchyntar waited a moment for the message to sink in.

"Tomorrow you will be starting your first courses at nine o' clock. You will attend six different classes, two each day. Then one free day at the end of the week. After your day's lessons you will work on the application of the lectures with your peers and Mentors in trying to comprehend the meaning of the lessons. You have all received an electronic copy of the *Terosian Science Academy Student Handbook* on your computers in your rooms, I encourage those eager to progress more quickly to read as much as you can. Please feel free to explore the grounds this evening and get to know the others in your class. May *The Creator* bless each of you and be with you as you undertake this new journey, dismissed."

The crowd erupted with applause and cheers. Aiden leaned over to Qendrin, Mariel, and Shendu and said, "Hey would you guys like to meet up in the Leisure Room at say....nine o' clock tonight?"

They nodded in agreement and each departed. Vyleah pulled Aiden aside. "So, how 'bout that game?" she said with a challenging smile. Aiden returned her smile and answered, "I'd love to."

He followed her back into the Main Chamber and they took the straight hallway to a set of lifts. They entered and she said, "Recreation Center." The lift rose up for a few moments then opened to a very large room spanning the width of the main academy building.

The room was filled with hundreds of floating chairs that had students reclined with strange headsets on. Each had their eyes closed but Aiden could tell they weren't sleeping.

"Let's start with something simple." Vyleah said and led him through the rows of chairs to a door in the back of the room. The door opened to a chamber resembling an airlock. She hit a button and Aiden felt that weightless sensation return and looked down to see himself floating. She hit another button and said,

"Zero-G training course, basic configuration, two players."

Aiden heard a hum from the other side of the door similar to the FPD when he made his steak. A moment later the door opened to a brilliant obstacle course with two tubes, one for each of them.

"Alright Aiden, this is a training course for Zero-G. We also use it for little races. Inside you will find various challenges that you must overcome. An experienced racer can do it in three to five minutes. Take your position over there and wait for the tone to sound."

He floated over and placed his hands on the starting grab spots. The first obstacle looked like a long tube he just had to fly down.

"Ready," he said. A few seconds later the starting tone rang. He pulled with all his might and began screaming down the tube, a bit faster than he intended to. A few times he had to put a hand out to try to steer himself back into the center, but then he started floating toward the other side.

The next obstacle soon approached; a square room with a zig-zag set of walls required the racer to kick off one wall to the next to get through. Aiden was able to do the first few with ease but he started to float to close to the ceiling and had to stop to right himself. He got back on track and finished the second room.

The third room had lots of spinning fans that each had four fan blades covered in pads spinning at various speeds. Throughout the room were small grab points that jetted out so that one could stop before flying into the next set of fans. Aiden did the first easily but the second was spinning a bit faster and he had to time it more carefully. He passed the next few then arrived at the fastest one. He pushed off too late and was slammed into the wall when the blade caught his foot and sent him spinning off into the next fan. That again sent him spinning and he was fortunate to bump into a wall. He struggled through the last and approached the fourth room.

This was an almost pitch black maze that took Aiden the better part of fifteen minutes to traverse. When he reached the end Vyleah was standing under a time of "*Four minutes, eight seconds*" and showing a victorious smile. Aiden's time was twenty-five minutes fifteen seconds.

"Well....could have been worse," she teased.

"Yeah yeah, when I have years of zero gravity experience, *then* we'll race again and see who wins." Aiden defended.

"I'm sure it won't take years, but keep practicing." She suggested. "I'm always here to accept a challenge."

They returned to the airlock and waited for the pressure to equalize. "So what are the floating chairs about?" Aiden asked.

"Those are the Neuro-Simulators," Vyleah explained as Aiden approached an empty set of chairs. "You can program anything you want in them and have an experience as close to reality as you want."

"That's what I'm talking about!" Aiden exclaimed. " Can we try those?!"

"Of course," she said lightly. "Do you have something in mind?

"Sophie, you said you downloaded all the games from Earth, right?" he queried.

"I have indeed, sir!" confirmed Sophie. "If you climb into the NS Chair I will interface with the computer and upload whatever you desire."

"Awesome," he said and looked back up. "Vyleah, can we have two-players on these too?"

"Yes we can," she answered with a nod.

They sat down in a pair of empty chairs and put their headsets on. Aiden immediately felt the strangest sensation he had ever experienced. His body became completely numb and was unable to move. His vision blurred and he felt like he was falling backward into darkness; a touch of nausea swam as the disorientation continued, but then he heard the familiar voice of Vyleah calling for him in the darkness.

"Aiden? Aiden you're going to have to talk with Sophie to load up the appropriate environments, otherwise your brain is going to have a hard time trying to keep track of what's going on, it needs a point of reference."

"Ok I'll try." He responded, still searching the darkness for the source of Vyleah's voice. "Sophie, can you access the game: Starship Creator 3?"

"Of course, sir. Would you like the program set to automatic or manual"

"Whats the difference?"

"Automatic means the basic programming of the original game is studied and exaggerated by the NS Chair's computer." Sophie lectured. "You will see everything from the original game but the computer will interpret the style of the scenery and function to allow a more complete experience. On manual mode you have to specify exactly what stays the same, and what is different. I would recommend automatic mode for now, sir."

"Ok let's do that," he agreed.

Aiden heard a tone confirming the selection and saw a speck of light in the distance. The speck rushed towards him with great speed and the next thing he knew, he was standing next to Vyleah wearing the uniforms of a *Starship Commander* from the game. They were standing in a room overlooking a hanger full of dozens of giant mechanical arms. Before them was a series of panels containing schematics for ship hulls, weapons, engines, and all other manner of customizable options.

"Wow...this is unbelievable." Aiden said as he ran his hands over the panels. "It's like we're *inside* the game. I never could have imagined technology would ever get this far."

Vyleah laughed, "Alight, so how do we play this?"

"Well, you have to pick a ship or create one from scratch," Aiden commented. "I'm going to use one I made a while ago."

"Okay," Vyleah replied. She studied the panels for a few moments then rapidly chose her options for each of the ship's systems. Down in the hanger the mechanical arms were fast at work bringing her creation to life. A short time later they finished and Aiden admired her design.

"Umm….gosh, you sure you haven't played this before?" he said suspiciously.

"Pretty sure," she shrugged. "But I've played similar games before."

"Alright hot shot, we'll bypass the tutorial then and get right to the flying trials." Aiden remarked with confidence.

They walked down into the hanger and climbed up into the cockpit of their ships. Aiden took a look around and quickly rememorized where all the controls were. After all it was a bit different sitting in the ship verses staring at it from a computer screen back home. He put his helmet on and pushed the *"Ship to Ship"* communications button.

"Check check, can you hear me?" his voice aired.

"Loud and clear," Vyleah answered.

"Alright just follow me out and we'll head to the advanced flight course."

"Can't wait."

Aiden started his engines and accelerated out of the hanger. The sensation was comparable to real flying; he could actually *feel* the vibration of the engine in his seat. He did a few barrel rolls and realized how easy it was to lose one's orientation.

"This should be interesting," he thought as they approached a series of small buoys with red beacons outlining the starting point.

"Ok so basically we're going to fly through an asteroid field towards a ringed planet," Aiden instructed. "Then we have to fly through a series of gates to successfully enter the atmosphere. They will lead us to a canyon we have to navigate through. The finish is at the end of the canyon."

"Sounds fun!" Vyleah commented.

They waited a few moments and the red beacons flashed green. Aiden fire-walled the throttle and shot forward. He checked over his left shoulder to try to spot Vyleah but couldn't see her. *"Poor thing, she probably forgot to switch off the take-off safety thrusters."*

"You looking for something back there?" Vyleah sounded through the radio.

"Wha-!" He shouted. She was on his right wing, easily keeping pace. "Oh no, just stretching."

"Right…" she mentioned in disbelief. "Stretching a back that doesn't really exist."

"Oh yeah, forgot." He said sheepishly.

She pulled forward as they entered the asteroid field. The thousands of rocks looked infinitely more vivid than when he played it on his computer. They approached a large chunk of rocks. She went high, Aiden rolled and ducked under. On the other side he noticed he was out front.

"Ooooo, Good move," she praised.He smiled and looked over his shoulder at her.

BANG!

He hit a basketball-sized rock and it skipped off his shields. A voice sounded and gave him a damage report,

"Shields are down to sixty-five percent, all systems functioning normal."

"*Damn it Aiden! Stay focused!*" he brooded and gripped the controls tighter.

They spent a few more minutes dodging rocks the size of cars and finally emerged to a clearing and saw the ringed planet rapidly growing larger. Once again he pushed his throttle to full, but Vyleah pulled in front and began to gain a larger lead.

Aiden reached over and activated the auxiliary boosters. The gap shrank again and he pulled past as they entered the first gate to begin insertion into the atmosphere. The nose of his ship began to glow bright as the friction met his shields. The voice sounded again,

"Reduce speed now, shields at twenty-three percent."

Aiden pulled the throttle all the way back and activated his speed brake. The glow was now covering his whole ship and he had to navigate using the radar screen.

"Shields down, hull integrity at ninety-one percent." said the voice.

At last the glow ceased and he could see the canyon; the new sensation of gravity pressed him into his seat. He followed the final gates and entered the canyon. He pushed his throttle up to sixty-five percent and began the first tight turn. The G-Forces smashed his body down, making him feel extremely heavy.

WHOOSH!

Vyleah screamed past and Aiden slammed his throttle forward again. A loud alarm blared and red lights flashed in the cockpit. His heart-rate doubled and the voice spoke,

"Speed brake failure! Critical damage has been sustained!"

"Son of a-!" Aiden cursed and hit the speed brake button and pulled up the *"Power Diversion"* screen. He transferred all remaining power from shields and weapons to his engines and rocketed after Vyleah.

A shortcut through a cave was coming up, that was his only hope now. They rounded another turn and Aiden saw it, the cave concealed behind a waterfall. She broke right and followed the canyon-- Aiden flew in and dodged the stalagmites jetting up from the ground. After a few seconds he saw the light at the end. He rushed out and checked his radar, Vyleah was right behind him! The finish line was just seconds away and he saw her begin to creep up again. He smacked his booster button once more and leaped forward one last time just as they crossed the finish.

"Whooo! I won!" Aiden shouted.

Vyleah laughed, "You sure did, that was so fun! Guess we'll have to do a rematch sometime!"

"Absolutely, anytime!" Aiden concurred. "Sophie can you get me out, think we're done for now."

"I'd be happy to sir!" Sophie complied.

Aiden felt himself being pulled back into darkness and thrown forward into his body. Everything was tingling as his senses rebooted; he opened his eyes and stood up, once again back in the recreation center. Vyleah did the same.

"I'm definitely gonna be visiting this place more often," he said passionately.

"Most people do, it is our most valuable asset in training. You can program scenarios that can help demonstrate the concepts and teach you how to use them." she replied. "I have to go give a debriefing to Tchyntar regarding today's orientation. I will see you tomorrow Aiden, good night," she said and gave him a hug.

"G'night!" he answered and walked back towards a lift. He checked his PCD display: "8:22". As he entered the Main Chamber on the way back to his room he saw Zayn standing with his arms behind his back, almost as if he had been waiting for him.

"Hello Aiden." Zayn addressed his pupil.

"Hi!" Aiden greeted back.

"So, what do you think?"

"This place is magnificent. I can hardly believe everything that's happened today."

"Let's take a quick walk, there's a few things I want you to know before you start tomorrow."

"Alright, But I asked the other First-Classes to meet me at nine in the leisure room."

"We'll be done by then. I'm glad you are getting to know them, each of you are part of the "Chosen Four". So the stronger you are as a team, the better example you will serve to the rest of the Academy."

"What do you mean chosen?"

"God gave you a unique set of circumstances to help you develop into the person you are today." Zayn said. "He does this with everyone. He gave you parents who love you and counsel you when you need help, and he led me to find you many years ago. He chose you to eventually train here. You, out of the billions of others on Earth. But I want you to be very careful about allowing those thoughts to corrupt your purpose. Remember that it does not make you better than those still there, or that you're better than the other classes here. Everyone has an equal opportunity to learn these things, but God must work with each individual's set of circumstances to bring about a successful relationship to Him, *The Beacon, and The Keeper.*"

Aiden let his words soak for a minute as they walked outside into the cool autumn night. He looked up and saw millions of stars splashed across the sky.

"Oh my...!" he breathed.

"Beautiful isn't it? The view from Earth would be a little better too if they fixed that pollution problem that's been increasing this last century," Zayn commented.

They walked towards the cliff overlooking the ocean and capitol city of Theron. Aiden turned and admired the

Academy, which had every surface lighted. He turned again and looked out toward the horizon; the city sparkled with brilliant colors and Aiden could see hundreds of ships flying around the skyscrapers. Every now and then a ship would dart away or arrive at the spaceport near the coast.

"Zayn?" Aiden inquired. "Vyleah spoke earlier about *The Keeper*. Could you maybe give me a simpler explanation?"

"Of course!" Zayn replied excitedly. "*The Keeper* is the infinite ocean of holy energy that saturates every inch of the universe. It existed with God before creation even began and it is his gift to all his creations."

"Okay...I get that, but she also talked about how we need to reconnect with it," Aiden acknowledged. "And once we do we can access tools such as being able to talk to anyone in any language. "

"Yes, in the Bible on Earth that was called the *Gift of Tongues*. But there are many others, healing, spiritual sight, teleportation, telepathy....those sorts of things."

Aiden felt that wave of confusion sweep through him again as he tried to comprehend the ideas of possibly learning how to teleport himself. It was at that time he looked at Zayn again since they had walked outside. His eyes were glowing!

"Woah! Do you wear some sort of... bio-luminescent contact lenses or something?" Aiden asked in surprise.

"What? Oh! You mean my eyes?" Zayn clarified.

"Yeah! What's the deal?"

"Okay, well you know that saying *"The eyes are the window to the soul."* Right?"

"Sure," Aiden nodded.

"Well, when one has the light of *The Keeper*, or Holy Spirit pouring into their soul it has the natural effect of making their eyes glow. This is a physical characteristic that you will notice until you learn to use your *Spiritual Sight.*"

"I... think I get it, but what is the difference between normal sight and *Spiritual Sight?*"

"When you learn to use it you will see creation the way *The Creator* does. Again this is difficult to explain unless you actually experience it for yourself."

"Whew, that's a whole lot to process."

"Just wait 'til tomorrow. You'll have a whole new set of ideas to ponder. But don't worry about that, just take everything day by day and you'll get through just fine." Zayn sat down and laid his back against the grass. Aiden did likewise. "I don't think I could ever get tired staring up there." Zayn commented in awe. "It's a bit different through when you actually start to explore all those tiny dots. You begin meeting people who could be at any one of them. A universe that was once full of mystery and loneliness suddenly has meaning."

"Zayn, what is the meaning of life?" Aiden asked with interest. It seemed like a perfectly acceptable question and he figured this was the person to finally give him an answer that made sense.

Zayn laughed, "You Earthlings love to debate that question. But in the end it comes down to one word."

"And that is?"

"Love."

"Love. That's it?" Aiden asked, he clearly was hoping for a different answer.

"No doubt you were expecting some hour-long explanation of the infinite complexities of our existence in a multi-dimensional state."

"Well, actually yeah," Aiden admitted.

"That is meaningless without love; without purpose, knowledge is wasted." Zayn resounded. "Love is the driving force of all things. But I guarantee you have not known love until you have experienced the love of *The Creator.* The great thing about love is that it can only spread and grow stronger when it is shared. That is the purpose of creation. God pours his love into his creations to strengthen it and make it greater."

"Wow, all this time I thought it was going to be something impossible to understand." Aiden said and looked back toward the sky.

"You'd be surprised how many answers are right in front of your face throughout your life, we see them and dismiss them." Zayn counseled. "Unfortunately our time must be cut short tonight. You have to go meet your classmates and I want you go get a good night's rest for tomorrow."

"Okay, thanks for the talk Zayn. See you tomorrow."Aiden got up and took one last look at the sky before heading back to the First Class Tower.

Chapter 8 - The Search for Answers

Aiden exited the lift of the First Class Tower and walked through the lobby into the leisure room. Seated around the fire pit were the three new recruits: Qendrin, Mariel, and Shendu. Aiden walked over and took a seat on one of the empty chairs. His attention was immediately drawn to the captivating performance of flames in the pit. The color of the fire would change every thirty seconds to something totally new and unique. First it was dark green, then bright purple, then blue. After a minute Aiden spoke, "Pretty cool fire, wonder how they do that."

"Nothing too special," Qendrin answered. "We have something just like it where I'm from. It's just a rotation of elements added to it so the flame changes."

"Interesting..." Aiden remarked. "So anyways, I wanted us to meet tonight cause I had a question about something. I was curious about why there are only four of us in the First-Class selection for this term. What have your mentors told you about being "chosen"?

Mariel spoke first, "I wasn't told exactly why I was chosen. My mentor told me that she was simply given my name and location by *The Creator*, and she found me when she followed his instructions. For whatever reason, I was picked out of the billions back on my world." Shendu nodded in silent agreement.

Qendrin, however, seemed to know exactly why he was picked, "It's no big secret for me, I have been reading about all this spiritual stuff for years. I've always suspected something like this would happen and sure enough, here I am. I wouldn't be surprised if I graduated in a few months."

"Graduate in a few months?" Aiden asked, "How long is it normally supposed to take?"

"As long as it needs to." Mariel replied. Shendu leaned forward and pressed a button on the firepit, making the flame rise higher. Then he said, "My mentor told me most First-Classes graduate anywhere from six months to a year."

"*A Year!*" Aiden pondered quietly the prospect of being away from Earth for a year. His friends, his family....his life – all were now a thing of the past. Zayn had warned him that this new life would be much different. And it wasn't like he didn't offer Aiden the option of refusing to come. Still Aiden wondered if the people from his formal life would even recognize him after his visit to Teros. Though he'd only been there a day he felt the amount of comfort he felt on Teros had come from decades of living there.

They all sat and stared at the fire for a few more minutes before they all agreed it would be best to retire for some rest before the first day of lessons. Aiden went back to his room and decided to take a shower before going to sleep. He unstrapped Sophie from his wrist and placed her on the desk then undressed and stepped in the shower; the water was hot and felt extremely comforting - after he was done the lasers perfectly dried him. He took one last look out his window and climbed in the ASDC; he pushed the *"Sleep"* mode button and felt himself float into the center of the capsule and became disoriented from the dark and silent atmosphere.

"This is a bit strange," he said and hit the *"Audio"* button. When the voice asked for his music preference he said, "Just something light and instrumental." A tone confirmed his request and a nice melody of harp and piano played quietly in the capsule. "That's better." After the initial strange feelings left him he fell into a deep sleep.

A tone sounded at eight o' clock exactly. Aiden exited the capsule and stretched his arms and gave a large yawn as he surveyed the beautiful view out his forty-ninth floor window. He put his uniform on and manifested a delicious toasted bagel with cream cheese in the FPD, followed by a glass of ice-cold apple juice. After a quick adjustment of his hair he was ready to go. He checked his PCD and noted the time, "*8:40*". "I guess we should head down there; Sophie, if you would be so kind as to point the way."

"Of course, sir!" She told him a few simple directions to get to his first class of the day: **Perception**. After a few minutes he was sitting in a large lecture hall with steep rows of seats; so steep, in fact, it required a small lift to reach each one. The room arched around a large display screen and floating platform containing a podium. From his estimates the room could hold nearly three-hundred people, although it appeared to only hold about two-hundred right now. Aiden took the lift to the middle level of desks and began to walk behind many students with hopeful glances at him to occupy the vacant seat near them. Sure enough he found that shy, pale boy with sunglasses: Kyon.

"So we meet again, mind if sit here?" Aiden said with a motion to the empty desk next to him.

"Of...Of Course." Kyon responded. He looked more nervous than ever. "So, Aiden, what do you think they're going to teach us."

"Not sure exactly, but I have a feeling we won't have to wait too must longer to find out." Aiden replied and pointed towards the bottom of the lecture hall. A young man with short ginger hair and a goatee took his place on the floating platform and the lights in the hall dimmed. A single light illuminated the instructor as the platform began to revolve slowly around the large display of an unknown symbol in the center of the room.

"Ladies and Gentlemen, welcome to your first lesson. My name is Pythas; as you are all new I will explain the purpose of this class. Perception; it is defined in a variety of ways, some say it is what you detect with your senses, others say it is your cognitive thoughts about the world around you. In short it is both. Perception is everything. It is what you see, hear, feel, taste, and smell. It is also what you think, what you believe, and any ideas you entertain about anything and everything. The focus for all of you will be to *change* your perceptions about everything you *think* you know about the universe. Are you all actually sitting here right now? Is what you're seeing, the same as everyone sitting next to you. It may surprise you all to know that how you see me right now has absolutely nothing to do with how I *actually* look. But I'm getting ahead of myself, when we get to that you will understand my meaning fully. Today we are going to start small." Pythas took a drink from a mug sitting on his podium and waited for the murmurs around the room to die down. Aiden noted the expressions of the students nearest him – a variety of confusion, boredom, and fascination. Pythas continued,

"We are going to discuss the role of material possessions and the value we place on these. Many of the planets you all come from have come to believe that life must be lived with *"things"*; that we *need* certain objects to survive from day to day. Now why is that I wonder? What is so important about possessing wealth, or vehicles, or anything? Well what I want you to learn is that these things aren't *necessary*. They are luxuries, nothing more. You can not define your life based off of what you have *gained*. When you die you don't take any of it with you. Even your body is a material possession. It won't last. You must all learn to rid yourselves of the value you assign your worldly belongings. They are not yours, you do not actually *own* them. If *The Creator* is responsible for making everything in the universe, then aren't all your possessions actually his? We are not worthy to take objects, and divide lands because essentially none of it belongs to us. You must show eternal gratitude to God because if He had not given *His* creations so many generous gifts, none of you would be here now."

Aiden's heart was racing, he had hated everything about his education at school for years. Being forced to learn things that didn't interest him was like being prodded with a hot iron poker every minute he sat and listened. This was by far the most interested he had ever been in hearing more of a lecture in a classroom setting. He sat up a bit straighter and waited for Pythas to continue.

"This brings me to another subtopic for today's lecture: The Body." Pythas began. "We are basically a collection of molecules held together in a number of organ systems, after we die there's nothing left but an empty shell. These bodies are merely *vessels* that hold our souls in a temporary state. You all have no idea the true awareness that exists outside of this fleshy-encasing." Aiden leaned to the edge of his chair. This was great, everything that Pythas was saying made Aiden believe the lesson was specifically designed for him.

"This is why it is impossible to create a clone of a *Child of God*. Scientifically it is perfectly possible to create a complete replica of a working, functioning body. But it will never be a person without the special ingredient: a Spirit. This is one thing that is given exclusively by *The Creator* to every one of us and cannot be created by artificial means. You all should take great pride in being given such a gift; it is a unique piece of *The Creator* himself, which lives deep within each of you. And when I say "within you" I cannot stress enough this has nothing to do with physical location. You may associate His residence within your heart but that is merely a physical manifestation of feeling love that comes from a place you *will* discover how to explore." Pythas continued to elaborate on the topics for another twenty minutes and Aiden knew that every soul sitting in that lecture hall was captivated by the newfound wealth of information flowing into them.

"...so in closing for today let me leave you with a profound attribute of perception. All it takes to change one's outlook of the world is the introduction of new knowledge. Just by hearing these concepts you have already begun to draw closer to a cognitive change. Later when you meet with your mentors, I encourage each of you to thoroughly discuss the finer points of today's lesson so that those perceptions embed deeper. Thank you all for listening, May *The Creator* bless you!"

As soon as Pythas left the podium a wave of conversation swept through the hall. It seemed Aiden was not the only one who was intrigued by the amazing lesson. He leaned over to Kyon, "Wow, great lecture huh?"

"Yeah...I feel kind of out of place." He answered.

"What do you mean?" Aiden questioned.

"It's just...I've never heard about any of this." Kyon said and looked down. "How can they expect me to believe such a radical change is possible?"

"My mentor told me something last night, "*Just take everything day by day and you'll be fine.*""

"I guess..." Kyon muttered and rose from his chair.

Aiden and Kyon walked back towards the Main Chamber and sat near a fountain, they had thirty minutes until their next class: **Fear**. Aiden continued the conversation they had been having while walking, "...so on Phobon they don't believe in *The Creator?*"

"This is all news to me," Kyon answered. "I think religion was sort of dismissed after my planet was nearly destroyed. Even now there are still very strong tensions between the remaining factions. I was never taught about anything regarding spirituality, and nobody ever spoke of it."

"Certainly you must have been curious about things though?" Aiden pressed. "Haven't you ever looked up at the stars and just watched?"

"Besides our sun we can't see any stars on Phobon, we were taught about our solar system and the fourteen other planets in it but by the time I was born the pollution and devastation from the last global war had damaged our atmosphere too greatly.

"Wow, and I thought things on Earth were bad." Aiden thought as he checked the time. "Let's get going, class starts in fifteen minutes."

Sophie gave directions and they followed. They took a lift down several levels underground and emerged into another lecture hall similar to the Perception one, but this one had steep edges that formed a triangle around the floating platform instead of the smooth rounded rows. It was very cold and very dark.

"I'm guessing we're in the right place," Aiden said and turned to see Kyon looking uneasy again. "Let's sit here."

Excerpt from TSA:SH

FEAR – 1

Everything that one has experienced in their life has happened for a reason and has led us to where we currently are. The good and the bad have both been tools to teach us and others. No matter where we get to in life, no matter how grave a situation may seem, it is critical to remember that we have the means available to us to take whichever road we want. If *The Creator* opens up an opportunity for something, and we make a mess of that opportunity, we must remain alert for the new paths our future will open up to us. The person who looks back on life and cannot point out any major regrets is someone who has seized their opportunities at the proper times, but greater still is the person who fails miserably over and over and comes to see the truth at last. Failure is nothing to fear or be ashamed of, it is when we are ruled by fear - and failure that we are not living as *The Creator* would have us.

They sat near the top and waited. And waited. And waited. Aiden was surprised how silent the room was, nobody dared speak. Then a sudden jolt of noise in the darkness made everyone jump in their seats. The teacher had entered and cleared his throat as he climbed to the podium; he was a shorter, older man with a scruffly white beard.

"Hello everyone, welcome to your first Fear lesson. My name Certus. I will not lie to you, in this class we will be discussing topics of a less than appealing nature. You will learn what true fear is, but fortunately, you will also learn how to deal with that fear and overcome it. So let's dive right in shall we?" A ripple of chills shot down Aiden's neck and he tried to look around to see the rest of the students but the intense darkness distorted the room too great to discern the reactions of the other cadets.

"**Fear is the absence of Faith**!" Certus said with a resounding echo. "It is the main cause of all the horrors many of you have heard about, maybe even witnessed first-hand. When you failed a test in school it wasn't because you didn't know the material, that may have contributed, but you were afraid of failure. This fear of failure wraps itself around us and chokes the very life out of us. It prevents you from boldly seeking new things and new ideas. It prevents you from speaking your mind about your true feelings in the presence of others. You fear judgment and thus refrain from sharing who you really are with the world. You learn about *The Creator* and you fear His disappointment in you. **BUT THIS DOES NOT HAVE TO BE SO**!"

Everyone jumped again in their seats. Aiden looked around and could barely distinguish a number people who were staring down at their laps, looking guilty and indeed, fearful. Certus continued.

"You do not need to live in fear! You can break free from these shackles and pierce the darkness to allow the light through. We will speak of the fear of failure again later this week. But now I wish to inform each of you of the invisible threat many of you have never known of. We have come to know them as *The Shadows*." Aiden looked around again and saw the level of fear in the room increasing by the second.

"...*The Shadows* are lightless beings that exist in contrary to *The Guardians*, which you will learn more of later. They were once luminous creatures that did the bidding of *The Creator*. But their leader, God's most beloved *Guardian*, decided to challenge God, and seize control of the universe for himself. We call him *Aphotician* – translated it means *The First who fell from the Light*." Aiden remembered a class he had taken in high school that talked about all the many names Satan had been given by cultures throughout history. Certus continued speaking,

"After his ploy failed he rallied others to his cause and they were exiled from *The Creator's* kingdom forever. Now their only purpose, their only motivation, is to see to it that every one of you share their fate. They know they cannot win, but they gain pleasure from causing even one *Child of God* to fail. They do not rest, they do not eat. They are completely invisible and silent, moving through darkness and causing evil in their wake. **But**!...We can combat them, which you will learn to do in your Defenses class. You will learn to see them, hear them, and abolish their presence. However, the threat of direct influence from them usually isn't the problem, they can influence and possess those creations which do not live within the light of *The Creator* and it is heartbreaking just how much they can destroy with a simple action."

"Now I know this is your first day, but you need to know what you're up against, it is a universal struggle and I'm sorry to be the one to say this, but everyone in this room is now a warrior on the front lines of this battle." Kyon sat up a bit straighter than usual and Aiden took note of the strange interest Kyon had taken at the word: warrior.

"Another topic of today is of the *Inner Shadow*. And first I will say this is not an outside entity living inside you. This is your conscious and unconscious self, absent of God's light. It is the voice in your head that guides your actions, but without guidance from *The Keeper,* this consciousness acts according to its own agenda. It is a fragile thing alone, vulnerable to influence from *Aphotician and his followers*. It will attempt to preserve itself if threatened - But it is not who you really are! Your lessons in your Practical Application class will test your will to wrestle this *Inner Shadow* to your control and allow *The Keeper* full access to your soul. But you must know that the darkness is in constant threat of resurfacing. From day to day, or situation to situation, it is a struggle you will have to learn on your own. But remember that together, we are most powerful, so ally yourselves with your peers and help one another. That is all for today, please meet with your mentors after lunch."

As the lights in the hall grew brighter Aiden looked around the room and saw every single face bearing a serious expression. He met Kyon's gaze and could almost feel the uneasiness radiating out from him. Aiden patted him on the shoulder, "Come on, let's get something to eat."

Excerpt from TSA:SH

LOVE – 1

Among the infinite possibilities that exist with *Spiritual Gifts* one must remember that those are useless without love; for it is the recognition of *The Creator and Beacon's* love that unlocks these abilities, freeing your soul from isolated numbness. Also remember that love always becomes stronger when you share it with others, you can offer them no greater gift because this is the greatest force in the universe. *The Creator* sent His Child, *The Beacon,* to pay the price of our sins in blood. He did this out of incalculable love for you – show your gratitude by showing the same love for Him and others.

Sophie told them the way to the Dining Hall. They took a lift up and emerged a moment later; this was a large round room on one of the upper floors of the main Academy tower. It had two decks that allowed everyone a view with their meal; it had a complete panoramic view of all angles from the Academy. In the center of the room were almost a hundred FPDs and many small hatches that Aiden assumed was the garbage disposal chute when several students tossed their dishes and leftovers in one.

"Sophie, isn't that a waste of dishes?" Aiden asked.

"Of course not, sir!" Sophie exclaimed. "Everything in the disposal center is broken down into individual atoms again and recycled into the FPDs so they can manifest new dishes."

"As always you Terosians seemed to have thought of everything." Aiden commented with a smile.

Sophie giggled, "Well, not *everything*, sir!"

Aiden thought of a delicious cheeseburger with grilled onions and a side of fries from his favorite burger restaurant. He followed it up with a root beer. He carried his tray over to a table facing the view of the ocean and *Stone Forest.* Kyon sat down without anything.

"You forgot to get food…." Aiden pointed out as he noticed the bare table sitting before Kyon.

"I'm not hungry, how could anyone eat at after hearing their entire world a lie." Kyon replied icily.

"Here…take mine." Aiden insisted, and slid the tray across.

"No Aiden, I'm not hungry." Kyon said, pushing the tray back.

"Just try it."

"I don't want to."

"Take one bite and I'll leave you alone." Aiden promised.

"Fine!" Kyon grabbed the cheeseburger and took a bite. "There! Are you Ha…" He continued chewing and the tense feelings began to slip away. He took a larger bite and swallowed. "Oh…what is this?!"

"I told ya! One sec…." Aiden manifested a duplicate meal and sat back down to enjoy his own.

"I haven't eaten since before I boarded the ship yesterday, but I can't believe how good this is." Kyon said, his mouth full.

"I know it's amazing right?" Aiden agreed and began to eat his own.

Kyon devoured the remains of his burger, then the fries, and chugged the root beer down.

"Geeze Kyon, If I had to guess you hadn't eaten for a week." Aiden himself had half a burger left. Kyon laughed, then resumed a slightly serious tone again.

"But back to what I was saying, doesn't it bother you hearing about having to *"be a warrior on the front lines"* and fight these *Shadows?"*

"Not really," Aiden said coolly with another bite.

"How can that be?" Kyon demanded, "Did you know about all this before?"

"Umm, bits and pieces," admitted Aiden. "On Earth we have a book called *The Bible* which sorta talks about the same things but in a bit different language. It's thousands of years old and gives a lot of history of the first civilizations on Earth and our fall from *The Creator's* kingdom. It also talks about our savior and Son of God, Jesus Christ - He pretty much gives the step-by-step guide to salvation."

"Wow, and does it mention *The Shadows?*" Kyon asked intrigued.

"On Earth we called them *Demons*, Or *Fallen Angels.*" Aiden clarified.

"Angels?"

"It's what we'll be taught are *The Guardians*," explained Aiden further.

"You already seem to know so much about all this, do all Earthlings?"

Aiden chuckled, "Oh hell no, I was one of the "weird" ones at my school. I never fit in and most people think believing in such things is crazy. I mean they believe in *The Creator*, as least some do, others believe in other religions, but anyway people have a really hard time taking in the full truth about things. I mean back on my planet we still think we're alone in the universe."

"Yeah so did us Phobonians." Kyon sympathized.

"Plus," Aiden added after a moment, "I play a lot of video games, so I've always kind of wanted to be a warrior."

"Video games?" Kyon asked looking positively lost.

"Yeah, you know, computer programs that are used for entertainment." Aiden elaborated.

"Never heard of them, I didn't have a computer back home."

"Oh, I'll show you them in the Recreation Center sometime." Aiden said with a last bite of his food.

Excerpt from TSA:SH

PERCEPTION – 1

We are only given the generous gifts of eternal life and spiritual gifts if we consciously decide to accept them. A gift may be received or rejected.

Sometimes people ask, "Why would God allow our family or friends to fall victim to illnesses or accidents?" It is not that God is solely responsible for those things to happen, he has allowed each of us to write our own destiny using this creative system he instilled when we ourselves were created. Sometimes we use the pain of a past event to become stronger or help others through the pain in their own lives.

They finished lunch and Aiden went to the Main Chamber to try to find Zayn for his first "in-depth study session". But he wasn't there, in fact, Aiden had no idea how Zayn seemed to show up at the perfect time when they met before.

"Sophie, can you tell me where Zayn is?" Aiden asked politely.

"I've been instructed to give you a message from him. Starting playback." Sophie answered and suddenly Zayn's voice emanated from Aiden's earpiece.

"Aiden, I trust your first day of lessons went well. But this day holds more potential for exploration should you choose to seek it. Let's call this a test of sorts. Our study time will not begin until you can find me. I won't be hiding too hard, but certainly out of sight. Do not be afraid to tread in unfamiliar places, you are welcome in all places on Teros. I want you to push the initial feelings you have aside and listen to the voice deep inside yourself. It will tell you how to find me. Use your instincts, and when you fail, remember that every failure is not actually failure; it is simply a solution to a different problem. Continue your search until you find the right solution, should you somehow not find me you will continue tomorrow, and the next day until you finally do.

Good luck Aiden, I have faith in you." Aiden stared at the screen for a few moments, blinking absentmindedly,

"Sophie, please tell me this is some sort of joke."

"I do not believe that was his intention, sir." She offered plainly.

"But he has been on Earth for a while; maybe he lost a few screws there." Aiden said in a less than joking tone.

Sophie giggled, "That is a possibility, sir, but nonetheless he has given you a task, and may I quote Tchyntar by saying "*...you are to follow the instructions of your mentors to the best of your ability, failure to do so has had fatal results in the past.*"

Aiden walked outside and looked around,

"*Great....just great.*" He gave a big sigh and began retracing his walk with Vyleah from yesterday. He checked the VHF (Vehicle Housing Facility) but couldn't find any trace of Zayn. He walked towards the *Stone Forest,*

"*Maybe he's in here.*" He walked for almost thirty minutes through the towering rocks before sitting down; he took off his left boot and rubbed the back of his heel.

"This is ridiculous, where does he get off testing me on my first day!" he hissed. Sophie's voice sounded from the PCD.

"Sir if I may be so bold, I do not believe he would have given you this task if he did not have confidence you could complete it."

"But he hardly knows me," Aiden whined, "How could he have such confidence?"

"Actually sir, he *does* know you," corrected Sophie. "He spent those all those years on Earth watching you. He was a neighbor of yours from the time you were born."

"What are you talking about?" he asked both angry and surprised. "How could've he have been a neighbor? I would have recognized him!"

"Would you sir? How often do you notice things unless you're looking for them?"

Aiden looked around and decided Zayn wasn't out in the stones. "Sophie, lead me back to the Academy. We'll check the gardens next."

Excerpt from TSA:SH

PRACTICAL APPLICATION – 1

Teleportation is a skill that would make the universe so much more convenient - luckily for you it exists! But just because it exists does not mean it is easy. The nature of *teleportation* carries more danger than most other skills you will use, this is because one can become lost in the vast expanse of space if their focus waivers. Now of course this applies to stellar distances, local *teleportation* from one point to another on a planet is much less dangerous, however people have unfortunately popped back into existence at the center of a planet's core. Become proficient in small steps, learn to travel from one side of a room to the next – then from one city to the next, continent, etc. Then you'll be ready to start exploring the cosmos!

To *teleport* one must have complete faith in *The Keeper* when they request a gateway to their destination – the gateway is only visible through *Spiritual Sight;* once it is fully formed one simply walks through it. Let your imagination create the most full picture you can of where you are going, and focus all your attention on that location. The smallest break in concentration can be dangerous, so only attempt to travel when you have preparation and few or no distractions.

He walked through the gardens and checked every hedge and walkway, but could not find Zayn. He walked back to the Academy and checked his classrooms, the coliseum, the recreation center, the leisure room, and finally ended up back in his room. His feet were killing him; after two hours of searching he had blisters the size of silver dollars on both feet and was no closer to finding his mentor.

"DAMN IT!" He yelled throwing one of his boots across the room. He walked over to his window, and crossed his arms while staring out at the city. He let his thoughts drift as hopelessness consumed him.

"What if you can't find him Aiden? What if it was wrong of him to bring you here? Maybe you don't have as much potential as they thought you did. If you don't find Zayn they might expel you. You would have to go back to Earth and lead a normal life - Away from all this, away from her. You two had started out so well, she seemed so interested in you. But that's ridiculous, you two could never be together, she's an alien for crying out loud. No, your life will be lived in regret for all you have lost, all you could have been but failed."

"Quiet! What are you talking about! You have seen more amazing things in one moment here than your entire

life! This is It, Aiden! God has answered your prayers, you are here and you aren't going anywhere! Look at that sky! Look at that city! Aren't these wonders enough to motivate you that this is real? Look at the water! It's beautiful! The red sand, the blue waves. Go Aiden, go and let the cool water ease your wounds. Go!!"

"Sophie, I think I'm gonna head down to the beach," he said with a deep breath. "Are there any shorts in my closet I can wear?"

"Yes of course, sir! Should be in the second drawer down on your left when you walk in the closet. There's also a sleeveless swim-shirt to keep you warm if you want to go for a dip."

Aiden unstrapped Sophie and placed her on the desk, then changed into a pair of black shorts with a blue stripe running down the side. He found the sleeveless shirt hanging with his spare uniforms. It was very form-fitting and warm. The material felt like shark skin. It too had blue stripes running down the sides.

Excerpt from TSA:SH

TECHNOLOGY – 1

Technology is a wonderful blessing – at least it starts that way. Millions of civilizations make the terrible mistake of taking a technology that begins as a means to ease the pain of everyday life, and then it transforms into a weapon, or something that can be used to promote one's status at the cost of others' suffering. Be responsible with new technologies – one bullet can change the galaxy forever.

He left his room and went down to the *Cliff-side Tram* Vyleah had showed him; it was a diagonal-shaped lift. He stepped in and it shot him down to the bottom. As he walked out the familiar spray of salty sea water tickled his face. He walked to the water and felt the sharp chill sting his damaged feet, but the pain ceased quickly and was replaced by a soothing tingle. He closed his eyes and felt at home once again, back in California, standing on the soft sand, connecting with the ocean; letting it wash away his unhappiness and fill him peace. Aiden stood for a few more minutes and began to walk down the shore towards a jetty in the distance. The waves were crashing hard against the rocks and splashing foam into the air. As he drew closer to the rocky peninsula he saw there was a shiny object on the end of it. He decided to investigate; so he walked all the way out, every now and then getting soaked with a series of large waves. As he approached the end he began to see the shape more clearly.

"Is that....no it couldn't be!" Aiden thought as he reached the object and picked it up. Within his grasp was a toy plane just like the one he had played with for most of his childhood. He turned it over and saw his six-year-old handwriting displaying his name under the wing. It was the very same plane from his childhood! What was it doing here?! Wave after wave of memories with the plane blazed through his mind; he held it up to his heart and closed his eyes as they began to well up with tears of joy.

"I see you have finally found me." Zayn said from behind Aiden. Aiden normally would have spun around in alert to a noise when he believed himself to be alone, but he thought about it for a moment before answering.

"I've never been alone.....Have I Zayn?" Aiden said and turned to see his mentor.

"No, you haven't. Not from the moment you were born, and you never will be. You have made me very proud today, you have exceeded my initial expectations and done in days what takes others months or years."

"And that is?"

"To trust *The Keeper* and allow him to guide you," said Zayn.

"I didn't do anything though, I found you by mistake," Aiden argued.

"Really? Because the way I see it, you were in a situation where you felt hopeless not to long ago, you were emotionally spent and physically too I see." Zayn said with a motion to Aiden's feet. "But what did you do? Why did you come down here to the water's edge? Think about it."

Aiden turned and looked back out at the ocean and pondered. How had he gotten here?

"I was in my room, I had just thrown my shoes across the room and I was staring out my window." Aiden recounted.

"And?" Zayn pressed lightly.

"I was thinking about how I had failed and how I would be expelled and sent back to Earth." Aiden admitted.

"Is that all?"

Aiden's thoughts about Vyleah flashed into his mind, about not being able to ever see her again. That smile, those eyes…. "Yeah, that's all."

Zayn continued, "But after those thoughts there was voice wasn't there?"

"A voice?" Aiden struggled to remember exactly what was going through his head, "A Voice! Yeah! Right after that it was as though someone else in my head was speaking in the same way I do when I'm thinking. I didn't realize it at the time because I thought I had done it by myself. But it told me to remember all the amazing things I've witnessed these past days and it drew my attention to the water. And for some reason I felt like the most important thing was to come down here."

"And so you did," Zayn said with a warm smile. "This is what it means to be guided by *The Keeper*. You don't need to understand why it suggests you to do something, just continue to learn to quiet your mind so you can better decipher what it is trying to tell you."

"Wow," Aiden sighed. "I would have never guessed it would be so simple."

"As I said," Zayn recited. "Many times we have the answers to things right in front of our noses, or in this case, right inside our heads. I will take this opportunity to also point out your encounter with your *Inner Shadow* during this exercise. That anger, that hopelessness, that fear was constantly sloshing in your mind as you went through this test. It was with you from the moment Sophie gave you the task, and it nearly led to you being defeated for today. But again I am very proud of you because you *let it go*. You let *The Keeper* get a foothold on your attention just long enough to lead you to me."

"But I don't understand," Aiden interjected. "You weren't here when I got here, just my plane was."

"Just because my body wasn't here doesn't mean I wasn't." Zayn replied nonchalantly. Aiden opened his mouth to ask about this but Zayn continued. "But that explanation is for when you get to that in your lectures. Trying to explain the finer points of quantum mechanics and its influence on the space/time continuum could take weeks so we'll get to that when we get to it."

They sat down and watched the waves roll in. Aiden looked back down to his plane. "Zayn how did this get here?

My brother threw it into a neighbor's yard when I was like six."

"That he did, fortunately that happened to my yard. It landed in a group of plants and I didn't find it for years until I did some changes to my backyard. I thought of giving it back to you but you had grown much older since then."

"How did you live near me this whole time and I never recognized you?"

"Well my home was on the hill above yours," Zayn explained. "Plus Children don't pay that much attention to their neighbors, or their parent's friends."

"Parent's friends? You know my parents?"

"Of course, I met them when I moved in; you hadn't been born yet."

"But they don't know….you know…that you're from Teros right?"

"I thought about telling them a few times. But it's always hard to know how someone would take the news, plus I didn't want them knowing so it could in turn influence how you grew up."

"So you've basically spent the last eighteen years waiting for me to be ready?"

"Precisely." Zayn said with a nod.

"Talk about your ultimate test of patience." Aiden mentioned as he looked back out to watch a bird dive into the ocean.

"I know, trust me it wasn't always easy. I had to remind myself every day, had to put complete faith that God knew what he was doing and here we are, taking the next step of our journey together."

"Thanks Zayn, this is definitely one of the most generous things anyone has ever done for me."

"No problem," Zayn replied and rose to his feet. "You could always get me a box of your mom's homemade cookies if you want to thank me." They shared a laugh and enjoyed the scenery a bit longer before heading back up the beach.

Chapter 9 - The Color Red

Zayn shared the lift with Aiden and parted ways. Aiden's feet were still bothering him, and he dreaded having to put his boots back on. He made his way back to the First-Class tower where Qendrin was just arriving from one of the lifts leading to the rooms.

"Hey Aiden, how was your first day? Mine was awesome, not too difficult, I knew most of the stuff they were talking about in the Technology lecture, the Defense class was entertaining though."

Aiden walked awkwardly as if he was trying to cross hot coals. "Not too bad actually, few hiccups this afternoon when my mentor, Zayn, decided to play hide and seek."

"Yeah….I haven't found my mine yet either. I heard they only do this with First-Classes and they almost always take about a week. I'm going back out to look again later, but I don't know where else he could be."

"I actually found mine about an hour ago….that's how I did this to my feet, I took a little hike through the *Stone Forest* while looking, but I ended up finding him down by the beach."

An unclear expression flashed over Qendrin's face for the slightest moment before he smiled and replied, "Oh, well, Great job! I'm heading up to dinner so I'll see you around."

"Ok, see ya." Aiden said with a grimace and approached the lifts.

Excerpt from TSA:SH

DEFENSES – 2

Be sure to use caution in deciding how best to use your spiritual gifts. Do not abuse *The Keeper's* trust by being selfish or bias with whom you choose to help. The nature of following *The Creator's* wishes will undoubtedly take you places or bring people across your path that are outside your comfort zone. Show everyone equal kindness, especially the people you have the hardest time interacting with for many times they are the ones in greatest need of our *Father's* love.

Aiden took the lift up to his room and changed back into his uniform. He tried to pad his heels with an extra pair of socks but as he slid one boot on he bit down on his lip hard and groaned with agony.

"Ow! Ah! Ouch!"

"Are you ok, sir?" Sophie asked, expressing a tone of concern.

"Yeah Sophie, just blisters on my feet," he assured her.

"Would you like me to notify a Medical CASE to help?"

"No thanks I should be alright." He replied. He stared at the other boot for a few minutes then closed his eyes tight and pulled it on. "Phew....Sophie can you send a message to Kyon?"

"What would you like to send, sir?"

"Just let him know I'm heading to the Dining Hall," he replied.

"Done, will that be all sir?" she inquired pleasingly.

"Yep, thanks."

Excerpt from TSA:SH

FEAR – 2

What is your greatest fear? Every now and then it is best to spend time evaluating what you worry about and what you fear the most; this allows *The Keeper* to provide guidance of how to deal with them. Strive to get to a place where you are no longer burdened by irrational cares for things that really aren't important.

Aiden arrived a few minutes later at the dining hall. It was more crowded than it had been at lunch, but he spotted Kyon sitting with Jaxcyn in a booth with a view of the city. He limped over to an FPD and recreated his favorite lasagna dish with a glass of cold milk, then joined them in the booth. Jaxcyn stood and greeted him with a handshake, "I guess we meet again sooner than expected!"

"Nice to see you again," Aiden greeted and gave a nod towards Kyon. "I thought it was a crazy coincidence when Kyon here told me you are his mentor."

"To the untrained it would seem like a coincidence," Jaxcyn instructed. "But to us there is no such thing as random, *The Creator* puts us exactly where we are supposed to be at just the right time."

"Well said," Aiden agreed. He began eating his meal and noticed Kyon's silence was for a reason. "How you doing over there Kyon? I see you still have your appetite."

Kyon was enjoying another meal of Cheeseburgers, fries, and soda. He looked up just long enough to acknowledge the comment with a smile before returning to his eating frenzy. Aiden had another bite of his mouth-watering lasagna and was savoring every moment of it.

The rest of dinner was spent chatting about various questions. Kyon continued to ask Jaxcyn about everything he could think of. Aiden finished his meal and excused himself; he told Kyon he'd meet him tomorrow for their Defenses class.

Excerpt from TSA:SH

LOVE - 2

Do not be afraid to tell someone, "I love you". In many of our cultures and societies it becomes a taboo to show open love for anyone other than our partner. This should not be! Begin to change this trend by making an agreement that will drive your ego to be less constricted by the cares of other's. Remember that it is not their judgment that matters – it is *The Creator's.*

He hobbled back to his room and delicately removed his boots once more; by some great misfortune his blisters were even worse. After he changed into his shorts, Sophie uploaded *Star Wars: The Empire Strikes Back* onto his computer screen. Aiden reclined in his hover chair and watched the words crawl upwards on the screen.

"This is what started it all Aiden, you would never have been so interested in all this weird stuff if you hadn't desired to learn about it as a kid. And look where it's led you! I bet my brothers would never poke fun at me if they saw me now. My brothers......My family......"

This was the first time he had spent time thinking of them since he had left. It's only been days but he felt like he'd been gone a month.

"I wonder if they're looking for me? I wonder if they think I'm dead? I could be here for a long time....maybe I shouldn't go back, it might be too painful for them if I keep leaving."

"You will go back."

"How the hell am I going to explain all this to them?"

"I will tell you what to say."

"What are they going to think about Zayn? He's been living near my family for years and they never had any idea.."

"That time will come, but for now just worry about your studies here. No good ever came from worrying about the future, or the past."

Excerpt from TSA:SH

PERCEPTION – 2

Be wary in your studies. Many may preach, "You yourself are a God!" but you must realize that this is another example of how Men can twist things to bring glory to himself, instead of to *The Creator*. We will never be a God, we may however, become more like God. Since we were created in His image, we must remember this more accurately means His *spiritual* image.

On the screen *Luke* had just crashed his snow speeder and was attempting to rescue his gunner. But suddenly a chime rang and Sophie notified him that someone was at the door. He walked over and the door opened to reveal Vyleah waiting with her arms behind her back. Her fiery hair curled every which way and her eyes....her eyes glowed brightly in the dimly lit hallway. Aiden's heart-rate doubled and he could already feel himself beginning to sweat.

"Hi there. Good to see you," he greeted.

"You as well!" She approached and gave him a hug. "I spoke with Zayn earlier this evening. He told me of your progress today, great job!"

"Oh, thanks." Aiden said sheepishly.

"You should be proud, no First-Class has ever passed the *Seeking Exercise* on the first day."

"I just got lucky, I had no idea he was going to be on the beach."

"Trust me, I should know," she smiled. "You would not have found him otherwise, he's great at hiding."

Aiden began to get confused again. "*How would she know?*" He thought, then decided to ask, "How long have you known Zayn?"

"All my life, of course, he's my older brother."

"Woah.....wait, what?" Aiden gasped.

"My older brother?" she repeated. "You know, the sibling born before you....."

"Why hadn't he ever mentioned it before? And how can he be so much older than you?"

"I don't know, maybe he didn't think it was relevant? And being thirty-nine years old is still very young for Terosians. We normally live just over three-hundred years."

"So….how old are you?" he asked, almost afraid of the answer.

"Me? I'm only nineteen." She replied lightly.

Aiden sat back down to absorb the new information. *"Great job Aiden, You've gone and formed a crush on your mentor's baby sister. But I didn't know! Well you do now so what are you going to do? You can't keep hanging out with her or Zayn would kill you. No…that's ridiculous, Zayn wouldn't kill anyone…..would he?"*

"Are you ok?" she asked and caught his gaze once more.

"Yeah! Sorry! Spaced out…."

"So anyway," she continued. "My brother told me you had a small incident concerning your feet today."

"Yeah they got a little screwed up while I was walking through the *Stone Forest*."

"I can help if you want…" she offered.

"Umm, ok?" Vyleah walked over to Aiden and took his hands in hers.

"Alright Aiden, I want you to close your eyes and try your hardest to imagine your wounds not hurting. Block out the pain. Try to not think about anything."

Aiden closed his eyes and tried to clear it, but his feelings about Vyleah kept resurfacing.

"Her hands are so soft. How am I supposed to concentrate. Ok ok, think about nothing, just count your breaths. Inhale...1.....Exhale.....Inhale....2......Exhale."

"Ok all done, you can open your eyes." Vyleah said suddenly.

"That's it?" he asked, he clearly thought whatever she was doing would take longer.

"That's it, have a look." Aiden looked down at his blistered heels but they were no longer blistered. The skin was just as new as it had been earlier that day.

"How did you....?!"

"Not too difficult to do, healing is just one of those tools we talked about, remember?" Vyleah answered. "You will learn to do it too, but just remember that many of the things you learn and experience on Teros do not reflect the actual amount of difficulty one would commonly experience when trying to perform such feats. You will be given a lot of help because you are surrounded by fellow practitioners; but when you are on your own your focus must be much stronger.

"I think I get it...."

"Excellent."

Excerpt from TSA:SH

PRACTICAL APPLICATION – 2

The first and most important tool one can learn to use is *prayer*. It is essential because it allows us to communicate with *The Creator and Keeper*. Learn to use your *Spiritual Voice* and learn to listen – then you will have the necessary skills to progress to more advanced concepts. *Meditation* is the next part of prayer, this requires you to quiet your mind and allow *The Keeper* to work within you. This is a very mysterious practice – it takes time to perfect and can sometimes be difficult to stay focused if/when the practitioner begins to experience strange phenomena. Initially one may see shapes, or shadowy scenes flash quickly then dissipate. One may also

---

hear things – voices of others connected to *The Keeper*, subconscious memories, or unidentifiable noises from somewhere in the universe. It is all very confusing at first so great **patience** is required as you develop.

They stood in an awkward silence for several moments before the sounds of *Chewbacca* growling in the background caught Vyleah's attention.

"Is this a movie from Earth?"

"Yeah, this is one of my favorites." Aiden admitted. "First movie that really got me interested in wanting to learn about the deeper aspects of life."

"Really? Mind if I stay for a bit and watch?" she asked.

"You've got to be kidding! Is she trying to torture me on purpose? What are the odds that a beautiful girl like her would want to stay and watch a movie like Star Wars."

"Sure," he responded.

"Great!" she added. "I've always wondered what my brother was watching on Earth all this time. He visited a few times a year and brought some of his favorite movies, music, and souvenirs back. Not to mention the stories but I was always curious to know first-hand."

"It's not that great, I mean, some of it is, sometimes...."

"Don't be modest, one should take pride in their home world," she suggested.

"I suppose," Aiden agreed. "There's just a lot that has happened that I'm not so proud of when it comes to people on Earth."

Just then a CASE opened the door and delivered a second hover chair. Aiden walked over to the FPD and created a bowl of buttered popcorn and a Sprite. After Vyleah sampled it and liked the taste he made another then they took their seats and Aiden restarted the movie. Every now and then he would glance over to see if she was enjoying it, to his surprise she looked extremely engaged in the viewing.

Excerpt from TSA:SH

TECHNOLOGY – 2

The ability to travel to distant worlds brings with it a huge responsibility. When you have the means of meeting

---

different civilizations you have the potential to change them and they have the potential to change you, for better or worse. Take caution to not provide a race of people with technology more advanced than they are capable of using. A savage and brutal group of people can bring greater destruction and darkness to the universe if they are not ready.

After the movie ended she proceeded to ask dozens of questions about everything she had seen. Being a knowledgeable fan he answered them as best he could. She finally gave a large yawn, (which Aiden of course copied since yawns seem to be contagious) and hugged him before leaving for bed.

"Thanks for letting me stay Aiden, I really enjoyed your movie."

"Anytime, you're always welcome," he added, instantly feeling like she would interpret that as meaning he was desperate for her to come by often.

"Thanks, good night!"

"G'night."

After she left Aiden walked around in an extremely cheerful mood and changed before climbing into the ASDC to sleep.

Excerpt from TSA:SH

DEFENSES – 3

Beware, Cadet! Every day will be a challenge, not only with your *Inner Shadow* but with the many *fallen ones* whose job it is to corrupt your purpose. They can appear in many forms and can be difficult to spot if one drops their guard. You must have constant vigilance to prepare your mind and soul to resist these beings and their deception. But you must never fear them, for through *The Creator, Beacon, and Keeper* you have authority to banish them from your presence.

He awoke at eight o' clock and followed his new routine of stretching and observing the view out his window. Today he made a plate of bacon and eggs with an iced coffee. While dressing he hummed a joyful tune and examined his heels again, noting their extremely normal appearance since yesterday. Sophie broke the silence while he put his boots on.

"In a good mood this morning, sir?"

"Very good mood Sophie, thank you for asking," he replied cheerfully.

"Kyon sent you a message, he says he'll meet you at eight-thirty in the Main Chamber at the fountain where you sat yesterday."

"Okay, thanks."

"My pleasure, sir!"

Aiden finished his last strip of bacon and styled his hair a little more fancy than the day before. He took the lifts down to the Main Chamber and met Kyon who was looking more confident than he had been after their first lessons.

Excerpt from TSA:SH

FEAR – 3

One of the greatest fears is that of death. It is our natural instinct to be afraid of what we are ignorant of. Some of us think we haven't lived a good enough life, some worry about the people they leave behind, and some fear the transition from this body to the next form. Try this – imagine a straight line; this represents your life so far. Now what comes to mind when you die? Did you imagine the line ending? Or did you

---

> imagine a gap forming and a new line starting? Both of these
> are misperceptions. Instead try to consider that there is no
> difference between this life and where we go when we
> transition. Being alive has nothing to do with this body, in
> fact, those who pass on are more alive than you are now.

"G'mornin' Kyon! Beautiful day isn't it?" Aiden greeted.

"Yeah….I guess…" They began walking towards the left hallway and took a lift up. "What are you so happy about?" He asked when Aiden's overly joyful mood continued.

"Oh nothing, Vyleah joined me for a movie last night."

"Who's Vyleah?" Kyon questioned, for Aiden had forgotten that Kyon had not met Vyleah or Zayn yet.

"She's the *orientation supervisor* for the First-Classes." Aiden explained.

"You're already trying to date a staff member?!"

"Psh! No! Well….I mean….I don't know," Aiden stumbled. "I suppose I would if she wanted to. But we just met so I don't think that's going to happen."

"Were you this popular with the ladies back on Earth?" Kyon said with a smile.

"Actually….no," Aiden replied. "Girls on Earth don't generally go for the nice guy, or one who likes to spend his free time playing computer games, or spending time talking about theories of the universe."

"Yeah, you're boring me already….." Kyon joked.

"Oh shut it!" Aiden scowled as Kyon broke a large mischievous grin. They entered a room with large windows on all sides and several hundred hovering NS Chairs just like the ones in the Recreation Center. Everyone was standing along the walls; Aiden saw that there were a number of Second-Class Alumni standing among them. Minutes later a very pretty woman about Zayn's age entered; she had straight, shoulder-length, black hair.

"Good morning class!" She said loudly. "Welcome to **Defenses**, I am your instructor, Rynoah (Ri-no-uh). If you would all take your seats, today's class with make use of the Neuro-Simulators." They all sat down and the disorientation filled Aiden's head as he fell backward into darkness; but this time he fell onto a grassy field surrounded by very old ruins. The crumbling stones looked like they once belonged to a temple of sorts; surrounding him were the two hundred other students; some looking a bit nauseous.

"Alright class! Everyone gather around here!" Rynoah gathered the students to a set of practice dummies.

"So today I want us to have a little fun just getting used to the NS Chairs and learning each of your backgrounds in defense. We will eventually move on to the *Spiritual Warfare* section of this class but we must first familiarize you with physical defense. This includes hand-to-hand combat and use of weapons and firearms. If you're all mastered in those you will hopefully have no trouble causing a city to burst into flames with a single thought when we learn spiritual combat." Aiden and Kyon looked at each other with mixed expressions.

"Just kidding..." she added. "I want each of you to practice the hand-to-hand exercises you know, or make use of the alumni students here to teach you some basics. I will make my way around and speak with each of you. Remember the safety rating for today is three so you will feel slight discomfort but not pain should you do something improperly. Let's get to it!"

Aiden knew his several years of martial arts would pay off someday; in middle-school he trained up to green belt. He normally would have stretched, but he remembered that this was a computer program and he wasn't going to injure a fake body. First he started with a few left jabs, then some stronger punches with his right hand. Next he worked on some kicks: front, side, back, and roundhouses. He was a little rusty but remembered the general guidelines for the moves. He looked over to his right, and to his disbelief saw Kyon giving his dummy some serious damage.

Excerpt from TSA:SH

LOVE – 3

Religion is a funny thing sometimes; on one hand it brings people hope and joy, and on the other hand it causes tension and can even lead to wars between peoples – both claiming they are in the right. So it is for this reason that it is sometimes best to take a step back and look at the bigger picture. It is not important who is right and who is wrong – the beliefs of a religion are essentially created to instruct its followers how to live a life that abides by the wishes of the object of their worship. But do not think that you must be a part of a religion to forge a deep and meaningful relationship with *The Creator*. No matter where you are in your journey, He is right there alongside you, waiting for you to seek Him.

Aiden continued on his dummy for a few more minutes before he heard Rynoah speak with Kyon. He kept exercising but listened to them talk. Apparently Kyon had extensive training in warfare, something Aiden would not have bet on in a million years. She told him to keep up the good work and approached him next.

"You are Aiden I presume?" she asked.

"Yes," he answered. "Nice to meet you."

"I see you have some fighting experience," she remarked.

"Oh, Yeah, just a little. I spent a few years doing martial arts and my step-father was in the military so he taught me about firearms when I was fairly young. And I play a lot of computer games so I've picked up some things there as well."

"Not bad," Rynoah commented. "Do you mind if I use you and Kyon over there for some demonstrations?"

"What kind of demonstrations?" Aiden asked suspiciously.

"Just for some sparing and to help a few of the less familiar students work on their technique."

"Yeah, sure." Aiden replied, with a touch of uncertainty. He walked over to Kyon after Rynoah had moved on. "Hey I heard you have a lot of training in this stuff." Kyon turned and addressed him with an aura of confidence Aiden was not used to associating with the shy boy he met on the ship.

"Yeah, unfortunately it's one of the few things they teach well on Phobon: Warfare. I think I was five the first time they put a gun in my hand and had me practice on targets."

"Five?" Aiden repeated. " Why so young?"

"Because everyone there has to be able to defend the city if another faction invades." Kyon explained.

"Are you telling me they expect a five year old boy to fight if your people get attacked." Aiden continued.

"They require anyone strong enough to hold a weapon to fight," Kyon answered and gave the dummy another swift punch. "Otherwise you are executed."

Aiden couldn't believe his ears, or at least, the artificial ones he was using in the NS Chair, but everything about Kyon and Phobon seemed so far opposite what he would have expected. *"Why was Kyon so afraid yesterday after the lecture about fear? Shouldn't he be a hardened soldier after growing up in a life like that?"*

Rynoah called from across the field. "Students please circle around the sparing ring, can I have Aiden and Kyon please come here?" They approached her and she gave them a brief lecture about the rules for sparing. "I'm going to turn off the pain suppressor for the NS Chair for you two so please go easy on each other."

Rynoah spoke to the rest of the class, "These two students will be sparing without the pain suppressors, I don't want you all to do this yet but I want you to see just how real this can be. Okay you two, take your positions."

Aiden stood with his left foot and hand forward and watched Kyon do the same. "Good luck," he said to him. Kyon nodded. Rynoah shouted, "BEGIN!" Kyon threw an aggressive right kick towards Aiden's head, but he ducked just in time. Aiden threw a right punch towards Kyon's chest, but was blocked. Kyon spun around behind Aiden and tried to get him in a head-lock. Aiden threw his elbow back hard and felt it collide with Kyon's ribs. They separated and resumed their stances, each waiting for the other to make a move. Aiden sprang forward and jabbed for Kyon's head, but it was deflected again and this time Kyon threw a punch to Aiden's ribs and swept out his leg causing him to fall with a thud. A few of the students watching gave cheers and some snickered. One last time they resumed their stances and waited for the other to strike. Kyon darted forward and threw a big right fist but Aiden ducked again and tossed Kyon over his back onto the ground. The crowd gave a collective, "Oooooo".

"STOP!" Rynoah called. "I now want you to use swords and you are going to attempt to disarm or yield your opponent. The pain suppressors will be set to shield you from feeling critical wounds only, that way you will have the surface trauma but nothing too excruciating."

They picked up a sword from the nearby rack and got in their stances for a fourth time. Aiden rubbed his false ribs for a moment. *"If that hurt I wonder what this is going to feel like,"* He thought as the anticipation began to build. Rynoah yelled once more, "BEGIN!"

Kyon, staying true to his former techniques, aggressively swung first. Aiden deflected his strike and tried to aim low to attempt to avoid causing him pain should he actually hit him. But Kyon blocked his attack as well and quickly flicked his sword back up catching Aiden's left shoulder with the tip of his blade. Aiden retreated back and kneeled in pain as he surveyed the laceration. Blood trickled out slowly but the pain began to numb as the adrenaline fueled him back to his feet.

Kyon called out, "Do you yield?"

"Not yet," Aiden replied and conjured a smile. They started again and this time Aiden was the aggressor. He calculated that Kyon wouldn't expect the less experienced to attack a more formidable opponent; the gamble paid off. Aiden swung right and spun left, as he came around behind Kyon the sword met its mark, cutting a diagonal line down his back. Kyon gave a loud grunt of pain. Aiden returned to his starting mark and reciprocated Kyon's offer, "Do you yield?"

Kyon returned a sporting smile as well and answered, "Not yet."

In the final round each were more cautious to avoid any more pain so they traded blows until at last Kyon made a more advanced maneuver that caused Aiden to lose his grip and drop the sword. Kyon held the point towards Aiden's neck and waited. Accepting his defeat Aiden smiled and said the magical words, "I yield."

The group of students gave a warm applause, Aiden walked over to Kyon afterward and gave him a pat on the back, "Great job man! Besides the agony of being cut with a sword that was actually pretty fun!"

"Thanks," he answered. "You're a great fighter."

"Me?" Aiden asked with a raised eyebrow. "Naw....Compared to you I'm hardly worthy to be called great."

Rynoah concluded the end of her lecture about the roles of physical combat and told the class to be ready to use firearms in a few days. As they awakened from the chairs and began to exit the room, Kyon and Aiden continued to receive recognition for their thrilling display in the virtual world. Aiden rubbed the areas where he had been injured; now they felt like distant memories of injuries, strange because they didn't actually happen, but he can still remember what it felt like.

Excerpt from TSA:SH

PERCEPTION – 3

Cadet, you must be wary of all that goes on around you that you cannot see. Do not fear these invisible activities, embrace the fact that there is more to this life and this universe than one can sense physically. Your *Spiritual Senses* are vast and much more complex than your physical abilities. You will *hear* the echoes of fellow children of *The Creator* from the greatest reaches of this universe; you will *feel* the joys and pains of the births and deaths of many worlds; and you will *see* the thousands of *Guardians* walking side by side with all of God's people.

They spent the break reliving the tale of their recent swashbuckling adventure. Kyon appeared to return to his normal shy self, although now Aiden knew if he ever had to fight, Kyon would be a worthy ally. They headed to the Vehicle Housing Facility for their first **Technology** lecture.

They descended into the hanger full of ships using the platform Vyleah had showed Aiden on his first day.

Following the other students, they entered a large circular room with nearly seventy-five circular tables, each with four chairs. Each chair had a touch screen and in the center of the table, a holographic emitter; the current hologram displayed very realistic model of a sleek delta-shaped craft with a pair of large engines that were built right into the wings. The cockpit was in the center and it too was built so that it rose out the delta shape of the fuselage but the aerodynamic properties remained optimal; the cockpit contained a single curved piece of glass to allow an unhindered panoramic view from within. Kyon and Aiden took a seat at one of the tables and were soon joined by two other second-class students.

One of them leaned in and spoke to Aiden, "So, is it true?" Aiden looked at Kyon for a moment and when he saw the same confused expression he responded,

"I'm sorry? Is what true?"

"Is it true you completed the *Seeker Exercise* in a single day?" asked the other second-class.

"Oh, yeah I guess, I kind of got lucky." Aiden said quietly. The second year elbowed his friend and laughed, "Ha! I told you it was true!"

Aiden, clearly puzzled, meant to question him further but just then a CASE robot the size of a normal human walked into the room and addressed the class in a male voice. "A very warm greetings to you class!"

Kyon and Aiden felt their mouths drop, looked at each other and said, "CLASS?"

The CASE walked toward the center of the room and continued, "I am the *Technical Operations Supervisor* here in the VHF and I assuming that by being here you all know this is your technology lecture. You may all call me *Toss* to keep things simple. In this class we will be discussing various technology systems from both primitive and advanced civilizations. As some of you may have already noticed the hologram in front of you, today we are looking at the *C.F.T.-One*. That is, *Cadet Flight Trainer, model One*. This is a short range, single seat scout vehicle, with twin combustion engines that utilize liquid fuel to burn and provide thrust. They have a maximum altitude of seventy thousand feet, so they are not space-worthy. They are unarmed and contain computer safety features that will override pilot control if you are in danger."

Toss continued to give a three-hour basic flight lecture. They learned how a jet engine works and about the properties of lift. They were all told to review the lecture notes over the next few days since they would be piloting their very own CFT-1s in a week. As they exited Kyon commented on the lecture,

"Bit soon to have us flying don't you think?" Aiden, who was extremely excited to get to the next technology lecture, couldn't wait.

"Are you kidding!?" Aiden exclaimed. "This is going to be fantastic, I've always wanted to be a real pilot. When I was younger my parents gave me a flight simulator game for my birthday. I learned it within a month, and when I was fifteen I got to go on a demo flight with an instructor in a real plane. He said I could easily pass the tests once I got some more actual flight time, but it was a bit too expensive at the time. I always promised myself I'd pick it up again though, someday..."

Kyon smiled, "Well I'm glad one of us is looking forward to it."

Excerpt from TSA:SH

PRACTICAL APPLICATION – 3

Telepathy is an extremely useful tool. One can speak with anyone, anywhere in the universe as if they were sitting right next to them. To perform this feat one needs to know who they want to speak with. A good recommendation for beginners is to start with someone physically seated next to them – the soul naturally radiates energy out and people pick up that energy subconsciously, allowing them to feel what one might be thinking. For longer distances it is also possible to imagine a picture of the galaxy, then as you focus your attention on one person *The Keeper* will connect the both of you; at this point the picture should begin to zoom in on that person's location. This way you can see and hear them, allowing for a more fulfilling conversation experience – however it must be noted that people can block their location. Advanced forms of this technique include the ability to send thoughts and feelings, as well as allow one person to see through another's eyes, but of course the person must be willing to accept this. Also the most proficient have been able to form imaginary "meetings" where numerous souls can meet in a telepathic location at once.

They had lunch in the Dining Hall again and parted ways for their one-on-one time with their mentors. A few minutes later Zayn met Aiden outside the *Stone Forest*.

"I see you're having a very good day," he began.

"How can you tell?" Aiden asked, but didn't deny his day was very enjoyable so far.

"I can see joy radiating from you," Zayn said with a piecing glance.

"You can?"

"Another benefit of using *Spiritual Sight*. One can see what emotional state others are in based off of the *aura* of light radiating off of them." Zayn explained.

"So what do I look like?"

"As with many spiritual concepts, it is hard to explain in words." Zayn thought for a moment then spoke again, "A person's aura is like a fingerprint, no two are the same. It is like a fire burning on the surface of one's true form, their soul. It contains a vast array of colors, some more prominent than others. And based on the current situation, that aura changes. Right now you are primarily emitting the color: red."

Aiden felt himself blush, he instantly tried to hide his feelings of fondness he had recently started to develop for Zayn's younger sister, Vyleah.

Zayn smiled and continued, "I also see that as soon as I said that, it switched to a much different color....that of someone who is trying to hide their emotions from others. And what might you be trying to hide from me?"

"I'm not trying to hide anything!" Aiden said, now feeling more defensive.

"You cannot fool me. Please, sit." Zayn said and took a seat.

Aiden joined him on a bench that overlooked the beach below. Zayn asked again, "As your mentor it is my responsibility to keep your best interests at hand. I also hope that you will come to trust that you can discuss absolutely anything with me, so let's have it..."

Aiden knew he had to speak about Vyleah but did not know quite how to bring the subject up, after a moment he finally spoke,

"Why didn't you tell me Vyleah was your sister?"

Zayn gave a large grin and leaned back, "So she spoke of me did she?"

"Yeah, she spoke of you. You're her older brother." Aiden frowned. "So why didn't I find out until last night?"

211

"Last night?" Zayn asked with curiosity.

"Yeah, we watched a movie in my room. She also healed my feet....But you're avoiding the question!" Aiden explained and felt like Zayn might get the wrong idea about having his sister over to visit so soon.

"Aiden relax, I understand I probably should have mentioned it before, and I apologize for that. I'm going to walk out on a limb here and guess you are beginning to have feelings for her?"

Aiden immediately looked back out towards the ocean, *"Oh no Aiden! He's on to you! Think up something quick! Deny it! Deny it!"* "No...." Aiden began to answer, "I mean, she's pretty, but....I....uh....don't....I mean I'm not trying to date her or anything...."

"Calm down! Calm down!" Zayn laughed, "Geeze you don't need to get all flustered. My dear sister is a grown woman, I would not dare interfere with her dating life. If you two want to hang out that's fine, I wish you all the success in trying to win her heart, but I will say this- I do not want anything to disrupt your studies here. You are a student first, girls are secondary."

Aiden felt his tension subside a bit then replied, "I know, as I said we just met and we just happened to hang out last night. But nothing happened....we just watched a movie. I swear. I promise nothing will get in the way of my training."

Zayn continued to laugh and gave Aiden a firm pat on the back, "I know, I have faith in you. Just be careful though, she's a sharp one, never met anyone quite like her."

After a few minutes they resumed their primary tasks of discussing the day's lessons. Aiden recounted his defenses lesson and sparing with Kyon. Afterwards he asked, "I'm curious about something..."

"Go on..." Zayn nodded.

"Why are we learning about fighting and firearms, and why do some ships have weapons on them?" Aiden asked.

"I assume you're under the impression that we are supposed to be a peaceful people?" Zayn interpreted.

"Exactly! Why all the training about warfare if we're supposed to be learning about harmony with *The Creator?*"

"You are forgetting that war has been an essential part of God's plan since the conflict with *Aphotician* began. As long as darkness has a hold on people, they will pose a threat to us all. We would all be destroyed if we had no way to defend ourselves. That's all we want to teach you, to defend yourself and others if you *need* to. Obviously you will learn to use a more diplomatic approach to avoid bloodshed, but there are people in this universe who are so lost there simply is no other way to reason with them."

"I guess that makes sense." Aiden responded. "Is it hard? To take a life?"

"I don't know, I've never had to, but I've spoken with others who have and they tell me it is never easy but again it is all perspective. If someone were trying to hurt me or my family though I don't think I would hesitate, and neither should you."

They concluded their discussion a while later and after a dinner with Kyon, Aiden returned to his room to get some rest. His third day would consist of lectures on **Love**, then **Practical Applications**. Aiden fell asleep that night and now faced a new challenge, perhaps even more difficult than learning to heal through supernatural means- trying to ask Vyleah out on a date.

Chapter 10 - The Sins of the Past

Aiden stirred violently while he slept; a number of disturbing images swept through his mind. He gave a large gasp and awoke to find himself in a cold sweat. He strained to remember the images but couldn't recall a single one. After exiting his ASDC he was surprised to see that the sun was just barely creeping up on a sky filled with dark rain clouds. Upon examining Sophie's display he learned it would be three hours until his *Love Lecture*. He showered and made French toast with sausage followed by a glass of orange juice. As he sat eating and staring out his window he could see a strong wind was blowing the trees far below; a light rain began to fall and Aiden found himself having a conversation with his head. *"Well this is going to be a gloomy day…."*

"I thought you liked the rain?"

"I do but it was something I dreamt about last night…."

"But you can't remember…"

"I know but I do remember the things I saw were so real, and apparently I didn't like it. I can't recall the last time I had a nightmare."

"Remember that book you read while doing your dream research? It said sometimes your subconscious creates dreams to help bring problems to your attention."

"Yeah I know, but this was different, they were things that couldn't have anything to do with repressed feelings about problems, I mean I don't have anything really bothering me at the moment."

"That's denial..."

"Oh shut up....But there was that other idea of course, that sometimes God gives people visions that are important."

"That's a thought; I mean he did do it before with Zayn and the lake."

"Well if it ends up to be the same thing I better ask Zayn about it."

Excerpt from TSA:SH

DEFENSES – 4

Also pertaining to Perception – You may find in your travels that you will come across individuals that show a certain distinction that makes them stand out among others. There are several variations of this. First you will see people like yourself, full of *The Keeper* and radiating with love; they too will notice you. Secondly you may come across *Guardians* in disguise; it is not uncommon for them to walk among us and to the untrained person, no one would ever know the difference. Lastly the *Shadows* retain the previously mentioned ability of *Guardians* to appear in physical form, but usually through possession of a host body – an unprotected soul they can use to accomplish their dark goals. You will know these *Shadows* if you are vigilant and you can dismiss them from their possession.

Aiden finished his breakfast and decided to put this extra time toward studying his technology lecture's extensive guide to safely operating the CFT-1. A couple hours later he put on his uniform and exited the First Class Tower to meet with Kyon on the way to their lecture. Kyon smiled unusually wide when he greeted him and spoke, "So.....you think of how you're going to ask out your instructor yet?"

"Hey!" Aiden gasped, "Keep your voice down! I've already told you, she's not my instructor, she was the *orientation supervisor.*"

"Whatever, she's still a staff member." Kyon rebutted.

"Well yeah, but it doesn't matter, Zayn already said he doesn't care if we hang out." Aiden remarked.

"Just as long as I get to be at your wedding, I wish you two a happy life together...." Kyon joked.

"Be quiet!" Aiden smacked Kyon as they entered the lecture hall. The walls were a bright maroon and the room was a similar type to the Perspective lecture hall, except it was completely circular. Just then Aiden's heart stopped, his mouth dried, and a chilling sweat made the hairs on his neck stand up. A familiar woman with fiery dark crimson hair took to the center podium and looked straight at him. "Good morning everyone! I hope you have been having a great week thus far! I would like to continue that today with an introductory lecture on Love. My name is Vyleah."

Kyon looked from Aiden to Vyleah several times before bursting out in laugher; this of course caused the entire room to look towards Aiden and Kyon. Aiden slammed his face into his desk and prayed he was dreaming. Vyleah floated over with her small podium and addressed the disturbance, "Aiden? Is there a problem over here?"

Kyon continued to giggle and Aiden elbowed him and and replied, "No, uh, Vyleah, everything's fine. My friend here, uh, Kyon was just remembering a joke I told him earlier."

"A joke huh?" Vyleah asked, "Well perhaps the rest of the class would like to hear it?"

"Maybe later….Please continue with the lecture." Aiden said, extremely short of breath.

"Very well…" Vyleah continued amidst a rumbling of whispers throughout the hall. She explained the purpose of learning the value of love. Meanwhile Kyon leaned back over and whispered, "So…..you were saying, She's *NOT* your instructor?" Aiden elbowed him again in the ribs and listened to the rest of the lecture. Vyleah had just started to speak about the main topics for the day, a topic she had briefly mentioned to Aiden during their walk,

"….Love is the most powerful force in the universe! It can withstand absolutely anything. When you share it with others it gains strength and spreads like a brush fire! The bond that forms between two people is inescapable! Have any of you ever heard about people who have sensed something had happened to one of their loved ones without any warning at all?" Several of the students muttered sounds of agreement.

"You see?" Vyleah continued. "And that isn't even Love in its most powerful form. Many of you have loved a woman or man, you have felt love for your family and friends, but so many of you have not experienced the Love of *The Creator*! I know this is hard to comprehend because you haven't developed that relationship with Him yet, but think about people who have children; the moment those parents see their child for the first time they feel something so powerful and intense no words can describe it! They also haven't had the chance to develop a personal relationship with the child, but they already feel overpowering love. Just like *The Creator*, he feels overpowering love for all His children and He is willing to show each of us how to do so as well if you open your hearts and minds to Him!"

Vyleah ended her lecture with some final words, "This week I want you to take notes on times you have felt a sensation of love and we'll share next class. We'll be meeting outside in the garden amphitheater. May *The Creator* love and bless each of you!"

Vyleah lowered her platform and exited. Aiden told Kyon to meet him outside while he spoke to her. "Good luck man!" Kyon shouted as Aiden descended to the bottom where Vyleah was taking a few notes on her computer clipboard. "Aiden!" She said with surprise, "So how'd I do? Don't be too harsh, It's only my first week of teaching."

"Oh, you did great!" Aiden quickly answered.

"Really? You're not just saying that?" She pressed with a sharp eye.

"Oh no! You were awesome, best lecture I've had yet." He said.

"Stop it! You'll make me blush." She giggled and brushed her hair back. The last of the students exited and Aiden wanted to take this opportunity to ask her out, but he couldn't sum up the courage. He ended up just looking extremely stupid by taking a deep breath and exhaling it.

"Are you ok?" She asked.

"Yeah fine," he said and started to feel his nervousness getting the best of him.

"So Aiden I've been meaning to ask, do you have any plans tonight?,"

"Uh.......no...." He automatically said, not realizing what was happening.

"Would you like to come to Zayn and my parent's house for dinner in Theron?" Aiden's brain didn't seem to be working properly, *"Did she just ask me out?"*

"He'd love to go!" Kyon suddenly shouted from up above where he'd been eavesdropping. Aiden and Vyleah both looked up to see Kyon's shadow running out the door. Aiden threw an expression of deep loathing and turned back to answer Vyleah. "Yes, yes I'd love to go...apparently." He said and looked back up towards Kyon's hiding spot.

"Excellent! I'll send the directions to your PCD. Just check out an AST (Autonomous Student Transport) in the Vehicle Housing Facility at around five o'clock and it will take you there. You're also welcome to bring your friend, Kyon? To come as well."

"Okay, thanks. See you then." Aiden concluded and left.

"See ya!" She waved and exited out a door behind her.

Kyon was waiting on a bench outside with a smug expression on his face. Aiden threw his arms up and vented, "What the hell was that?"

"What?" Kyon innocently defended.

"I was going to ask her out and you're up here shouting things!" Aiden said with more frustration.

"Sounds to me like she was doing the asking." Kyon started laughing again.

"Not cool dude! You can't mess with someone's conversation like that, it's Guy-Code!"

"Guy-Code? Whatever, so when are we going to dinner?"

"WE? Hell no! You're not going!" Aiden said a bit too loud. A pair of second-class girls turned to look at him before walking off briskly.

"Come on! She said I could go!" Kyon complained.

"Yeah, she said *I* could bring you, not you can invite yourself!" Aiden defended, lowering his voice.

"Okay...So can I go?" Kyon asked playfully.

"NO!" Aiden shouted once again.

"PLEASE!? Come on! I swear I won't make any more trouble! Listen! I want to go see Theron too! Look I'll leave right after dinner and you two can go have a nice night out on the town! PLEASE! PLEASE!"

"Alight! GEEZE!" Aiden agreed reluctantly.

Excerpt from TSA:SH

LOVE – 4

Many times we find it hard to be generous to others; this can be from greed, or perhaps a lack of abundance. To the greedy – remember that wealth is temporary, money can buy many things, but the more you have the more you rely on it to fulfill what only *The Creator* can provide. To the poor – remember that being generous has many variations; one can always donate time, advice, and service to others. What are your talents? Bring glory to *The Creator* by sharing them with the universe.

They took a lift to the top of one of the towers and emerged in a large circular room that was empty except for hundreds of cushy pads scattered everywhere. The room had large windows all around it and on the ceiling. Outside the weather had cleared for a brief time and the sun was peeking through from behind some large dark cumulous clouds. Their instructor had already arrived and was seated directly in the center of the room. Aiden was feeling bold after his successful conversation with Vyleah and approached the man. The man had a goatee and long brown hair just below his shoulders; he was sitting cross-legged with his eyes closed and appeared to be completely unaware of the hundreds watching him.

"Maybe we're just supposed to sit?" Aiden thought when the man didn't acknowledge him standing close-by. Aiden decided to sit on the pad near him and assume a similar cross-legged position and wait. The rest of the class followed suit and took a seat on the pads. Kyon sat next to Aiden and leaned over to whisper, "You think he's asleep?"

"No, he looks like he's meditating."

"You are correct, Aiden," said the man, eyes still closed. After a moment he opened them and spoke to the rest of the class. "My name is Arthanis, and while you are in this class you will do exactly as I request, nothing more, nothing less. You will not ask why, and you will not ask for clarification from a classmate, all questions will be directed to me. Do we have an understanding?" Everyone nodded in agreement and Arthanis continued.

"I realize that sounds like a harsh introduction but in this class you will be dealing with forces more powerful than any single person can possibly comprehend. We will be learning to take all lessons you have learned and applying that knowledge, hence, we call this your *Practical Applications* lecture, but make no mistake, this is a hands-on course and each of you are expected to try your best at all times. If you come to class and I feel you are in an unstable emotional state, I will kindly ask you to leave. Others have lost their lives because someone was "having a bad day.""

The tension in the room was almost palpable. All around people were wondering why they would be put in such a dangerous situation. Arthanis must have noticed this too and spoke again, "Do not worry yet though, today we are starting small. We will be learning *Meditative Prayer* today, the only difference from normal prayer being that you are completely stopping all you are doing to submit your time and focus to *The Creator*. Can someone tell me the purpose of prayer?" A Second-Class student a few feet away said, "To ask for things you want from *The Creator*?"

Arthanis smiled and responded, "Sometimes we do that but no. Anyone else?"

Aiden looked around and everyone seemed to want to avoid providing another wrong answer. The instructor smiled and spoke again, "No one? Very well I shall educate you. The purpose of prayer is to have a conversation with *The Creator*. But do not only pray for things you want, be humble. Share with Him your fears, your doubts, and your flaws. He will not judge you because He already knows, but He wants us to recognize our shortcomings so He can provide guidance. But go ahead, tell Him those things you want, and do not be afraid to ask for great things."

Arthanis looked around the room and made each student feel like he was addressing each one, "Another thing we so often overlook with prayer is that since it is a *conversation* with God the most important part is to *listen*. If we're constantly praying for answers but we do not quiet ourselves to hear the answers, the meaning is lost, isn't it?"

The class nodded in agreement and the instructor continued, "Now that you know about prayer we will discuss meditation. Meditation is a tool we can use to quiet ourselves and set our ego aside so we can get a clear signal from *The Keeper*. Look outside for example, you see the sunlight, yes?" Everyone nodded. Arthanis closed his eyes, held out his hand and an enormous cloud formed outside and blocked the sun. The class gasped, some in awe, others in fear.

"When those clouds gather you cannot see the light clearly, in essence we have poor reception. Those clouds are also in our minds blocking our ability to hear our *Father*, they could represent one of a billion things that are distracting us from being able to listen. So by using meditation, we are going to attempt to clear those clouds....." As he said this, he once again held out his hand and the cloud outside was miraculously pushed aside. "Everyone understand?" The students' mouths hung in disbelief.

Aiden's heart was racing and the story of *Jesus* calming the sea suddenly flashed into his head. Arthanis let the commotion die down; he then stood up and walked through the students and continued, "Alright I want everyone to sit comfortably and close your eyes. Sit quietly for as long as you can, ignore absolutely everything. Clear your mind of all questions, all thoughts. And eventually you may start to notice a change; but do not be afraid. You may perceive sights and sounds from *The Keeper*, you won't be able to control these just yet, but you may hear voices, or see people and places. It's possible these are people throughout the universe connected to The Keeper as well, or God may be guiding your experience directly. Using this method of meditation you may eventually learn to speak with others telepathically, but that's a different lesson. Today just clear your minds."

Aiden and Kyon exchanged awkward glances and began their meditation exercise. Aiden struggled for the better part of twenty minutes to stop his brain from bringing all manner of gibberish to his attention, but he couldn't seem to do it. After a few more minutes, Arthanis gently spoke,

"Okay, good job everyone. You may not feel like you made much progress but this is something that takes time to learn so don't be discouraged. Now let's implement prayer into the exercise. First you need to know *how to pray*. Many people do not understand that just speaking words or thoughts is enough, but you must speak using your *Spiritual Voice*. This is not as difficult to do as you may think. To use your soul's voice you must be sincere in what you're saying, the words must have feeling behind them. We are going to have one more thirty-minute session but this time I want you all to pray to *The Creator* for help in achieving some tangible evidence of *The Keeper's* presence within you. You may begin."

Aiden closed his eyes again and knew what he wanted to say but let it resonate within him for a moment. He let the desire to know *The Creator* more personally build and focused on his longing for the void in his life to be filled. When he felt he was ready he prayed,

"Father, I have seen first-hand that this is all real. I now know I no longer have to doubt that you can do great things through us and I wish to be a part of this much more magical world I have seen. Allow the Holy Spirit, or The Keeper to access my soul and allow you and I to have a conversation. Amen."

Somehow as he let the words flow through his thoughts he felt assured that God heard him and would provide an answer. For the next few minutes he struggled again to clear his thoughts. *"It didn't work….God didn't hear me…But I was so sure…."*

"It's ok, you don't need to worry about it. Hey! Remember your date with Vyleah is tomorrow! Cheer up!"

"That's true, she's so awesome."

230

"Yeah she is....plus you'll get to see Theron....wonder what kinds of things you'll learn."

"Yeah.....WAIT A SEC! I'm supposed to be clearing my head..."

"You don't need to, it's the first day, you gave it your best shot."

"Do not let your Inner Shadow win your attention. Focus Aiden!"

"There is was again, the voice! It's working! Come on Aiden, focus!"

He finally felt a sense of freedom and let his thoughts go. As he sat there he suddenly began to become aware of voices that were not his. They sounded like echoes from a distant place; they were barely audible and almost felt like a memory....but they couldn't be, because Aiden remembered that voices in his memories are usually recreated with his own voice. These were different....

"......They're Coming!............"

".....Help!...Someone!........"

".......No! Please!........"

"......AHHHH!........"

231

Aiden heard dozens of cries for help and could hear the screams of women and children. He also saw images every now and then. They were quick flashes of scenes; some were of explosions, some showed hundreds of people lying dead in the streets. It was a cold place; a place that despite having two suns in the sky was still very foggy and dark. He could see what looked like a mixture of snow and ash falling everywhere. Now he saw people walking in a large caravan away from a city that was in ruins. Two people, Aiden assumed were leaders, were arguing. "We must continue north!" The first said. "We can't! These people won't survive if we don't stop and rest!" The other shouted.

"I understand your concern but we have to keep moving while there's light, otherwise we won't find shelter and many will freeze during the night! Phobon's people must endure!"

Aiden's realization of what he had just witnessed suddenly hit him hard. He lost his concentration and the image, along with the voices, dissolved. One final voice echoed,

"Remember the sins of the past, they will be repeated!"

"Aiden! Hey Aiden! Are you alright? Arthanis come over here! Aiden won't wake up!" Kyon yelled over to the instructor.

By now the class had circled around Aiden and were chattering amongst one another, each one speculating what could have possibly happened for such a seemingly harmless exercise. Arthanis reached the center of the circle and quieted the class,

"Everyone calm down! He's fine! Just as you saw me earlier when you walked in, it is very easy to lose one's touch with the outside world when you give your complete attention to *The Creator*, but as these things sometimes last a varying amount of time I will ask that you all please move along and head to lunch."

The class did as he asked and began to exit, but their mutterings continued. Kyon waited outside the door and refused to leave until Aiden returned. Meanwhile Arthanis was patiently pacing around the prayer room. He was not worried, this was perfectly natural for every student he'd ever met, although he admitted to himself that only a few students had ever achieved this level of success on the first day of lectures. He walked over to the window and stared out at the thunderclouds in the distance.

The echoes from Aiden's vision faded away and he slowly opened his eyes, feeling like he had just awoken from a very long and deep sleep. He looked around the room and saw his instructor leaning against the window with his arms crossed.

"Welcome back, Aiden."

"What happened? Where is everyone?" Aiden asked, getting to his feet.

"They left a few minutes ago, I believe your friend is still waiting outside for you though."

"What happened?" Aiden followed up.

"I am confident you can find that answer yourself. You have greatly exceeded my expectations for someone just starting here at the Academy." Aiden recalled the disturbing scene he had witnessed, he wanted to ask about it but Arthanis spoke before he could,

"Aiden I must urge you to discuss your visions with your mentor, he will know how to best help you in determining their significance." Aiden nodded and turned to leave. Just before he reached the door Arthanis called out once more, "Oh and Cadet, I insist that you do not share what you experienced until told to do so." Aiden swallowed hard and nodded again. Outside, Kyon rushed to meet him.

"You alright? What happened?" he asked.

Aiden continued to walk towards the lift, "Nothing, it's fine, I'm fine."

"What are you talking about? I saw you, you wouldn't wake up. That's not fine, did you hear something? Or see something?"

"Yeah, I did, but it doesn't matter, let's just grab something to eat."

"Come on! What was it!" Kyon urged.

"Listen! I can't tell you until I've talked to Zayn. Okay? If he says it's ok to tell you then I will, but this is important, just don't worry about it, let's just go out tonight and have a fun time in the city."

Kyon sighed, "Alright, just as long as you promise to tell me if Zayn says it's okay."

"I promise," Aiden responded, but he couldn't imagine how he would explain what he saw.

Excerpt from TSA:SH

PERCEPTION – 4

What do you think happens after death? Did you have the illusion that you will be instantly rushed to your billion-dollar mansion waiting for you in heaven? Well it's time to change that thought because it's not all lounging around and partying. When you die you won't automatically be given all knowledge of the universe - that would not make much sense; we simply must continue to explore. As beings in this life we are given *The Creator's* Word through our written languages, but that Word is only the first chapter of an infinitely long story that is now available to you. The only catch is that you get to spend an eternity getting to know and understand that story. Don't worry though; you won't be given any written exams to test your comprehension of creation.

Little did Kyon know that Aiden did not think he would be having a fun time that evening. He barely touched his chicken sandwich during lunch and couldn't get the images and sounds of screaming Phobonians out of his head. Feeling that some fresh air would do wonders, he decided to walk down to the beach to try to clear his head, where to his surprise, Zayn was surfing some impressively-sized waves. Aiden stood perplexed at the odd scene before him. There, in bright yellow and orange board shorts, was his mentor, looking like any average beach-goer. He wanted to let the humor of the situation wipe away his worries but a fresh wave of images replayed in his mind, washing away all traces of his desire to laugh. A large wave slammed Zayn off his board and he decided to paddle back to shore to greet his pupil.

"Aiden, I just spoke with Arthanis about your successful lesson. You continue to amaze me, you may very well be our most distinguished graduate if you keep this up." Aiden did not respond. He was not sure how to bring up the topic of his visions, or if he even wanted to relive the horrors again. Zayn took his silence to mean just that and didn't press the subject, "It's alright, we don't have to talk about that today."

But Aiden finally spoke, "No...I do want to talk about it, but can I first ask why I would be shown something so horrible."

Zayn showed a slight hint of surprise, "What did you see?"

Aiden breathed hard recounted the vision as best he could, several times his throat tightened and he had to pause to regain himself, but when he had finished Zayn gave him a hug and gave his reply, "I'm so sorry, I understand why this would disturb you. We may not know the reasons why God shows us certain things."

"Is this what life is going to be like Zayn? Am I destined to have nightmares every time I close my eyes? Is that all this is out here?" Aiden could feel his blood boiling, he felt anger and betrayal for believing life would be so much better once he embarked on this journey. "For years I've wondered what mysteries awaited beyond the stars and am I supposed to accept that it's all just death and destruction?!" He turned and began to walk away.

"No, Aiden, Of course not, You must understand that..."

"LEAVE ME ALONE!" Aiden suddenly felt himself say, feeling that being alone would be the most comforting way to cope with his emotions.

"Aiden! Wait!" Zayn called, "**CADET SHEPHERD! YOU WILL TURN AND FACE ME AT ONCE!**"

Aiden froze in place, he'd never been yelled at like this before. And he would never have believed the thunderous voice that just ordered him to turn around could have come from Zayn.

Zayn spoke again, "THAT WAS AN ORDER, CADET!"

Aiden's eyes welled with tears and he turned to face his mentor. Zayn continued,

"Now as I was trying to say, You need to understand the very reason you are here. It's true that you may see much death throughout your career with us, that is part of living in the dark state the universe is in right now. But we are doing this to help the *other* people find God because otherwise they *will be lost*, you get it? They will miss out on the greatest gift ever given: an eternity to spend with our Creator.

Aiden took another deep breath and answered, "I get it....I'm sorry."

Zayn walked forward and put his hands on Aiden's shoulders,"It's alright; you've gone through a lot in a very short time. I want you to go back to your room and get ready for this evening, you've earned a night out."

Aiden nodded and answered, "Yes, sir." He wasn't even sure why he addressed him that way, ever since he met Zayn he had treated their relationship so much like a friendship that he forgot his role as a student. On the way back to his room he recounted the comments Zayn made about his vision; he had advised against telling Kyon until they had fully interpreted the meaning of the events witnessed, and the eerie warning, *"Remember the sins of the past, they will be repeated."*

Excerpt from TSA:SH

PRACTICAL APPLICATION – 4

Learning to use *Spiritual Sight* will provide the user to see many unseen things. For example, you will see *Guardians* (Angels) everywhere as bodies of light. They differ in appearance from others – should you look at another soul you will see a unique aura for each person. No two are alike and this aura will usually reflect the bearer's emotional state, unless they are consciously hiding it. It should also be known that this technique is very useful in the detection of *Shadows*. When looking at *Shadows* one will note a distinct lack of color and most are surrounded instead by a wispy dark fog – hence the name, *Shadows*.

This skill, just like the others, is acquired through request of *The Keeper*. It is most commonly used for brief periods of time rather than remaining active at all times.

After a quick shower he got dressed and spent extra time styling his hair, he definitely wanted to make a good first impression with Vyleah's parents. For now he decided to put the vision, and his feelings of uncertainty concerning his desire to continue learning these spiritual gifts, aside. At a quarter to five he met Kyon in the VHF to check out the Autonomous Student Transport. It looked like a sleek sports car from Earth, despite the fact that it floated without wheels. The interior contained four spacious seats and no steering mechanism. All the glass panels had built-in HUD displays that provided information on any object selected from the passenger's point of view.

They descended the thousand-foot hill and sped along a very beautifully decorated highway. It was lined with various trees and plants, (a far different look than Earth's asphalt and concrete), and they did not see very many cars on the road. They zoomed toward the towering buildings on the edge of the city and Aiden felt the last cares of his vision melt away as they were replaced with the awe of Theron. Despite a great number of vehicles parked in vast vertical parking garages, rising as tall as many other skyscrapers, people flooded the sidewalks and didn't mind walking. All of them looked pleasantly content, wherever their destination. Kyon pointed at a row of restaurants on their left and they both took note of the amazing amounts of variety of each. They also noted that many buildings had architecture much different from the Terosian style. They did not know that on Teros, hundreds of peoples from all across the galaxy had come to seek business opportunities, escape persecution, or start a new life; whatever the reason for their visits, Teros had become a great mixing bowl of cultures that spanned billions of light years.

Whenever someone arrived, they received a warm welcome and were given a PCD like Sophie so they could communicate and find anything they needed. Teros had a very odd economic structure. People did not have to pay for food, it was given freely. The same went for clothes and housing. However, most houses would share a similar format as Aiden's room back at the academy. It would usually be in one of the towering spires, and contain enough rooms for the number of occupants.

If people desired extra luxuries, they would have to be purchased with credit. A person accumulated credit based on their good deeds toward one another, providing service to others, really anything that contributed their time toward a meaningful effect on the people around them. So for example, if someone desired a custom flying vehicle, it may take weeks of charitable contributions before they could acquire one. The reason such an economy could function is for two main reasons: first, people took only what they needed, since there is no value of wealth on Teros people do not seek to have an abundance of anything. Secondly, many years ago the Terosian people had discovered a means of finding virtually unlimited resources.

Aiden and Kyon parked in an underground structure a few minutes later and took the lift to the one-hundred and twenty-sixth floor. When they emerged they were greeted by Vyleah and Zayn. They escorted them through the living room, common room, and finally to the kitchen. A man and woman were cooking on what looked like a stove top and laughing heartily. The man leaned in and offered her a passionate kiss, which she reciprocated.

"They're here!" Vyleah announced. The woman gave a gasp of pleasant shock and rushed over to greet them.

"Oh, Phealix! They're here. Stop cooking and greet our guests." The man put his spoon down and followed his wife. Vyleah continued introducing her parents as her mother swooped in and gave each an uncommonly strong hug.

"This is my mother, V'ena and my father Phealix." Her father also hugged both and wrapped an arm around his wife as Aiden and Kyon introduced themselves. V'ena's eyes were a piercing shade of violet and Phealix shared a brilliant blue set like his son, Zayn. Despite the fact that they were old enough to be grandparents, each looked no older than their mid-thirties.

"Vyleah would you be an angel and go grab your sister, she's been talking all day on her PCD to that boy.... What's his name, Orecus?" V'ena asked.

"Yeah I'll get her, come on guys." Vyleah said with a chuckle as she led them to a set of glass panels that retracted to allow passage to the balcony. The view was of course, breathtaking. Only a few buildings nearby rose as high but they had an unhindered view of the ocean and city around them. To his right Aiden saw a large hot tub, which he thought should have surprised him but somehow did not. To his left were lounge chairs and an umbrella made of materials to allow varying amounts of sunlight through. Seated on one of these chairs was Vyleah's fifteen-year-old sister, Shara.

"Mom says it's time to get off that thing and get ready for dinner," Vyleah proposed. Shara threw her a look of defiance, then turned and continued talking.

"Don't make me do it, Shara. Five….four…three….two…one." Vyleah leaned over and pushed the "End Call" button. To which her sister looked as though she'd had a bucket of icy water poured over her.

"You'd better pray he calls me back." Shara gritted through her teeth.

"You'd better pray, that your food's still warm by the time you change for dinner, now get." Vyleah rebutted, without skipping a beat.

They returned to the kitchen where Zayn and his parents where singing *"You've lost that lovin' feeling"*. As per Zayn's usual routine, he answered before Aiden could ask. "They just saw *Top Gun* last night; it's one of my favorites on Earth." He said as Aiden broke into a large smile.

"If you boys want to have a seat, food will be ready in a minute." V'ena suggested. Aiden and Kyon took their seats and Zayn brought a set of champagne glasses followed by a large bottle of vintage 2001 Dom Perignon. With a loud "*POP*" the cork shoot out and a stream of fizz trickled down the side of the bottle.

"Care for a little bubbly, Gentlemen?" Zayn asked with the bottle ready.

"Sure," they both answered.

"I am told this is especially good, so we shall see if it was worth the extra cost." Zayn added as he filled the rest of the glasses around the circular table.

Excerpt from TSA:SH

DEFENSES – 5

Many times we find that when someone wrongs us in a particular way - we feel it only fair to repay them. **Do not give into revenge**. It is not your place to judge those who do evil, unless you are without flaw. But since *The Beacons* are the only among us that have ever been perfect, let *Them* judge those wrongdoers. Practice this exercise to help ease these poisonous emotions – imagine your body filled with a dark vaporous fog, then watch the fog become displaced by a

---

white refreshing fog. Let the dark thoughts drift away from you and redirect your feelings elsewhere.

Aiden took a seat left of Kyon; Vyleah was seated across from Aiden, Zayn sat in between her and Shara, and Phealix sat to Aiden's left, across from his wife. The feast before them looked and smelled delicious. They said a prayer for the meal and began eating. A soothing melody of Lute and Cello resonated in the background and Aiden suddenly remembered a question he meant to ask when he had arrived,

"V'ena? How come you were cooking? I thought people here just use the Food Processing Devices to get meals."

"That's a fine question, dear. Most people here only use those to create the ingredients to cook the meal. Unless they can't cook, in which case they are very lucky to have one." She laughed, as did the rest of the table. Most of the meal was spent talking about the experiences Aiden had on Earth, Kyon disarmed most questions about himself and his past quickly.

"You just finished your primary education? Shara's got one more year before she graduates, then she starts secondary school.....Shara... please don't do that at the table, it's rude." Phealix said as Shara finished sending a text on her PCD.

"So, Aiden, How are your classes going? Zayn says you have the potential to get on the *Director's List of Most Distinguished Graduates.* Is that true?" V'ena asked.

"Oh, umm....I don't know, I'll leave it to him to make those kinds of judgements." He answered, and grabbed his glass of champagne.

"I bet it was a real shock to meet Vyleah again huh?" She continued.

"Again? What do you mean?" he asked, feeling like another mystery was about to hit him smack in the face.

"You don't remember? You two used to be best friends till you were about seven years old."

"Excuse me?" he gasped.

"On Earth, she lived with Zayn for about five years while Phealix and I were on an assignment for the Terosian High Council. We were able to come and visit a few times, you two were inseparable." Aiden felt the strong desire to drink his champagne faster to help slow his head from spinning off his shoulders. V'ena continued, "You remember the first time we were visiting, Phealix? Those two were in the backyard by the pool and Zayn was videotaping them." Phealix nodded in agreement and sipped his own glass. "Then you remember what they did next?" she asked, but Vyleah made a loud cough and groaned,

"Mom, please don't. "

"What do you mean? It's a funny story." She pressed. "You two wanted to go swimming so you both threw off your clothes and jumped in, naked!" She laughed.

Aiden had taken a swig of his champagne and with these words choked on it followed by an embarrassing few moments of coughing as he regained his breath. Zayn roared with laughter along with the rest of the table, all except Vyleah.

"Great job, Mom!" Vyleah was blushing a matching shade of red with her hair and quickly got up to put her dishes in the sink (which did not contain a faucet but a laser which vaporized the food instantly).

"I still have the tape, over here!" motioned Phealix and everyone stood up to take a seat in the living room, everyone but Aiden, who was still recovering from almost drowning.

"NO! DAD, COME ON! THIS ISN'T FUNNY!" Vyleah protested, running from the kitchen. But it was too late; the wall-sized screen was already replaying the scenes from a day long forgotten by Aiden. He recognized himself but Vyleah didn't have her red hair yet, instead a girl with long dark brown hair was running around, followed closely by the child version of him. A moment later they had stripped down and jumped in the pool- The laugher on the screen mimicked the laugher coming from the living room. Aiden turned and saw Vyleah chug almost a full glass of champagne and pour herself another. She then walked back outside where the sun was quickly falling behind the sea. Aiden followed, believing he'd use the opportunity to hide his own rosy-cheeked embarrassment.

Excerpt from TSA:SH

PERCEPTION - 5

Learn to change your weaknesses into strengths. This is easier said than done but that's why we have *The Keeper*. He is here to assist us with anything and everything.

Vyleah was leaning against the rail and looking out, Aiden walked up and did the same. She spoke first, "I'm so sorry, I meant to bring this up at some point, but you know Zayn and I didn't want to bombard you with all this your first week getting here, but I guess it's best you know."

"No, it's fine. Now that I think about it I actually do remember running around with a girl. And when I saw you the first day on the ship talking to Zayn I knew I had seen you from somewhere, but I couldn't remember ever seeing someone with red hair. But I definitely remember the eyes." He responded, and she looked over at him just over a foot away. Realizing he had just said something to put him in an awkwardly romantic sort of situation he quickly changed the subject and prayed Vyleah didn't catch it.

The door opened to admit Zayn and Shara, "So I think we're gonna jump in the hot tub, you guys wanna join? You can borrow a pair of board shorts from me, Aiden." Zayn asked.

"Uh, ok." Aiden nodded.

"Yeah I guess," Vyleah shrugged.

Shara gave a mischievous grin and added, "Or you guys don't need a swimsuit, you can just strip down here and go naked again!" Vyleah chased her into the house and Zayn giggled with a shake of his head.

Excerpt from TSA:SH

PRACTICAL APPLICATION – 5

Healing is among one of the noblest gifts *The Keeper* can distribute. Its potential ranges from the tiniest irritation of the body to resurrection of the dead. It must be noted; however, that acts of resurrection are always performed at the request of *The Creator* Himself – it is not for you to decide if a person is to return to this form of living.

Healing works on the principle of filling your soul full of *The Keeper*, then transferring that healing energy to the patient. If *healing* yourself, be sure to concentrate on what you want healed. When healing another, physical contact is recommended and both should concentrate on the location or ailment to be corrected. Technically, this feat could be used to constantly rejuvenate one's body, but this is unlikely since anyone who is able to heal through *The Keeper* will undoubtedly understand that it is not *The Creator's* wish for us to live past a certain point.

As an additional note, should you be in the presence of a

healer at work, use *Spiritual Sight* to perceive one of the universe's most beautiful phenomena.

Kyon and Aiden sat for a few minutes in the extremely soothing water before Vyleah and Shara emerged from their bedrooms. Shara sported a conservative swimsuit Aiden believed to be more traditional of Terosian women, Vyleah however, as if trying to torture him without mercy, fashioned a revealing bikini that Shara was quick to criticize,

"You might as well have just gone naked! Zayn, why did you get that for her?" She blabbed.

"I think it looks nice, you're just not used to it, Shara. Everyone wears them back on Earth." Zayn commented.

They spent nearly an hour in the steamy water, sipping a second bottle of champagne and admiring the glowing city all around. Zayn dried off and went inside to talk with his parents. Shara had gone back to her room to continue her conversation with Orecus. Aiden was watching a particularly large spacecraft taking off from a nearby rooftop when Vyleah splashed him.

"Hey! So what do you guys wanna do tonight? Watch a movie? Go for a walk?" She began but Kyon butted in,

"Are there any clubs? Where we can have drinks and hang out?"

"Yeah, is that what we want to do?" She looked at Aiden.

"Fine with me," he responded, figuring anything would be interesting…after all, he was billions of miles away from Earth sitting in a hot tub. *"I'm just gonna go with the flow tonight."*

Ten minutes later he and Kyon were back in their uniforms and Aiden was re-styling his hair, which wasn't cooperating. He decided to shake it and accept the result. Vyleah was stunning. She wore a beautiful black mini dress and high heels and around her neck was a necklace holding the academy's symbol in silver. Kyon and Aiden said goodbye to her parents and thanked them for their hospitality. Zayn gave him a nod that felt to Aiden like he was saying *"Have fun, but not TOO much fun."* Aiden returned the nod and followed them out to the lift. The Automated Student Transport vehicle took them a few minutes away to a cozy, curved building that contained three floors. Bright lights and fog were pouring out of the entrance, which had a line halfway down the street.

"Geeze this looks just like back home." Aiden thought. As Vyleah approached the bouncer she didn't have to say anything, he let them in, to the moans of many disappointed people still waiting in line. The inside was meant to look like an industrial factory of sorts, or perhaps that is what the building once was. A conveyor belt ran through the middle where people were laying down to be *rolled* through a gauntlet of alcohol.

"SO, UH, I GUESS TEROSIANS LIKE TO PARTY?!" Aiden tried to shout at Vyleah over the blaring music.

"NOT USUALLY THAT HARD! MOST OF THESE PEOPLE ARE FROM OTHER WORLDS. YOU NOTICE THE EYES?" she shouted back.

Aiden looked around and noticed indeed that the majority of people were lacking the distinctive glow that Vyleah had in her deep indigo eyes. Kyon had already vanished into the crowd and Aiden would have looked for him but it was far too crowded. He followed Vyleah to a lounge seating area near a bar and she ordered them drinks.

"HERE! YOU'LL LOVE THIS!" she yelled and handed him a glass of swirling red, yellow and orange liquid. He took a swig and felt as though he might flip inside out with a burning citrusy after-taste. "IT'S CALLED A *SUPERNOVA*! DON'T WORRY IT'S SUPPOSED TO FEEL LIKE THAT. TRY THIS ONE!" She handed him another that was crystal blue. This one tasted like having your head slammed into a bucket of arctic-cold water, with a sweet and sour after-taste. "THAT ONE'S CALLED *THE SEAS OF TORON*, IT'S ONE OF OUR MOONS, MADE OF MOSTLY ICE AND WATER."

He decided to stick with the second drink. They sat and watched the crowd, every now and then looking around for Kyon and drank several more *Seas of Toron*. At long last Aiden spotted him....in line for the conveyor belt.

"OH MY GOSH, LOOK!" he laughed and pointed for Vyleah to see. She turned just in time to see Kyon roll along the belt to the screams of approving partiers. A slow song began playing and after consuming a great amount of *liquid courage* Aiden got to his feet and took Vyleah's hand, "May I have this dance?" he asked confidently.

"Yes, you may." She smiled.

They danced for several songs, Aiden could feel eyes on him from all around but he did not care. After all, he had earned this night and he was fully intent on enjoying it. After the third song Vyleah leaned in and whispered, "Thank you the dance, Cadet. I'll see you tomorrow," and kissed him on the cheek before exiting. His spirits soared through the roof, he looked all over to find Kyon and tell him the news.

Excerpt from TSA:SH

PERCEPTION – 6

Pertaining to the mention of unseen forces only available through *Spiritual Sight,* the *Guardian* is the loyal servant of *The Creator* that serves as his messenger, warrior, and your protector. These are the untainted forms of *Shadows*, the one's that did not rebel against *The Creator* and serve Him without question. *Guardians* are tremendously complex to understand. They are individuals but do not necessarily act according to their own agenda, in essence they are permanently linked to *The Keeper* and receive all instructions from Him. There may be times when your *Guardian* may appear to you and offer you council, physical aid, etc. Take comfort that you have a powerful ally at your side at all times, Cadet.

It took the better part of thirty minutes before Aiden heard a pair of people yelling at a bar nearby. He pushed through the crowd to find Kyon and Qendrin on the verge of throwing fists. The music ceased and Qendrin saw Aiden burst into the ring around them. "Ah ha! Here he is now! The sidekick of this Third-Class piece of garbage!" Slurred Qendrin.

"Woah, what's going on?" Aiden asked, wondering what could have possibly provoked such a cold insult from his fellow First-Class.

"Nothing's going on, I was just having a friendly chat with your buddy here about the difference between him and I are. I advised him that he should really listen to his superiors, after all, he listens to you." Qendrin hiccupped.

"Superiors? What are you talking about? We're all the same. We're no better than any other class!" Aiden defended.

"Well if that's how you feel perhaps you should be in Third-Class as well." Qendrin snarled.

"You will never be as good as Aiden!" Kyon shouted and waved a finger at Qendrin. "He finished the *Seeker Exercise* in less than a day! Aren't you still looking for your mentor? ....And he saw a vision today, what have you seen, besides the dust of being left in second place?" It was with this insult, and the resulting laugher of Kyon and the crowd that Qendrin's fist slammed into Kyon's temple and sent him to the ground in a spinning disorientation. Aiden rushed to help his friend up and carry him out. Considering if he should return the favor, but the small voice inside him urged against it.

"Don't do it Aiden, there will be another day." Heeding the advice he hoisted the disoriented Kyon up and a fellow Third-Class, who was also at the club, helped shuffle him towards the door. Qendrin's taunts continued until he finally shouted something that made Aiden stop in his tracks.

"What's the matter, Earthling? In a hurry to go get some one-on-one lessons with our Love Teacher? She is terribly attractive, perhaps she'll tutor me as well." With this Aiden spun around and cracked Qendrin across the chin, breaking his jaw and sending him unconscious onto the bar. The crowd gave one last jolt of gasps before breaking into applause and allowing Aiden to carry Kyon outside to their car. The drive back was uneventful, Kyon was passed out in the back seat and Aiden was tending to his hand, which was swelling up and almost certainly had one or two broken knuckles.

When they arrived back in the VHF, Aiden asked Sophie for some way of helping carry Kyon back to the

Third-Class tower. She called a human-sized CASE robot to assist him, when it arrived Kyon was thrown over its shoulder and it led the way. The leisure room was nearly identical to the First-Class tower, with the exception of everything being red instead of blue. Feeling it would be frightening for anyone to wake up in a capsule under these conditions Aiden opted to leave Kyon on one of the comfortable couches. He returned to his own quarters and fell asleep in no time at all.

Chapter 12 - Zayn's Task

Aiden's capsule opened and he groggily climbed out
and headed for the restroom. Two of his knuckles were
extremely swollen and the pain was excruciating. He rinsed
off the staleness of the night before and dressed in a fresh
uniform from his closet. After making a cup of coffee he was
surprised to hear a chime come from his door. As it opened
his eyes met with his mentor's.

"Morning, Zayn. Didn't expect to see you so early.
You want a cup of coffee?" Aiden asked, trying to sound as
innocent as possible.

"No, I'm afraid our presence has been requested by
the Director of the Academy." Zayn replied with a burning
seriousness. "Come with me."

Aiden followed his mentor to a set of lifts that lead
to the main tower; they took one to the very top and
emerged at a room with a large crescent-shaped table and
thirteen people sitting around it. In the middle, sat Tchyntar.

"Cadet Shepherd, perhaps you would be kind enough
to shed some light as to why one of my First-Classes woke
up this morning in the infirmary with a broken jaw and

covered in blood." Tchyntar said calmly. Aiden took a deep breath and recounted his tale of the previous night,

"Well, we got to the club just after eight..." Aiden began. " Vyleah and I lost Kyon within a few minutes and we spent most of the time just sitting at the lounge and had a few drinks..." He then thought if he should tell them about his dance with Vyleah and her stolen kiss, but quickly decided to skip ahead. "After Vyleah left I heard Kyon and Qendrin arguing near the bar. I went over to break them up and Qendrin hit Kyon after Kyon insulted him. I picked Kyon up and tried to walk away but Qendrin kept trying to provoke me. So I...."

"You indulged those feelings...." Tchyntar said, interrupting him.

"Yes, but I only did because he said something disrespectful about Vyleah." Aiden defended.

"Very well, we will take your statement into consideration. Please wait outside while we determine the course of action to take." Tchyntar responded, still maintaining a curiously cool tone. Out in the hallway Zayn spoke,

"I hope you realize the seriousness of the situation. An attack on a student most always results in expulsion."

Aiden said nothing. Fear had tightened its icy fingers around his throat, allowing him just enough mercy to continue taking shallow breaths. A minute later he shifted his hand in a manner that made him grunt with a fresh wave of searing pain.

"Is there something you can do to fix this?" Aiden asked, raising his wounded hand.

"Yes," Zayn nodded, then turned away again.

"Ummm....so will you?" Aiden asked again, wondering why he was being ignored.

"No, your price for your hot-headedness is that hand. For now you'll just have to deal with it." Zayn replied, sounding bored.

PRACTICAL APPLICATION – 7

Prophecy is a very unique skill. It usually occurs involuntarily during meditation and possibly during sleep – also, it can carry several meanings that may include literal or symbol contexts. To experience a *prophecy* almost always means *The Creator* is showing you the future for the sole purpose of

---

changing it. This is why one will notice that certain elements are always left out of a vision – particularly the consequences of one's actions; this is because we will not be able to see the results of a choice we have not made yet. Do not fear what you do not know, for no matter what the future holds, *The Keeper* will be with you to guide you through it.

The worst thing one can do is waste a *prophecy*; they contain critical pieces of information that many people go their whole lives without experiencing.

After ten more minutes the door to the council chamber opened and allowed them to enter once more.

"Cadet Shepherd, I trust your mentor has informed you of the consequences of an action such as this. We cannot allow students to harm each other. We also cannot allow our Cadets to act in such a barbaric manner in full view of the public, as a member of this academy you are its representative not only while you are here, but out there. We have decided, though, on this particular case, that you were indeed provoked, and since Zayn has reported your vision yesterday afternoon, you have given this council a most important piece of information regarding the planet known as Phobon; we have decided to close this matter and none of the participants will receive disciplinary action."

Aiden's heartbeat finally returned, "Thank you, all." He managed to utter.

"You also acted admirably for choosing to help your friend and attempt to leave, before being provoked back. All things considered we feel that you are a special case that deserves special attention. In your first days of being exposed to all of this you have shown a tremendous talent in all fields that required you to invite *The Keeper* into yourself to accomplish your goal. This is something no other student has accomplished so quickly, and as such, we believe you can reach the more advanced levels of training ahead of the others. You will be given the *Enhanced Edition* of *The Terosian Academy Student Handbook*. Contained within are much greater details as how one would be able to use the multitude of gifts accessible through *The Keeper*. But a word of caution, to be exposed to such advanced material can be dangerous. You must read carefully and work harder than anyone else here. You will have private tutoring lessons with each of your instructors to help you grasp these higher techniques. Have a good day Cadet, May *the Creator* bless you and be with you at all times." Tchyntar said with a bow.

"Um, th-thanks?" Aiden spurted, completely unsure what just happened. One moment he was contemplating how horrible his life would be after experiencing all this then being forced to return to Earth and try to lead a normal life. Now he was being offered supplementary instruction to learn more advanced knowledge. He turned with Zayn and departed. On the walk back Aiden asked what he hadn't dared to ask the council,

"Hey, what did Tchyntar mean about Phobon, what information did I give them?"

"I am forbidden from discussing it, and you are not to speak of it to anyone, especially Kyon," Zayn replied.

"What? What happened? You can't just leave me in the dark about this," Aiden protested.

"Run along now, you're already late for your Perceptions lecture, we'll talk later." Zayn said, apparently deep in thought.

Excerpt from TSA:SH: Enhanced

PERCEPTION – 7

The future is not set in stone. The pages of time continue to flip back and forth, rewriting themselves as people make

---

choices for their lives. Do not despair, Cadet! No matter where you are, what you've done, or how you feel – *The Creator* is always there, setting new opportunities in motion to allow you to jump back on track and carry out His plan for the rest of creation.

Aiden arrived halfway through his lecture, Pythas, his instructor, gave a curt nod as he took his seat beside Kyon, who looked dreadfully hung-over. He was as pale as ever, unshaven and his lip had a thin line of dried blood on it. The lecture consisted of an exercise requiring the students to close their eyes and imagine meeting yourself in the future. Then the second exercise was meeting your past self. Pythas said that many times this can help us sort out the conflicts we may have had before, and prepare us to by mindful of what the future will bring.

During break before their next lecture Aiden noted an increase in the number of strange looks he was getting from people walking by. Everyone seemed to be whispering about something. Kyon informed him that nearly the entire academy heard what happened last night and people are talking about *"The Chosen Four"*. Before Aiden could consider any of this, they had to hurry off to their cold, dark lecture hall to receive more education about Fear. Their instructor, Certus, stopped them from taking their seats and took all of them to another lecture hall full of NS chairs similar to their defenses room.

"Everyone take a seat," he ordered.

They were soon in a barren landscape, all the trees were dead and the air was chilling. The sun was hidden behind thick storm clouds and most of the students took on an expression of anxiety and uneasiness.

"If one wants to learn fear, they must experience it; get comfortable with it. That way you can recognize its ugly face and overcome it. Each of you will enter your own scenario where you will be confronted by your greatest fear. And you will remain with your greatest fear, until I have seen some form of progress of dealing with it, or you are simply too terrified to continue the exercise." Certus said plainly. Of all the people Aiden had met since arriving, Certus was unmistakably the least comforting. Perhaps this was done on purpose, but whatever the case, it appeared most everyone else agreed.

"Alright here we go, three, two, one." Certus shouted.

Aiden felt the nausea hit him for a moment as the scene warped into a house much resembling the one he lived in with his father. Except part of the roof was missing and the inside was empty. He looked around, debris littered the street, and many of the houses had fully collapsed. *"What's going on? Where is everyone?"* He jogged from his neighborhood to the nearest shopping center. Cars were all over the street, some abandoned, and others were in charred ruins. He forced his way into the market, where most of the shelves were empty. He shouted, "HELLO!" but received no answer.

Everyone was gone. There was no explanation of what had happened, there were no bodies, no traces of where they had gone, nothing. Aiden looked around and knew that he was completely and utterly alone. He had never considered his greatest fear, nothing had ever really scared him, but this was certainly formidable. He walked for about twenty minutes and though he was extremely lonely he was coping. Night began to fall and he approached a deteriorating hospital. The sudden noise of broken glass put his senses on alert.

He jogged into the entrance of the hospital and a wall of icy air encased him. The interior was much colder than outside and Aiden could not understand why this place was the only place he had been to so far where he didn't feel alone. There was something, or someone here. A second loud crash of broken glass echoed from one of the floors above but this time a blood-curling scream from a woman rang out for a few seconds before complete silence permeated the air.

Aiden tried to move in the direction of the scream to go help but he was suddenly rooted to the spot. His legs would not move and the level of fear grew considerably. Another piecing cry rang out, whoever was screaming was in danger and needed his help but he couldn't get to her- and eventually whatever was attacking her would come for him as well. So this was what he feared the most, not being able to help another in need. Whether he lacked the courage to move or the NS Chair deliberately disabled his legs he did not know, but as tears began to stream down his face Aiden felt the familiar sensation of being pulled back to reality and thrown back into his body.

He opened his eyes and saw the classroom once again. Many of the students were sobbing in the corner, attended to by alumni. One walked up to Aiden and spoke,

"How you doing? Alright?"

"Yeah," Aiden replied, wiping his face. "I'm fine."

Excerpt from TSA:SH: Enhanced

PERCEPTION – 8

Cadets, throughout your travels you will find yourself being called to a wide variety of roles. If you are a leader now, perhaps you will soon be the follower. Do not feel you must continue to follow the same path throughout your entire life. Be open to new experiences and new challenges. A baker may someday become a blacksmith; then perhaps that blacksmith will become a politician; then should his path come full circle – he will once again return to his bakery.

Aiden headed off to lunch to wait for Kyon to finish his own fearful ordeal. *"I wonder what he had to experience,"* Aiden thought as he made a plate of pulled pork sandwiches. Kyon turned up twenty minutes later, looking morbid.

"You alright, man?" Aiden asked, knowing perfectly well he wasn't.

"I'll be ok, quite a lesson, eh?" Kyon responded grumpily. "How's your hand, I forgot to ask earlier."

"It's...well...broken. But that's not important, what did you see?" Aiden answered.

"Tell you what, you tell me what your vision was about, and I'll feel more up to sharing." Kyon said, a faint trace of a grin appearing on his face.

"Come on! I can't! I'm under orders to not tell anyone." Aiden whined.

"What a shame..." Kyon said, staring out the window. "I gotta get going, Jaxcyn and I are going to talk in the gardens today. Catch ya later."

"Alright, take it easy." Aiden said, feeling disappointed.

He finished his lunch and met with Zayn in his Practical Applications classroom. The room was bright and today, only two squishy pads sat on the floor.

"Have a seat." Zayn commanded. Aiden did so. "I want you to understand that I'm not angry with you, not many people would have resisted the chance to strike against someone who'd just injured their friend. However as part of your new training curriculum, I am required to push you much harder than any other student here. It pains me to do so, but understand that you have the chance to do something very special here. So..your first assignment, is to learn to heal your hand, alone."

"You're joking, right?" Aiden asked, clearly believing this to be a ridiculous prank.

"Afraid not, the staff in the infirmary have been instructed to refuse you treatment and you are not to ask anyone else for help. It's just between you and God now." Zayn replied casually.

"This is bull! I only hit Qendrin because I was defending your sister!" Aiden said, raising his voice a bit higher.

"Yes you did, and I believe she will be very grateful for that." Zayn replied. "But this is not about why's or who's. You have an injury right now, in this moment, and you need to repair it, right? It doesn't matter how you got it and for what reason. You have something that is broken and you have a desire for it to be fixed. That is all you need to focus on. Belief is a funny thing. It doesn't require you to be an expert at something to be able to do it when it is needed. Moses probably hadn't parted too many seas before he was asked to, or turn the *Nile* into blood. But when he was told how to do these things, and he had a purpose for them, he did them. So now here you are, you've seen amazing things these past few days, in particular, you've seen that it is more than possible to heal a wound. You are to spend the next few hours listening for instruction from *The Keeper*. Listen for him to guide you in how to fix your hand, *believe* he'll show you the right way, put faith in the miracle and it will serve you. You are to do the same for each day until you succeed, until then we will not meet." Zayn finished, sat up and gave Aiden a friendly pat on the shoulder then began to walk away.

"Wait! Zayn! What if I never figure it out!?" Aiden shouted.

"You determine your own level of success. I'm confident you can do it." Zayn offered without stopping, then he vanished into the lift.

Aiden waited for a few minutes, wondering if Zayn would return. When he didn't, Aiden got up and began pacing around the room, every now and then stopping by the window to look outside at the rest of the cadets enjoying the day down at the beach or playing games on the lawns. He sat back down and thought hard about what Vyleah had asked him to do.

"Ok, she took my hands and asked me to think about nothing, to block out the pain. So I counted breaths." He tried this technique again in several variations over the next twenty minutes but nothing happened. *"Hmm, maybe I have to do what I did yesterday in here, pray before I quiet my mind..."* He prayed and continued his breathing method, but nothing. Two hours later, though he'd only been sitting, he felt exhausted and admitted defeat for the day.

He had Sophie direct him to the infirmary. Not to try to get his hand healed, but he wanted to apologize for the fight between himself and Qendrin. He emerged into a long hallway with nearly two-dozen rows of beds, instead of anti-gravity capsules. A young, and beautiful woman with orange hair and freckles walked over to greet him. She wore flowing white robes and wore an expression of warm comfort.

"You are Cadet Shepherd, correct?" She asked.

"Yes, yes I am," he answered, peering around for Qendrin.

"I'm afraid we've been told to refuse you healing, I'm sorry." She said, her expression growing more consolidating.

"Oh, no, I know that, I was trying to find Qendrin, he's a first-class that had a..."

"Broken jaw? Yes he was released almost two hours ago. I'd steer clear of him for a while if I were you, didn't seem very happy at all." She explained.

"He's alright though? You were able to fix his...jaw?" he continued to ask.

"Oh yes, good as new, although we can't repair the psychological trauma one experiences from their injuries." She said.

"I see, well, thank you for your help. I'll just catch him later." Aiden said and turned to leave.

"Have a good day!" She called.

"Thanks, you too!" He called back. Aiden was determined to find Qendrin, but everywhere he looked turned up with more dead-ends. He decided to skip dinner and go to bed early.

Excerpt from TSA:SH: Enhanced

PERCEPTION – 9

Education is among the most important things one can seek to gain in life. But to not believe that some fields are more useful than others is naïve; some are more often drawn upon but everything has its uses when the time comes. Whilst in school you will be subjected to studies that you may feel are not worth learning – this is a sign of the fallen state of the universe; as long as *Aphotician* is allowed to roam free, he will spread chaos and discord wherever he is given the opportunity. But do not fear, for *The Keeper* has come to bring you into all knowledge and wisdom. All of eternity is a learning experience, so get a head start by learning all that you can about the wondrous worlds around you.

A week passed and Aiden felt no closer to solving the puzzle of how to heal his hand. It was now an ugly mix of green and purple and he was sure something had to be done soon because it had reached a point where he was waking every hour when his hand would twitch in the night. He spent those sleepless nights reading feverishly through the *Terosian Academy Student Handbook: Enhanced Edition.* He was learning much more, he felt, from reading it than from the actual lectures. But some of the exercises contained within bordered on completely impossible. A particular lecture discussed the finer points of summoning a sustaining food called *Mana.* He recalled a similar food being described in *The* Bible when Moses led the Hebrew people through the desert for forty years, eating a food that fell from the heavens every day. Aiden and Kyon speculated further ideas of Aiden's studies over meals and the free time Aiden should have been spending trying to heal his hand.

During his last Love lecture, in the outdoor amphitheatre, Vyleah had thanked him for his "heroics" and apologized for being the object of his provocation, which led him to be in the suffering state he's currently in. She also told him that she promised Zayn to not spend "personal" time with him outside of official classes to minimize the amount of distractions.

Although this had an undesirable effect on Aiden's mood, he grudgingly agreed it was for the best. During this time, to his bewilderment, he had been unable to find Qendrin to apologize. But he did have a notable conversation with Mariel and Shendu.

"We're worried about Qendrin," she said one afternood. "He has been a bit distant in classes lately and he supposedly spends all his free time in his room."

"Well, I guess that would explain why I haven't been able to find him..." Aiden muttered.

"I spoke with his mentor, but he said Qendin has just been studying extremely hard since the incident," Shendu added.

"Thanks guys, hopefully I'll catch him around soon. It's just all my free time is supposed to be spent fixing this...." Aiden responded, holding up his injured hand.

Excerpt from TSA:SH: Enhanced

PERCEPTION – 10

Often times we mortals are too short-sighted to see the great plan that exists. The universe seems chaotic and random – leading us to believe that we are either lucky or misfortunate. But wise is he who understands that God has control of your life, not to direct it for you, but to work with you based off of each decision you make. Many times we will experience failure of epic proportions but this should not discourage you or cast doubt on your faith in Him. Strive to remember that every second, every minute, every hour of each day – He is working tirelessly to orchestrate the grand drama that is your life.

Another week went by and Aiden was now feeling as though his health was getting worse by the minute. He had come down with a fever and a nasty cough. Most nights he would wake up sweating and shaking. When he saw Vyleah after a Love lecture, she had caught his glimpse and he could have sworn he saw tears in her eyes. He was beginning to fall into a mild depression in which his remedy was creating several *"Seas of Toron"* to help take the edge off his pain. On a brighter note, his technology lectures had been consisting of letting the students fly their very own CFT-1s. Even with the pain of his hand, Aiden was one of the best pilot's in the class.

Aiden spent his afternoons trying everything he could to listen to *The Keeper,* but all he heard was silence. Zayn had stuck to his promise of refusing to return until he succeeded. Aiden was now too sick to attend classes, Kyon sent text messages to offer words of encouragement and the recorded transcripts of his missed lectures, which Aiden was very grateful for.

So it continued until one particularly stormy night, Aiden had just finished his sixth alcoholic beverage and was staring out into the distance. Bolts of lightning were striking the ocean in the distance and Aiden felt he had reached his limit. With a sickening *"CRASH!"* he collapsed, cracking his head on the side of his desk and breaking the computer as he flailed to keep himself steady. Blood trickled out of the fresh cut above his eye and he lay motionless on the floor.

Chapter 13 - The Prophecy

Zayn walked over to the kitchen and took over his mother's preparations for the last bit of dinner. Over these past two weeks his parents had grown increasingly worried over their son's apparent lack of consideration for his pupil, but Zayn was convinced he was doing the right thing. Vyleah usually got home with tears in her eyes and had, on several occasions, pleaded with her brother to stop this display of "manly" pride that he was so hell-bent on seeing through. This evening Vyleah had stormed in, with fury in her eyes and addressed her brother, who seemed perfectly calm stirring the pasta in a foaming pot.

"How many more days are you going to do this!?" She demanded. "Kyon says this is the sixth day he's missed, the entire academy is whispering about how you've lost it and you're trying to kill its most promising student. Even the instructors are starting to worry you've taken this too far."

"As you have yet to learn dear sister, it does not matter what everyone else thinks. I *know* what I'm doing. Aiden hasn't been complaining to anyone, even Kyon." Zayn rebutted, continuing to tend to his pasta.

"Yes because he doesn't want to disappoint you!" she continued. "He's only been here mere weeks, we wouldn't ask any other First-Class to try something like this for at least another month. And even then we wouldn't force something like this on them." She said, tears now streaming freely down her cheeks.

"Aiden is not like any other first-class that has ever come to this academy!" Zayn said a bit louder. "He's different. You think I want to do this to him? This is as much a test for me as it is for him!" His temper was clearly beginning to rise.

Vyleah could always tell when it was time to stop an argument and she knew just how far she could push her brother. She walked out on the balcony and stared up at the academy in the distance.

"Something's wrong, I can feel it." She wiped her tears away and walked resolutely back inside. She grabbed her uniform coat and headed for the lift.

"Wait! Vyleah!" Zayn called.

"I'm going to see him!" She called back as the lift door closed.

Zayn threw his spoon, knocking down one of the pots hanging over the stove. He grabbed his own coat and made to follow. Vyleah's car was already gone so he jumped onto his Hover-bike and sped up the ramp leading out of the underground parking garage and onto the main street leading back to the academy. He sped along, weaving in and out of cars, and reached the long stretch leading up to the thousand-foot cliff. He could already see Vyleah's car climbing the steep rise. Rain was pounding his face hard and in the distance, bolts of lightning collided with the ocean's surface. He hastily parked in front of the entrance and dashed in, took the lift up to the First-Class tower and barely caught a glimpse of Vyleah's fiery hair as she took the second lift from the leisure room. He boarded the other one and emerged a moment later. Vyleah had overridden the door to Aiden's room and just as Zayn was about to stop her, he turned and saw the life-less body of his student lying in a puddle of blood.

"No…" He whispered under his breath. Vyleah had already swooped to Aiden's side and checked his pulse.

"He's alive!" She said with great effort. At these words Zayn knelt down beside her and examined Aiden's forehead, wiping his face clean of blood. Strangely…he couldn't see any wound where the blood had erupted from. Next he checked Aiden's hand, which had been turning a horrible shade of brownish-purple. But to Zayn's astonishment, the hand was in perfect condition.

"He..He did it!" He whispered.

Aiden gave a low moan, and Vyleah excitedly asked, "Aiden! Aiden can you hear me? We're here, I'm here!"

Aiden slowly opened his eyes and spoke a very exhausted, "Ouch...." Then grumbled, "D'you mind getting off my knee?"

Vyleah, who had been completely unaware she was crushing his leg, jumped up and, with the aid of her brother, helped him to his feet then into the hover chair. Aiden sat in silence for a moment and enjoyed the pleasant sensation of breathing.

"Can we get you anything?" Zayn asked, looking back at Aiden's hand to verify that it was indeed healed.

"Yeah...I'm like..REALLY hungry." He said with a great sigh. This was an understatement, he hadn't eaten for nearly three days and felt as though he would break the FPD trying to provide enough food to satisfy his hunger.

"He's coming home for dinner then." Vyleah commanded, eyeing her brother in a way that no wise person would dare argue with. Aiden got to his feet and after stumbling, walked with Vyleah's support.

They arrived at their family's home ten minutes later and Aiden cleaned himself up as best he could. He still felt very weak but was much better than he had been. During dinner, he ate as if he had lived his entire life without ever having a meal. He helped himself to a fourth helping of pasta and did not care to wipe his face, which was covered in sauce. Shara giggled every now and then, this spread to Zayn and Vyleah, and eventually Aiden, who finally realized his manners had gone unchallenged by his accommodating hosts.

"Thank you all, this hit the spot." Aiden said with a pat of his stomach. "I'm guessing you guys have a few questions for me?" He asked and looked over at Vyleah and Zayn.

"Only when you're ready," Zayn replied.

"Alright, well as you can see I finally figured out how to fix this, "Aiden said and raised his right hand up, "but it only happened a moment before you guys got to me. I had been staring out at the storm and my legs gave out, I reached for anything nearby to steady myself and I ended up pulling the computer off the desk, and I smacked my head. It must have left me unconscious because I don't remember hitting the floor. It was weird though, it was like being in a lucid dream. I thought for a moment that I was dead, but I heard that familiar voice that had spoken to me in my visions. I saw a blinding light that told me to not be afraid. I responded that I wasn't, in fact, I can't remember ever feeling so peaceful and calm. I told it I'm ready to be healed; I think I had reached a point where there was no more room left to doubt that it couldn't happen. It was either do it or I'd bleed to death right then and there. The light told me I would be healed for not only my faith, but the faith of those coming to my side. Then I opened my eyes and saw you two, but the pain was gone and I immediately knew it had worked."

Zayn wiped a tear from his eye and gave a joyful smile. "I knew you could, everything is going to change for you now. You've opened your heart up to *The Keeper* and replaced doubt with faith and now you *know* that you can do anything."

Aiden got up and placed his dish in the sink, then asked, "So what happens now?"

Zayn raised his eyebrows and chuckled, "Well you keep doing what you're doing. Tomorrow is a free day but you've fallen behind on your one-on-one sessions with each of your instructors, I'll arrange for you to meet with each throughout the day."

Aiden gave a nod of approval and thanked everyone for his extremely satisfying meal. Vyleah agreed to drive him back to the academy. As they zoomed along, Aiden posed the question he'd been unable to ask since the night at the club, "So....why'd you kiss me that night."

Vyleah did not look over at him, but she seemed instantly ready to answer this particular question.

"I don't know, we grew up together, I've spent every year since then hearing about you, my first friend, growing up on some world thousands of light years away. I didn't know if you had any idea who I was or if I would ever get to see you again. I suppose I've always had a bit of a crush on you. The time finally came when you were ready to take your rightful place out here where you were meant to be. I guess you can't blame a girl for being interested after twelve years of waiting." She said with a shy smile.

"No, I guess you can't," was all Aiden could respond with. He continued looking out the window for the duration of the drive, unsure of how to continue any kind of normal conversation with her. He felt different though, a change had taken place within him that he had not noticed when he first awoke from his dance with death. He was filled with a confidence he had never known. It seemed the world was completely new to him. The feelings he once had as a child were flooding back into his consciousness. He had feelings of carefree happiness and a curious passion about learning everything about the world around him. A sermon from a particular day at church flashed into this mind; the pastor had spoken about living life with a child-like wonder. It wasn't until now that Aiden understood exactly what that meant. He felt born again. Tomorrow he would devote himself entirely to his goals of being the best student he could....no...not tomorrow, he would start tonight, right now.

They rolled to a stop outside the main entrance and Aiden thanked Vyleah for everything, he was about to close the door when he seemed to be possessed to speak his mind,

"Would you like to have dinner, with me, just the two of us?"

"Sure," she said, trying to hide her excitement.

"Excellent, tell you what, give me a few days to look around and find the perfect place, in the city I mean." He proposed.

"Alright, it's a date." She answered. "See you around."

"Okay, see ya." He replied and gave a small wave as she drove off.

Aiden slept uninterrupted for the first time in weeks. He awoke at midday to the sounds of Sophie's beeps. Kyon had sent him a message demanding what had happened the previous night. Apparently the entire academy had, once again, discovered that Aiden had performed his first healing and were raving about his near-death experience.

"How does everyone keep finding out?" He wondered while he showered and dressed himself. Kyon met him in

the main chamber and was positively livid about his miraculous change overnight.

"This is amazing," Kyon exclaimed, "I can't believe you actually did it. People are talking about it you know, and I don't mean one or two people, *everyone* can't seem to shut up about it. I did a little eavesdropping earlier; the Director himself was talking about you to one of the other council members."

Excerpt from TSA: SH

PRACTICAL APPLICATIONS – 8

Sin is a part of our lives, there is no getting around it. Either we are the ones sinning, or we are surrounded by others who are. This is why we have developed the *"Sin Exercise"*. Take a moment at the end of today and evaluate the day in its entirety. What have you done that may be in conflict with the will of our Creator? Learn to root out thoughts and actions that are against His wishes and you will soon reap a harvest that is fresh and pure.

After a short lunch, which was spent with Kyon warding off inquiries from fellow students, Aiden joined Kyon in the academy's shooting range. They had been practicing with firearms in their Defenses class but Aiden had been unable to properly grip his due to his injury. But he wasn't far behind the curve; his lessons with his stepfather back on Earth had given him the proper instruction to provide him with the necessary skills to be able to use a variety of guns.

Some time later Aiden met with two of his instructors to catch up on his extra lessons. His fear instructor, Certus, helped to clarify the role that fear played in his ordeal in trying to perform his first healing.

"You see, fear prevented you from being able to do it, but you finally got to a place where you had nothing more to fear and look what happened, *The Keeper* showed up right on queue." Certus explained.

He also met with his robot teacher, Toss. Toss piloted a CFT-2 with Aiden. This was a bigger version of the CFT-1 and was designed for reconnaissance missions where the pilot may be required to stay on site for longer than a day. It had faster-than-light speed capabilities and could travel from one end of the galaxy to the other in about a week.

After an early supper with Kyon, he was back at it. He met with Pythas to further his change in Perception, and discuss these feelings Aiden was experiencing regarding his new outlook on the world; his bold attitude towards being able to take on anything. Pythas warned against letting these feelings cloud his ability to still discern what's right and wrong and Aiden did his best to heed the advice.

But it was his final meeting of the day that Aiden looked forward to eagerly. His Practical Applications lessons with Arthanis were always the most interesting. Arthanis showed Aiden the more miraculous things that he normally did not show the rest of the class in normal lectures. Today they sat in the classroom with two squishy cushions and he demonstrated his ability to levitate a third cushion from the corner of the room to just above Aiden's head, which he then let fall so that it gave a friendly *"Plop"* as it bounced off and to the floor. Aiden pleaded with him to learn this particular skill since it was the dazzling feats like this that were so fascinating for him to see in the movies as a child. But Arthanis promised he would another day; for today, they were continuing the exercise Aiden had performed on his first day of lectures: listening for auditory or illusory messages from *The Keeper.*

Although disappointed, Aiden closed his eyes and cleared his mind of all thoughts and emotions. He had become quite good at doing this now, without the pain of his hand this seemed almost easy. It took only minutes before he heard faint whispers and a few murky images swam by, but the trouble was trying to maintain his focus and unbiased concentration so that he could see and hear them more clearly. After failing on several more attempts, he took a very deep breath, and held it for as long as he could, then began to exhale as slowly as possible.

He could feel his heart pounding inside his chest. It beat with an entrancing loudness; it felt as though his whole body reverberated with each cadence. He let the rhythm take him away, back to the place he had last had a vision: to Phobon. This time was different, he wasn't simply witnessing a scene; he had control over his actions. He walked around, examining his surroundings. He saw dozens of settlements scattered in all directions, small lights zipped from one to another, and thick smoke was rising from one of them. Then he realized that those lights were cannon shells being fired! The scream of a rocket sounded from the closest settlement and a missile lifted off and flew over Aiden's head high above. He followed the smoke trail and turned.

As he finished turning a sharp shot of adrenaline exploded through his veins; a CFT-2 recon ship was spiraling

293

out of control in the sky; smoke billowing from its engines. It was heading straight for him! But before he had any time to react, it crashed with a roar of splintering metal and a wall of dust blasted forth, landing just short of Aiden. He ran towards the ship, now in pieces, and looked for any survivors; But the cockpit was empty. Aiden looked towards a nearby settlement and saw a group of people coming toward him. It sounded as though they were cheering.

Aiden was suddenly thrust forward into a new scene. He was face to face with Kyon, each of them were holding a weapon at the other's face and Kyon was speaking words that Aiden could not hear, this was also the first time Aiden had seen Kyon without his dark sunglasses on; his eyes were a reflective silver. The vision changed again and a third, unknown person was standing before Aiden, this figure was shrouded in darkness and was bent over an unidentifiable object. The scene changed once more and Aiden was running along-side Kyon. As he turned to see what they were running from, the vision ceased and he opened his eyes to once again reveal the room of squishy pads, but Arthanis was gone.

Not knowing if he was supposed to wait for him to return, Aiden decided to leave and continue to nourish his appetite once more by meeting Kyon for a second dinner. Aiden's feelings about his visions this time were quite different than the last time. He found himself determined to understand everything about what he just seen. He had read in his handbook that visions may sometimes be literal and sometimes symbolic. But he was unable to understand which this was.

"*It had to be symbolic,* Aiden thought, "*Why wouldn't the ship have a pilot in it, and why would Kyon point a gun at me. And why couldn't I see who the third figure was.*" Kyon had just thrown a pea at him, apparently trying to bring him back from his ponderings.

"You okay?" he asked, amused. "You're doing that thing again when you go into your own little world."

"Yeah, I was just trying to remember something Arthanis and I were working on." Aiden answered.

"How's that going by the way? Any more visions?" Kyon inquired.

"No," Aiden lied, "But did I tell you he would teach me how to levitate objects sometime soon? Man that would be awesome..." He said and let his thoughts drift for a moment. "So I need to get into the city this week to find a good place for my date with Vyleah. You want to come?" Aiden asked.

"You kidding? Of course!" Kyon responded.

"This is just to go *look* for the right place, I'm not inviting you to come along on the date...." Aiden clarified.

"I know, I know..." Kyon laughed.

Chapter 14 - Rivalry

Aiden and Kyon sped along the buildings of Theron for the fourth afternoon, seeking to find the perfect location for Aiden's upcoming date. They had found very promising spots each day and Aiden was enjoying getting to see the city more, but he kept telling himself, *"This looks great, but there's got to be something a little better out here."* Kyon, who was enthusiastic about joining the search initially, was now starting to grow tired of what seemed like an endless stream of rejected ideas.

"Let's just go back to that place downtown, it had great live music," he insisted.

"No, I don't want to go somewhere that I'll need to struggle to have a conversation with her. We need somewhere with a view, but quiet, and sophisticated. Maybe soft music... You know, romantic-like." Aiden said as they walked along a string of restaurants resting along the shore.

"Those kinds of restaurants don't exist on Phobon..." Kyon said under his breath.

They had just walked past a mound of rocks with an opening, but as Aiden did a double take he realized that this "cave" was in fact a restaurant but there was no building behind the pile of rocks - Just an opening. Intrigued by the odd advertisement they walked in and found themselves on a moveable floor, like the people movers at an airport on Earth. The ramp lowered them down for almost twenty seconds before they were moving horizontally again. They found themselves gliding through a tube that was *underwater!* Fish were swimming all around them and the light above pierced through the surface in brilliant white rays as it reached them nearly fifty feet below. A few moments later they arrived at the front desk where a young woman, eyeing their uniforms, greeted then with a curtsy.

"Good afternoon, gentlemen." She said. "Just you two for lunch?"

"Uh, no." Aiden replied. "You see, I have a date with a very special girl and I would like to make reservations if I can."

"Awww, that's so sweet!" she exclaimed. "Okay, do you know what time?"

"I'd like to get some of the sunlight still shining through if I can." He suggested.

"Very well, I have an opening at...five-thirty?" She asked.

"Yeah, that would be great." Aiden thanked her and returned to the academy with a grateful Kyon.

Over the next two days, Aiden could think of little more than his date. His lessons usually flew by too quickly for him to remember what was talked about and Zayn was beginning to take notice of his lack of focus during their study time.

"How was your Defenses class today?" he asked his pupil.

"Bit boring, I mean we've been down at the shooting range for the last week and it's always fun to compete with Kyon, but he's much better than me." Aiden said in an uninterested voice.

"It's not about trying to be better than anyone else; it's about how *you* are progressing." Zayn insisted.

"I know," Aiden defended, "I am excited about starting the Spiritual Warfare section though in our one-on-one lessons, the rest of the students won't start for a few weeks but she thinks it's time I started learning about putting on my "spiritual armor".

"Well, that's good, I'm glad you are progressing. Is there anything else you would like to talk about?" Zayn asked, eyeing Aiden a bit closer than usual.

Aiden had been ready for this question; he had been practicing his first Spiritual Warfare exercise with great success- guarding one's emotions. One can learn to bury their surface feelings so that another seeing them through "spiritual eyes" will be unable to determine if they are being untruthful about something. This is a useful technique against *Shadows* since they can take advantage of one's feelings and turn them against a defender. Aiden pushed his feelings about his recent vision into the darkest recesses of his soul and masked them with a feeling of common disinterest. This must have worked because Zayn, as if scanning him with an infrared beam, failed to detect his lie and departed for the day, wishing Aiden a good day and offered a wink for his upcoming date with his sister.

Aiden awoke from another sleepless night, caused by either his excitement of date in....thirteen hours, six minutes, and twenty-two seconds- or his reliving of his most current vision concerning Phobon. He took advantage of the extra time this morning to get a good workout in. He went for a jog around the grounds for a half an hour, then spent an hour and a half in the physical fitness center. Upon first glance this looked like any average gym, but the vast numbers of machines were almost perfectly designed to work every muscle intensely. CASE robots roamed around, offering to "spot" students and giving instruction on the best way to use each piece of equipment.

After he finished his post-exercise stretches Aiden caught a brief glimpse of a student in navy blue athletic gear departing.

"Was that..." Aiden wondered as a got up to chase after the young man he had been searching for nearly three weeks. He jogged down the corridor, passing his Fear Lecture classroom but couldn't find the student.

SLAM!

Qendrin erupted from the shadows and pinned Aiden against a wall, pressing his forearm hard against Aiden's neck.

"Stop looking for me." Qendrin hissed coldly, "Just leave me alone..."

He released Aiden and swept away, back into darkness. Aiden collapsed to his knees, coughing and gasping for breath.

"What the hell just happened? I seek to apologize and the next thing I know I'm hanging by my throat." Aiden returned to his room, pondering what could cause Qendrin so much anger, and risk getting expelled. *"Unless he's trying to get **me** expelled, he wants me to fight him again. But why? What am I supposed to do? Tell Zayn or Tchyntar? No...this is between me and him. I'm not going to run away and taddle-tell because some meany was bullying me."*

Sophie, as if reading Aiden's inner struggle to decide what to do, broke the silence, "Sir? Would you like to file a report against First-Class Cadet: Qendrin?"

"No, no" Aiden quickly said, "I'll handle this Sophie, but can you please send Kyon a message to meet me for breakfast A.S.A.P.?"

"It is still fairly early, he will most certainly be sleeping in on his free day," she informed.

"I know, just do it, I need to talk to him." Aiden ordered.

"Yes, Sir" Sophie said with a beep.

Kyon emerged from the lifts on the dining hall and met with Aiden. Still looking half asleep, he dragged himself over and lay down along the pad wrapping around the booth.

"Alright, Aiden. What was so important that you had to pull me out of bed on the one day we get to sleep in," he asked resentfully.

"I just had a run in with Qendrin," Aiden said plainly.

Kyon shot up and instantly looked more awake, "WHAT? You finally found him?"

"You could say that..." Aiden said, rubbing his neck.

"And? What did you say?" Kyon questioned.

Aiden lowered his voice to a whisper, "I didn't say anything...He jumped me out of a dark corner and almost strangled me." Kyon was speechless, his mouth simply hung open.

"That slimy..." Kyon cursed a number of things that didn't translate, "So what are you going to do?"

Aiden stared down at his plate of unfinished pancakes, "I don't know, I have this theory that he wants to force me to fight him, that way, I get expelled."

They continued discussing the matter for another twenty minutes before Aiden had to prepare for a private lesson with his Perception Instructor. He met Pythas on one of the benches near the cliffs that overlooked the beach. He gave his ginger goatee a scratch and examined his clipboard,

"Alright, you have been moving right along, I see. Today we'll have a short discussion on prayer and *The Keeper*." He asked Aiden a series of questions to define a baseline for his lesson then began, "Okay, so first off let me shine some light on the proper method for prayer using your *Spiritual Voice*. You see, when we speak to *The Creator* most people talk to him in their language, for me it's Terosian, for you it's English. But you must understand that *The Creator* doesn't speak either of those languages. He speaks in the language of the spirit. So fittingly, *we* must speak in that language as well. *Our* language is really so we can organize our ideas."

"So how does one speak in a *Spiritual Voice?*" Aiden asked.

"It happens quite easily actually," Pythas had a sip from a mug he brought with him then continued, "Imagine everything you were praying about converted into feelings, and you let those feelings resonate within your heart. Then you allow them to radiate out of you so *The Keeper* can sweep them up and present them to *The Creator*."

Aiden nodded his head in understanding, this did seem to make sense, though he'd never heard it described this way before. Pythas took another sip and checked his clipboard, "Next we address the issue of what you're saying when you pray - have a clear and definite idea of what you're saying, and know *who* you are saying it to. If I want to thank *The Creator* for his blessings, I pray to him. But when I want to do this for example...."

Pythas held out his palm and what looked like a pair of flaming marbles materialized out of thing air and orbited around each other, floating just above his hand. Aiden was ecstatic over the display, but Pythas closed his hand and the flaming spheres disappeared.

"When I desire a miraculous work I go to *The Keeper*. It was, after all, designed for that. Many cultures we find do not emphasize the role of *The Keeper* strongly enough and as a result people do not realize what is possible and that they are praying to the wrong *body* of the *Trinity."*

They concluded their discussion and Aiden returned to the leisure room, today he remembered that he wanted to design his own holographic banner to post on the wall in the leisure room to represent Earth. He began with one that had the United State's flag on it, and then realized that the banner was supposed to reflect the whole planet, not just one nation. He altered the design and finally came up with one he approved of an hour later. A First-Class alumni emerged from the lift and admired his banner,

"Not bad, what do all the parts mean?" he asked.

Aiden explained each - in the upper left was a rotating picture of Earth with a small moon circling it. The borders looked like white marble, (which reminded Aiden he would have to visit the monument in the *Stone Forest* soon), and a faded symbol of the academy was behind the names listed, currently *"Aiden James Shepherd"* was the only one recorded. He put the academy's symbol because he felt it represented a bonding of the two worlds.

At five-thirty Aiden showered and dressed for his big night. The oddest sensation of complete relaxation had overcome him. Normally he felt he should be nervous about going on a date, but everything felt perfectly ordinary tonight. He headed for the Vehicle Housing Facility and, instead of requesting the land vehicle he and Kyon had been using all week, took advantage of his recently acquired permission to fly planetary leisure craft. The sleek twin-seater shuttle shot out of the hanger and assumed an automated route to Vyleah's building. He landed on the roof in one of the *"Ten Minute Parking"* spots and took the lift down to the one-hundred and twenty-sixth floor.

Shara answered the door and, looking mischievous as ever, shouted over her shoulder, "Mom! Tell Vyleah her boyfriend's here!"

Aiden smiled and said, "Thanks, Shara."

She smirked and went back towards the kitchen. V'ena greeted Aiden with another of her famous bear hugs and told him Vyleah would be out in a minute. Several minutes later, Vyleah emerged wearing an elegant dark blue dress – its straps hung off her shoulders. It ran down to her thighs, and as Aiden's eyes continued to survey her beauty he had to remind himself that he wasn't dreaming. This was the first time he had ever seen her wear her hair up. Her silver earrings complemented the ornate necklace of silver and what looked like sapphires.

V'ena aided in breaking the silence, "Doesn't she look gorgeous?! Quick, get the camera!"

Vyleah protested, "Mom! Please, no!"

"Oh don't be silly, it's not every day you go out on your first date..." V'ena insisted, accepting the camera from Vyleah's father. V'ena pulled Vyleah over to Aiden's side and posed them both. "Alright....3...2...1..." The picture was immediately uploaded to an empty frame sitting amidst a number of family photos on a table near the entryway.

"There we are!" V'ena admired her new picture and bid her daughter and Aiden a good night.

As Aiden helped her into the shuttle she admitted that she was impressed with his acquisition of flying permissions. They jetted through the buildings and arrived a few minutes later in a parking structure near the ocean. Beautiful waves of birds glided over the shoreline and white frothy mist sprayed up as waves crashed onto the red sand. Down on the beach children were making sand castles, chasing birds, and dashing into the waves. Aiden and Vyleah arrived at the cave opening with the ramp leading down and stepped upon it. As they descended Aiden asked,

"Have you ever been here before?"

Vyleah shook her head and glowed with an excitement comparable to the children they'd just passed outside. She was absolutely fascinated with the short trip through the tube to the entrance of the restaurant. The same woman from before gave a small curtsy and seated them at a table overlooking a beautiful coral reef. Fish of all kinds swam by, as if putting on a show for their spectators. The golden light pierced through the dark blue water and shimmered with unpredictable radiance upon everything around them. Aiden looked around, besides the fact that the floor, ceiling, and walls were made of glass, the restaurant looked just like any other he'd been in – though he admitted they were never this fancy.

All of these wonderful things paled in comparison to Aiden's guest for the evening. Vyleah was glowing, and for the first time ever, Aiden could think of nothing else he could want more than to be here with her.

"Are you ready to order?" said a young man with a small electronic notepad.

"I'll have the shrimp salad to start with, then the seared Toma-Toma fish entrée," Vyleah answered. "And for desert can you mix a piece of Shutan Cake with Boream ice cream."

Aiden was unsure what most of that was, but it sounded good so he shrugged and said, "I'll have the same." While they awaited the main course they discussed Aiden's lesson earlier that day concerning prayer.

"You know I really think I'm starting to get it," Aiden commented, helping himself to another bite of his salad.

"Oh?" Vyleah said, having a sip of her water.

"Yeah, I feel different, like internally. Almost like that void I've been trying to fill for all these years if finally starting to get smaller." Aiden explained.

"That's excellent, that's a great sign that you're well on your way. I still find it hard to believe how much you've accomplished in so little time." She offered.

"Time is all relative, it is not constant and when we see the universe as The Creator does we will finally see the uselessness of keeping track of it." Aiden recited in his best teacher-sounding voice.

"Perception: Chapter Six – Section Four...." Vyleah laughed. "You've been doing your homework."

"Everyday...." Aiden nodded.

"Well I'm glad you're so dedicated, if more students put that kind of work into their personal studies they would be graduating in half the time." She complimented.

"How much time does it take, to graduate?" he inquired.

"Only one's mentor knows that, it's different for each person," she answered.

"So...has Zayn said anything about when he thinks I will?" he continued.

"No...he has not, and even if you did you should know I couldn't tell you..." she said light-heartily.

Just then their main course arrived, looking and smelling delicious. The fish tasted like salmon, and Aiden believed it to be so enjoyable due to the visual experience of sitting in the ocean. The sun was finally fading behind the horizon and the restaurant atmosphere grew much more dark and sensual. Candles were lit at each of the tables and the music became more entrancing. The desert arrived and was deliciously satisfying. The cake tasted of chocolate and the ice cream, Aiden thought, tasted like a hybrid of tea and coffee.

Across the table Vyleah's eyes, due to the darker conditions, were now visibly illuminated as she tracked Aiden's every move, almost as if they were urging him to reciprocate her gaze. A month ago Aiden would have shyly looked anywhere but back at a girl staring so blatantly at him – but he was indeed a changed person, for his own piercing green eyes stared back unflinchingly.

"Would you like to go for a walk?" Vyleah proposed.

"I'd love to," Aiden answered, still refusing to break his stare. He followed her lead as she thanked the waiter, chefs and hostess for their wonderful service, then exited.

The night was dazzling, one of Teros's moons: Toron was silhouetted against the vast clouds of stellar dust and nebulae – Almost like seeing a solar eclipse at night. Vyleah walked toward the ocean, the waves were no longer crashing, instead the water was calm like a recently disturbed lake. She removed her shoes and let the water wash up on her feet.

"You coming?" she asked.

"Where? I thought we were going for a walk," Aiden asked confused.

"We are, out there...." She giggled, pointing to a lighthouse sitting on a small island almost a half-mile away. Aiden stared blankly, looking as if he were trying to understand a complex math problem.

"Take your shoes off and get over here..." she demanded playfully.

Aiden did so and approached the water and closed his eyes, *"You can do this, you can do this. Remember what Pythas taught you today...Know what you're praying for and who you're asking...Holy Spirit, I pray with all my heart that you help me do this. Don't make me look like an idiot on my date...please.....Amen."*

Vyleah had already started walking backward over the water's surface, "Come on, don't leave me out here all by myself..." she called.

Aiden was clearing his head of all doubt, he knew he could do this, after all, she clearly just demonstrated it was possible, as did a fellow named *Jesus* a very long time ago. He closed his eyes and stepped out...his feet did not sink! He took another step, then another and he was indeed standing upon the water. He wiped away his joyful tears. He was literally following in Jesus' footsteps! Although he took a few moments of careful treading to feel confident to walk normally, he reached Vyleah at last.

"You are truly amazing." Vyleah said in wonder as she took his hand.

"Shall we?" Aiden motioned to the lighthouse. They walked along and he found it relatively easily to stay concentrated, the key was to not think about the fact that one should sink in water. He did this by keeping his eyes fixed on his destination, and distracted himself in conversation with Vyleah.

They reached the island and Aiden's heart had never felt so full. He said a short "Thank you" prayer and sat down on a bench facing the city. He felt he had to do something, there was no hiding it anymore, Vyleah wasn't hiding her interest in him and he knew there was no reason to do so either.

"I forgot to mention when I saw you this evening how beautiful you look." He felt himself say, not realizing he had said it aloud. He could not tell but the sheepish smile that crept over her face made him imagine her blushing as she did that night at dinner with her family.

"T..Thanks.." was all she could think of to say. He had exposed her weaknesses, this was the first time she looked away.

"Kiss me! Kiss me!" She pleaded silently. He must have heard her somehow because he reached over as if possessed by an invisible force and guided her lips towards his.

Chapter 15 - The Pains of Love

A month passed since Aiden's stroll with Vyleah across the waters to the lighthouse. They tried to spend as much time together as they could, but Aiden's studies were becoming increasingly taxing of his time. He was now able to demonstrate several gifts with ease and was progressing to the more advanced lessons with Zayn and his instructors. He and Kyon had also become much closer friends, spending hours at a time In the recreation center – playing dozens of virtual reality versions of Aiden's favorite games from Earth.

Aiden became accustomed to life on Teros and the traces of his former life began to slip away as he looked forward to what seemed like endless possibilities. Though at times his thoughts drifted upon his family and the life he once lived, he longed to see them again and tell them about his experiences.

Although frowned upon, the academy staff permitted Aiden's relationship with his instructor to continue on the condition that they behave in a professional manner during classes and in the presence of cadets.

Aiden still experienced tension with Qendrin over this time but the extent of this was represented in dark expressions they exchanged whenever they met. He was reluctant to bring these to his mentor's attention, feeling he was adult enough to deal with these matters alone. The real conflict he was having was trying to decide the right time to tell Zayn about the visions further concerning some issue regarding Kyon's home world. He also felt the time would come when he could no longer stay silent about these visions and would have to confide in his friend.

One particularly cloudy day Aiden flew a shuttle over to Vyleah's for lunch. She greeted him with a passionate kiss and skipped back to the kitchen to continue cooking.

"So, I have a meeting today with the council," Vyleah said casually. Aiden raised his eyebrows and she instantly understood that he was worried. "I don't think it's anything to do with us, we often have meetings scheduled to review the lesson plans and discuss the progress of *certain* students." She said with a wink. They finished their meal and Aiden returned to meet with Kyon, today they were finally getting around to visiting their monuments in the *Stone Forest*.

"Why don't we just fly out to them!?" Kyon demanded.

"Because I haven't gotten to work out in a few days and I need to exercise...so do you." Aiden rebutted. Kyon scowled and they set off to hike through the towering pillars of rock. It took them an hour to reach the halfway point, at which point they took a break.

"How'd that lesson go the other night, the one with Arthanis?" Kyon said. Aiden's heart swelled and the feelings of euphoria swept over as he recounted the memory.

"I finally did it," he answered.

"You did!?" Kyon gasped, "Show me! Come on!"

Aiden closed his eyes and cleared his mind, he said a short prayer and he opened them, staring intensely at a small rock a few feet away. He held out his hand and visualized the rock raising upward and floating to him slowly. As he did this the rock lifted and glided to a point in between himself and Kyon. Kyon's mouth hung open in complete disbelief as the rock slowly rotated, as if it were a small planet. Aiden's concentration waivered as a bird flew overhead and the rock dropped.

"Only been a few days, I gotta work on it more. But awesome huh?" Aiden laughed, getting to his feet.

"I can't even believe it." Kyon said, still shocked.

"I'm confident you'll get there too, just stay positive." Aiden said, helping Kyon to his feet. They continued on the path for another hour and reached the beginning of the last row of pillars. Each one had a plaque containing the planet and students associated with it. By a pleasant coincidence, Earth was right beside Phobon – though the two looked very different. Earth's was a bright white slab of marble, whilst Phobon's looked like a pillar of rust. They took a carving laser out of their packs and wrote their names into the rocks. Aiden added a quote offering advice to any future student from Earth, *"Through God, All things are possible."*

The hike back seemed considerably shorter, but as they emerged from the final row, Aiden's heart burst into pain. He steadied himself against one of the pillars and closed his eyes in agony as the pain spread. But this was like nothing he had ever experienced, it was not *his* body that ached.

"Hey, you ok?" Kyon asked, unaware of what was happening.

"Yeah...it's not me...it's..." Aiden said through gritted teeth. He closed his eyes again and did his best to ignore the searing torment. The pain subsided and he saw a flash of a woman's face, "It's Vyleah...Something's happened."

Before Kyon could ask what was going on Aiden was already dashing across the grounds. According to Sophie, Vyleah was on her way to the First-Class tower. He ran recklessly, almost knocking over a pair of Second-Class boys that had just gotten off a lift. As he arrived at his room the door opened to reveal a distraught Vyleah, sitting on the hover chair sobbing vigorously – her head in her hands. Aiden knelt down and embraced her, allowing her time to regain her composure before he asked her what happened.

"It was....*sniff* it was the meeting with the council." Vyleah said, wiping her face dry.

"What'd they say?" he asked.

"They...*sniff* they said that after a recent report from a student...I am...*sniff* being reassigned to my next post ahead of schedule." She answered, fresh tears streaming down.

"Report? From who? What'd it say?" he asked, wiping a tear off her cheek.

"They wouldn't...*sniff* say who...but the report said *"I seem more distant and distracted during lessons and my free time should be spent more with other students, instead of you,"* she said, her voice growing less shakey.

"That's ridiculous, it's ok though, I can still come see you where ever they assign you." Aiden assured her.

"You don't understand...my next assignment after my year as a teacher is to go to a planet and spend time getting to know the culture, then I can decide to stay and find a pupil to watch until it is time to bring them back to the academy. Just as Zayn did with you." She explained. Aiden did not know how to respond. All that mattered was that the girl he had become so close to these past two months was leaving, and he was not leaving with her.

"Do you know what planet you have to go to?" he asked after a few minutes. Vyleah gave her first smile since hearing the news.

"Yeah, Earth." She said.

Although he was displeased at the news of Vyleah's approaching departure, Aiden dealt with the feelings over the next few days, spending every moment he wasn't in class with her. She was in much better spirits and though saddened to leave, a hint of excitement was discernable as she packed her things. To Aiden's surprise he learned that she would be living in the same house Zayn stayed in for all these years as one of Aiden's neighbors.

"That means she'll see my parents!" he thought, gazing at the city from the balcony of Vyleah's parent's home. He walked back in the house and found some paper to write with. Then began to transcribe a letter to his parents.

"Dear Family,

As you know I have kinda disappeared off the face of the planet these past months, but there's no need to worry. I can't explain where I am right now but you can let my father know I finally found a career to pursue and he doesn't need to worry about paying for college anymore. I'm sorry I can't give you guys more details but I promise I'll see you all when I can.

With lots of love,

Aiden

P.S. Get to know your new neighbor, Vyleah."

He sealed the letter just as Vyleah rolled another bag from her room and placed it by the entryway. She kissed him on her way back to get the last of her things, and just as she was out of view he attached a note to the letter, addressed to Vyleah, asking her to deliver it to his parents when she finds it. He quickly stuffed the note in one of the side pockets and hoped it would reach his parents.

The next day he and Kyon went with her family to see her off at the spaceport. Her uniform was now replaced by a pair of sandals, jeans and a red shirt that matched her hair. She cried again as she hugged and kissed her family. She gave Kyon a hug and as she finally reached Aiden she hugged him and whispered something before kissing him furiously.

"*Hem Hem...*" coughed Zayn.

They broke apart at last and she reluctantly boarded the ship. Minutes later it rose up gracefully and disappeared in the blink of an eye.

Once back at the academy Aiden joined Kyon for drinks to help take the edge off the sting he felt in his heart as the memory of seeing her ship leave replayed itself over and over. As a tribute to their first night out he had *Supernovas* and *Seas of Torons*. After several hours, and several more drinks a wave of anger finally broke through the surface of Aiden's barrier of guarded emotions.

"You know what I wanna know..." he asked and prodded Kyon, whose head was face down on the edge of the table, looking as if he were going to be sick. "I WANNA KNOW WHO THE HELL REPORTED HER! She didn't do anything wrong! She didn't seem distracted in the least bit, if anything the lectures were better than before!" He shouted. Kyon slowly leaned back and offered his agreement.

They did not have to wait long to discover this answer. The next day Aiden and Kyon were walking through the Main Chamber when he overheard someone from a group of Third-Classes say,

"...Yeah, he claims he's the one that got the Love instructor reassigned. Serves her right, teachers shouldn't date their students." Aiden confronted the young man and seized him by the arm.

"What did you just say?" he asked, scorched with anger.

"I'm sorry, Aiden, I didn't mean to offend you, it's just an opinion," the boy said, cowering.

"No, the first part, who's claiming credit for reporting her?" Aiden asked sharply.

"Tha...That First-Class, over there..." the boy pointed to a group of Second and Third-Class girls giggling around a very smug looking Qendrin. Aiden's fists clenched tight and he thought only of the satisfaction of inflicting as much pain as possible to his enemy.

The next thing he knew he found himself in the infirmary. Looking around completely puzzled. Kyon was sitting next to his bed reading something on his PCD.

"Wha..How did I get here?" Aiden asked groggily.

"Ahh, finally woke up, believe I overdid it a bit." Kyon responded.

"Huh?" Aiden moaned.

"Really sorry, man. Had to stop you, couldn't let you get expelled now could I?" Kyon said. Aiden was still very confused. "I've been carrying around this sedative in the event that you discovered who reported her. I had a hunch it was Qendrin but I didn't want you to do something rash so I made sure if you found him I could stop you."

Aiden laughed, "Kyon that's just about the cleverest thing I've ever heard you do."

"Yeah...you can thank Zayn later, he's the one who gave it to me." Kyon mentioned.

Although he was grateful for the actions of both his mentor and friend, Aiden struggled over the next week to deal with the loss of Vyleah, and the rage he felt for Qendrin. When he had finally mastered these feelings he resumed his studies with intensity like never before. He figured if he could learn all this as quickly as possible he would be able to return to Earth to see her again. He was rapidly gaining proficiency levitating objects from around his room. Sometimes during lectures he would float his pen in front of him and make it do all sorts of maneuvers, as if it were a dancer in a ballet. This performance gained hushed "Oooo's" and "Wow's" from students nearby, but eventually the instructor would eyeball him, which meant it was time to get back to the lesson.

It was just before sunrise one chilly morning when Aiden was awoken by the chime of his door and the frantic calls of Kyon as he sought to wake him.

"Aiden! Open up! Aiden!" Kyon yelled as banged hard on the door. Aiden opened the door to find Kyon sweating and his hands covered in blood.

"What's going on, what happened, are you ok?" Aiden said shocked.

"Yeah, it's not mine..just...get dressed." Kyon said breathlessly. Aiden dressed and followed Kyon outside to the Cliffside Tram. Several hundred students were gathered near the edge. Kyon and Aiden butted through to the front where two of the staff guarded the entrance to the tram. They allowed Aiden and Kyon to enter and ride it down to the sand. As they reached the bottom they were escorted to the rocks where the other First-Classes, Mariel and Shendu were being questioned. Aiden reached them and gasped sharply as he saw what they were huddled around. The body of an unknown staff member lay mangled upon the rocks.

"It's Qendrin's mentor..." Kyon whispered. "I came down here this morning to go for a jog and I found him. They went to find Qendrin to question him only to find signs of a struggle and a small trace of his blood on the floor. They're still searching for him but no luck yet."

"Wait...so Qendrin didn't do it?" Aiden asked.

"Kill his mentor?" replied Kyon. "I don't know, that sounds pretty harsh. If he did he sure tried hard to make it look like someone else...But they're questioning all the First-Classes to find out if they saw anything suspicious lately....Aiden...there's something else." Kyon said and nodded toward the lifeless body. "There's a note carved into his back..."

Aiden looked down and read the ominous words poorly etched, *"DERTH MOT."*

"What does it mean?" Aiden asked, trying to remember if he'd ever seen the word before.

"Nobody knows, it's not in the library of languages. And if no one on Teros knows of this language, who would?" Kyon replied.

As they walked back up the beach they determined several things. First, the person had to have permission to be in the academy; otherwise they couldn't get through the many force fields. Second, the person had to be connected to one of the First-Classes or else they couldn't have gotten on the lift from the leisure room. One must have permission from whomever they're visiting to use those lifts.

Over his shoulder Aiden saw the figure of Zayn emerge from the tram. He walked over to the body, and no doubt discovered the message carved. He then walked over to Tchyntar and the other council members present and spoke a few words Aiden could not hear. A moment later he approached Aiden.

"Do either of you know anything about all this?" Zayn asked plainly. Both of them shook their heads, though a moment later Aiden felt he had to voice his opinion.

"I may be out of line, but could it be possible that Qendrin killed his mentor and faked his own kidnapping?"

"That is unlikely, the computer logs show Qendrin entering his quarters and leaving sometime after the time of his mentor's murder." Zayn answered. "Whoever it was, they went through a lot of trouble to carve that note, and I fear none of us are safe until we determine the person responsible. Please follow me, both of you."

Aiden did not ask why, he had seen Zayn look this serious only a few times before and Aiden knew it was best

329

to not ask too many questions. Zayn led them to the armory, a highly guarded and secure vault on one of the lowest levels of the academy. It was lined with hundreds of firearms and weapons for all kinds of combat. He took two pistols and two holsters and handed one to each of them.

"I have been given permission for the first-classes to be armed at all times until this situation is resolved, Kyon since you're always with Aiden you are to be armed as well. The ammo is self-replenishing bolts of concentrated plasma surrounded by an electro-magnetic field. One shot could stop an elephant dead in its tracks. The lowest setting will stun for several minutes, the highest will burn a hole through just about anything. You both have considerable experience with firearms so I trust I don't have to explain how to use them. Kyon, your mentor is waiting for you at the lifts, please allow Aiden and I some privacy." Zayn said sternly.

Once Kyon had left, Zayn looked at Aiden as if trying to understand a complex hieroglyphic.

"You've been keeping something from me, something hidden very carefully, you've been successful until now, so I'll only ask once...What is it?" Zayn said with a fatal stare.

Aiden drew a breath and mentally removed the barriers guarding his secret. He revealed his vision to Zayn, whose burning expression transformed to surprise and worry. Without speaking another word he swept from the room and boarded the lifts. Aiden stayed put until he received a message from Zayn on his PCD.

"Stay in your room, do not leave, speak to no one."

Aiden went back to his room and paced around for several hours, wondering what possibility could be so bad about this vision. After a while he received another message, this time from Kyon,

"Hey, something's up...Zayn had to speak to my mentor about something urgent. You know what's going on?" Staying true to Zayn's word, he didn't respond to Kyon; though an hour later he heard a bang on his door.

"Aiden! You in there? What's going on?" Kyon yelled. He could not ignore him any longer, Aiden opened the door and permitted his friend to enter.

"Have a seat..." Aiden said nervously. Kyon did so and Aiden finally revealed both visions of Phobon to him. As he finished the second, Kyon said nothing at first then asked,

"So… I don't understand. What does that mean?"

"I don't know, but Zayn looked worried and council had told me that I had given them important information about Phobon," Aiden responded. Kyon was about to ask something else when their PCD's both chimed. A message from both of their mentors appeared reading, *"Meet in conference room number 28 in five minutes."*

As they arrived in a room containing a large circular table surrounded with hovering chairs, Aiden and Kyon saw their mentors looking positively upset about something. They each took a chair and Jaxcyn spoke first,

"Civil war has broken out again on Phobon."

"WHAT?" Kyon shouted.

"It began several weeks ago and we've just learned that….that one of the factions has plans to deploy a nuclear weapon over every major settlement," Jaxcyn continued, his voice quivering.

"We have to do something! You have to help stop this!" Kyon demanded.

"We tried to convince the council to allow us to lend aid but they are sticking to the policy of not interfering with a culture's development, especially if those people are not prepared to handle such a drastic change as accepting that other people exist in the universe." Zayn replied. The door behind them opened and an administrative staff member addressed Zayn and Jaxcyn,

"The council would like a word." They both exited with her and Kyon paced furiously around the room. Aiden was unsure what to say, but after a minute Kyon had silently deduced something that made him turn sharply and stare directed at Aiden.

"You've known about this for months...."

"What do you mean?" Aiden asked.

"You knew there would be a war, you saw it. That means you could have stopped it!" Kyon said in a louder more accusatory tone.

"No I didn't, How could I have known it would turn out like this?" Aiden defended. But it was too late, Kyon moved determinedly toward the door and Aiden moved to stop him.

"Where are you going, we have to stay here!" Kyon caught Aiden off guard and threw a hard fist into his left cheek, causing him to fall with a thud before blacking out.

As he regained himself the first thing Aiden noticed was that Kyon was gone. And though he did not understand how, Aiden felt as though he knew where Kyon was. He ran down to the Vehicle Housing Facility and caught sight of a missing CFT-2 recon ship. Convinced Kyon had taken it, he entered one himself, and took off – setting a course for Phobon.

Chapter 16 - The Rain of Fire

"You are in direct violation of official orders and academy protocol concerning the proper usage of military resources, sir." Sophie warned.

"I understand that Sophie, just send a message to Zayn apologizing and tell him I have to bring Kyon back. If he gets himself killed because of me I don't know what I'll do."

"Very well, sir" Sophie complied.

Aiden sat in quiet contemplation, watching the hundreds of stars flying by and trying to determine how he would get Kyon to come back.

" *I never should have kept it a secret...*" Aiden thought.

"*You did what you felt was right...*" whispered *The Keeper*.

"Is there anything you can do to help him?"

"*I am doing something..Sending my servant to help.*"

"Servant?"

"Yes, you are my servant. And I will help him through you."

"Wouldn't it just be easier to transport us back to the academy in the blink of an eye?"

"Easier yes, but you should know by now that it doesn't work like that. You have free will, so I could indeed help a willing person, such as yourself…but Kyon is not there yet."

Aiden opened his eyes to the sound of a warning chime. There in front of him was a rapidly growing Phobon. Its surface was obscured by thick clouds of smog and dust. He switched the auto-pilot off and guided the ship through the atmosphere. He knew there was a canyon somewhere around where they had landed when Jaxcyn first brought Kyon aboard the large ship months earlier.

Suddenly a second alarm blared and the cockpit flashed red. A red circle appeared on the glass in front of him, outlining a small dot labeled *"Incoming Missile"*. Aiden instinctively pulled up hard and rolled. The missile passed just beneath him and exploded, rattling the ship violently. He leveled off and to his horror saw six more dots light up on his screen.

"You've got to be kidding!" He shouted.

He pulled up again and turned hard to his right –
firing countermeasures as he did. The first five took the bait
but the final missile exploded and tore apart the rear of the
ship. Aiden checked the panel on his left and saw that all
engines were failing and a significant piece of the tail had
been destroyed. He checked out the windows and
confirmed that smoke was billowing out of the four engines
set in the wings. He set the best glide angle he could and
rode the ship in to an extremely violent landing – skidding
along the harsh sand and rock.

A few minutes later he opened his eyes and realized
he was still alive. He removed his seat straps and climbed
out of the now shattered windscreen. Although he sustained
a few cuts and bruises, he was not seriously injured - though
his PCD was completely smashed. He got to his feet and
examined this foreign world. Kyon had not been lying about
how dark it was; whether due to them being in the polar
region or the extremely dim suns. The planet greatly
resembled Mars; everything was red and rocky, and he
couldn't see any plant life among the barren landscape. In
the distance he could see small settlements scattered
around – from one of them a group of people were headed

straight towards him. Aiden turned and surveyed the wreckage, suddenly remembering that everything in his vision was happening. He sat down and prayed, asking for the ability of the Phobonian people to be able to understand him. A few minutes later the mob arrived, cheering over their victory. All of them were armed, including four children no older than twelve. Aiden stood with his hands raised and one of the men approached him, his rifle pointed carelessly towards Aiden's head. The man's face had several deep scars stretching the length of his face. His eyes were a devilish black and without warning he swung the butt of his rifle across Aiden's face, knocking him unconscious.

Aiden awoke some time later hanging shirtless upside down from the ceiling – his arms hanging freely, but bound at his wrists. He looked at the floor beneath him and saw the stain of a dark red puddle. He had a feeling he knew what substance caused the stains. He looked around and saw two men sitting at a table near him, the man who had struck him, and another battle-worn soldier that was taking a drink from a bottle of what must have been liquor. The first noticed Aiden's stirring and got to his feet, then slid his chair before Aiden and sat on it.

"What faction are you with?" asked the man.

"I don't know what you mean," Aiden answered.

"Where did you come from?" said the man.

"A ....planet called Teros..." Aiden responded.

The men looked at each other then broke into laugher. He slapped Aiden fiercely and knelt down, his black eyes as cold and dark as space itself,

"You think this is a game, boy? You think I won't put a hole through your head right here and now?" he said, raising his gun to Aiden's temple. Aiden matched the man's intense stare before letting his eyes dart quickly to the table behind his captor – noticing that his pistol was sitting several feet away. There was no chance of getting it now, but he tried vigorously to think of a plan for escaping.

"I'm not lying, you shot down my ship," Aiden said, turning his eyes back to the scarred face of his interrogator.

"How do you explain then that you speak perfect Phobonian?" pressed the man.

"I..." began Aiden. But before he could answer a knock came at the door. The man answered it and exchanged hushed words with another soldier before returning to the room with Aiden, when he spoke he addressed the battle-worn guard keeping watch.

"The eastern wall has been breached; Caldonian soldiers are making their way here. No doubt coming to save their pilot!" Shouted the man, he stomped back to Aiden, now holding a long thin stick. "You are Caldonian, yes?!" Before Aiden could say anything the man cracked the stick violently against his back. The sting was much worse than he could have prepared for. The man snapped the stick again on his bareback and the pain grew with each swing.

"When did the Caldonians start building those kinds of aircraft?!" *CRACK!* "What other weapons have they been making!?" *CRACK!* Warm blood trickled up Aiden's neck and soaked his hair. Aiden did not know what to say, he didn't have the answers the man wanted. After another twenty minutes of lashings Aiden finally passed out.

Outside the building the streets were now filled with the shouts and screams of soldiers giving orders and innocent people calling out for loved ones. Explosions rocked the building every now and then and the pops of bullets hitting the walls raised the level of tension a hundred fold. Aiden was left alone in the room for almost an hour before a large blast shattered the windows in the room.

Aiden finally came to and barely caught sight as the guard watching him swept from the room to find out what was happening - the sounds of more shouts and gunfire erupted from the floors below.

Aiden surveyed the room and noticed the chair the first man had left now contained a few shards of glass from the recent explosion. He stretched out and could only get a fingertip on the top of the chair. He swayed himself a little and was able to grasp the chair. He pulled it just beneath him and took up the glass and began cutting at the ropes holding his feat to the ceiling. The pain on his back had subsided a bit and a numbing coolness flowed over his wet wounds. He was almost through the rope when he heard the guard outside yell,

"No! WAIT!" then a burst of bullets ripped through the walls, missing Aiden by inches – the roped finally broke and with a sickening crash he fell onto the chair below, smashing it to splinters. The pain returned and he gave an agonizing grimace as he climbed to his feet and grabbed his uniform coat. Then he heard the footsteps in the room next to his quicken towards him. Aiden's pistol still lay on the opposite side of the room and as the door opened, he reacted instinctively, reaching his hand out and "pulling" his weapon to him as if magnetized to his grip. Aiden dashed to the balcony and jumped to the next rooftop then slid down to the rubble filled street below. He hesitated to put his uniform coat back on as his back very tender. But a series of mortar explosions fuels his actions and he blocked out the pain. He made his way to the side of a home with one of its walls collapsed. He made to move on to the next house but the frantic screams of a woman within glued him on the spot, just like his fear exercise. He gave himself only a moment to be afraid and made up his mind to investigate. He hopped over the remains of the wall and was dashing up three stairs at a time, he tried the knob of the second door on the left but the lock held steady. The desperate sobs continued to sound as Aiden took a step back and kicked the door into pieces. It took only a second for Aiden to realize what was happening - a soldier was standing near a young woman, whose shirt was torn in places. The soldier turned and drew his weapon but Aiden was already squeezing the trigger of his own. Two lethal shots burst forth from the barrel, the bright blue glow of the plasma bolts passed easily through the man's torso before continuing on through the wall. The soldier's lifeless body fell to the floor and the young woman cowered in the corner of the room, still sobbing. Aiden holstered his gun and walked over to her,

"Are you okay?" he said softly. She didn't answer. "Look, I'm not going to hurt you, but if you want to survive you have to come with me!" Aiden said with more authority as he knelt down beside her. The girl's sobs grew lighter and she finally withdrew her face from her hands. "Come on," he said again and offered his hand once more. She looked from his eyes to his hand and finally accepted it. As she rose to her feet the sounds of someone climbing stairs creaked from behind him and Aiden turned just in time to see a Caldonian soldier enter the doorway. He prepared to fire but the soldier yelled suddenly,

"Wait!" Aiden kept his pistol pointed steadily as the soldier holstered his gun and began to remove his helmet. It took Aiden several seconds to recognize the now visor-less face of Kyon staring back at him.

"Kyon?" he said, now lowering his gun.

"Found you at last, I got a warning on my PCD when your ship was getting near, but after a minute the signal went dead; it wasn't until thirty minutes ago that we intercepted a message saying a "pilot" was captured and being held here in Edath." Kyon said, his expression was difficult to read. As Aiden stared into his silver eyes he was able to see the most brief glimpse of light blue light surrounding Kyon, Aiden interpreted the emotion instinctively as sincerity and relief. He approached Kyon and embraced him with a great sigh of relief.

"Who's this?" Kyon asked with a nod towards the girl.

"No time to explain, we just have to get her to safety" Said Aiden.

"Fair enough," Kyon said with a nod.

"Look Kyon, I'm sorry I didn't tell you sooner about the vision, I was trying to understand it myself." Aiden said truthfully.

"It's alright; I regret what I did but I had to come, I can't just sit by while everyone here tears themselves apart. You ok? Looks like you've been dragged through hell and back" Kyon replied.

Without warning, a flash of white exploded into the room, illuminating everything much brighter than Phobon's suns. Kyon and the girl covered their eyes and Aiden turned to see the horrific and impressive sight of a mushroom cloud rising up in the distance. As thousands of lives were extinguished in the blaze Aiden could almost feel the loss of life sink deep into his heart. Kyon walked over and stood next to Aiden, staring at the destruction.

"I've failed….." Kyon whispered.

"We need to get out of here… Kyon, KYON!" Aiden said loudly, shaking him back to his senses. "We have to get back to your ship!" Kyon wiped his eyes free of tears and gave a sharp nod.

"It's in the canyon, we have maybe fifteen minutes to get there before the missiles get to us," said Kyon sadly. As he did this another flash of light erupted in the distance, slightly closer than the first; another enormous cloud rose up from the inferno and Aiden knew it would only be a matter of time until the city of Edath was the next target. They ran from the ruined home and cautiously hurried through the winding narrow streets. Complete chaos had taken possession of the people in the city. They were shooting at everyone they saw, whether friend of foe, It didn't seem to matter to them anymore. Bullets whizzed past their heads as the three of them made their way to a former marketplace. Aiden sat for a moment and closed his eyes, the scenes of what he had just done replayed over and over in his mind, almost as if he were watching it in slow-motion. An explosion across the street shook Aiden out of the memory and he refocused his attention to the task at hand – they had to escape the city before it was too late. The woman he had just rescued lay shaking a few feet from him. Kyon was laying down suppressive fire on the building across the street and the screams of men confirmed that he was hitting his targets.

Aiden did not want to move; he wanted to sit there and close his eyes and wake up from this nightmare. How did he get here, and how could this be happening? Kyon looked back at Aiden.

"Alright!" Kyon shouted, "On the count of three we're going to make a break for those motorcycles near the entrance." He grasped the girl's quivering hand and looked her dead in the eyes,

"You run with me, okay?" She gave a nod and Kyon began the countdown, "One….Two….THREE!" Kyon led the way, firing wildly at the last men remaining within the shattered building. Aiden did the same and followed closely behind. The whines of bullets enveloped the three of them like a pack of angry wasps. They were only a hundred feet from the bikes when a sudden rush of air blew Aiden off his feet. Then the deafening sound of the mortar clogged his eardrums as shrapnel peppered his left arm. Aiden landed with a sickening crunch and felt unable to move. His head rang and the dim red of the sky began to fade into darkness.

"Was this what it felt like to die?" This didn't seem like the way it should end. He closed his eyes and let the sounds of the battle slip away from his mind; all that was left was silence and darkness.

"Aiden...!"

"Aiden!"

"AIDEN! GET UP!" Kyon shouted and dragged Aiden to cover nearby. Aiden finally opened his eyes and coughed.

"Ouch..." he said more lightly than the situation called for. Kyon gave a grateful laugh and sat up him.

"Oh, man I thought you were a goner!" he said and gave Aiden his pistol back. A few feet from them was a small parking area containing several rows of primitive motorcycles. Aiden got to his feet and jumped on one; though his arm should be hurting he could hardly feel any pain. The girl sat behind Kyon on another and they throttled the bikes up and exited the border surrounding the settlement, heading in the direction where Kyon's ship awaited in the canyon.

"Can't these go any faster!?" Aiden shouted after several minutes. Kyon didn't answer; his eyes were focused on the canyon ahead. The woman held Kyon as tight as she could, her black hair waving behind her like ten-thousand angry whips. Another flash lit the sky and as Aiden turned to look he saw the settlement they'd just left disappear into a pillar of ash. They were just outside the heat blast but the shockwave rushing outward from the rising mushroom cloud would surely reach them in moments. Aiden turned and saw they had reached the canyon, Kyon and the girl slowed and jumped off the bike, then disappeared over the edge.

Aiden knew he had only seconds to act, he knew he wouldn't have enough time to stop before the wall of sand and rock reached them. Just before the cliff he slammed on the brakes and jumped – sliding harshly along the last few feet before skidding off onto a small plateau some fifteen feet below. The bike flew forward down an additional hundred feet, erupting into a shower of flaming and twisted metal. They lowered their heads and took cover as the wave washed over them, threatening to dislodge their grip on nearby boulders. Then the wave ceased and the ground grew calmer. They climbed down the cliff as fast as they could, and arrived at Kyon's ship. Aiden took the pilot's seat and took off, flying as fast as the engines would permit. Kyon stood looking out the window; as they rose higher it was possible to see no less than fifty nuclear blast areas. He turned, teary-eyed, and sat down opposite of the shocked young woman; she had just realized that they left the atmosphere and were accelerating into a "faster than light" speed. Aiden put the ship into autopilot and went to a locker and removed a first aid kit. He sat back down in the pilot seat and began to tend to his wounds, first injecting himself with anti-radiation medicine, then with a pain reducing substance.

She took the seat near Aiden and stared at the rush of stars. He took note of her dirt-stained face, disheveled black hair and silver eyes, so much like Kyon. Under different circumstances she would look quite beautiful. She caught Aiden staring and asked shakily,

"Who...are you?"

"My name is Aiden, Aiden Shepherd. And that's Kyon." He answered, pointed back at a clearly disturbed Kyon. "What's your name?"

"Aerilla." She said, it was several minutes before she spoke again. Aiden was attempting to pull a large shard of shrapnel out of his left arm but was struggling. "Would you like me to help?" Aerilla offered.

"Oh, thanks" he responded graciously. She continued to work on the various wounds, pulling at least eight pieces of metal from his arm; he fidgeted uncomfortably and bit down hard on his knuckle while she worked.

"You... are not from Phobon are you?" she questioned.

"No...well Kyon is, but...maybe I'll just start at the beginning..." He responded painfully. He tried as best he could to explain his story of being offered to leave Earth and attend the Academy on Teros. The expression of incomprehension seemed permanently etched on Aerilla's face the whole forty-five minutes to Teros. But her fear replaced it as they descended into the atmosphere and a voice sounded over the speakers,

"Cadet Shepherd, you will land in hanger four immediately."

When they arrived back in the hanger of the VHF a line of armed CASE guards stood waiting, along with the council, Jaxcyn, and Zayn. As they departed the spacecraft Aiden stood as tall as he could, refusing to show remorse or regret for his actions. Despite the stony look on his face, Zayn did not burst into screams of rage at Aiden, in fact, he did the opposite. He rushed forward and embraced him as a parent would embrace a lost child now found.

"That was a very stupid thing you both did," Zayn began, but was cut short by a council member.

"Zayn, if you please, we need to debrief these two young men." Said Tchyntar.

"Of course…" replied Zayn. Aerilla stepped out of the ship behind Kyon and drew the attention of the crowd of people. She refused to leave Kyon and Aiden's sight and after a small argument between Jaxcyn and Tchyntar, she was allowed to sit in on the debriefing.

The boys followed the council and their mentors back to the room with the crescent shaped desk Aiden had started to associate with a sense of uneasiness. A medical CASE had begun to treat each of their injuries and The thirteen members of the council took their seats and Tchyntar wasted no time.

"Alright, let's hear your version." He said calmly.

Aiden and Kyon exchanged looks and Aiden spoke first, beginning with when he had been awoken to investigate the murder. He finished his tale, leaving no detail untold. He knew there was no more reason to keep anything a secret. Kyon's version of the story was basically the same; he spoke of when he returned to his city of Caldonia they welcomed him back, and assumed he had been captured by a warring faction for these past months. As Kyon was speaking to the military advisor Aiden's PCD signal was able to be tracked to a spot somewhere just outside of Edath before being lost, then Kyon led a squad to find him.

Tchyntar sat up a bit straighter and spoke, "You realize under normal circumstances you both would be expelled," he said, then looked at Kyon, "but it is most unfortunate that Phobon will be unable to sustain life for some time once the fallout has spread. I also feel this council must share some of the responsibility of this tragedy; we were unable to determine the extent of Phobon's destructive potential, and we should not have decided to remain silent about Aiden's prophecy. For this you are cleared of your wrong-doings. Cadet Kyon you are dismissed."

Kyon gave a sharp nod and left with Jaxcyn and Aerilla. Tchyntar turned to Aiden now and continued,

"Cadet Shepherd, I'm not really sure where to begin. With your apparent disregard of orders and protocol, or your foolish, though heroic acts in following a fellow Cadet into a grim situation. We do not place blame for how your friend acted, the truth of the deteriorating state of Phobon should have been revealed to him. You have shown an unnatural competency these past months. We have no doubt that you will be a great addition to this academy. Just please do try to follow orders every now and then." Tchyntar said plainly. "You are dismissed, Cadet. Please visit the infirmary at once." Aiden gave a small bow and left with Zayn, feeling as though he'd just dodged another bullet.

Zayn escorted Aiden to the infirmary and sat with him as the healers cleaned him up, Aiden drifted into a deep sleep for almost a day and a half, then was startled awake by flashbacks of atomic explosions and gunshots. Zayn comforted him, and let him return to his room. He had the rest of the week off to gather himself. This was the first time he actually had time to slow down and think about what had happened in the past few days. He traced his thoughts,

"Okay, so Qendrin goes missing, Phobon's people just exterminated each other, I killed someone...." These thoughts hollowed themselves into the pit of his stomach and he struggled to control his feelings of rage and sorrow that those people had died, moreover he empathized with Kyon's loss.

Aiden tried to message Kyon for lunch over the next few days but there was no answer. When he bumped into Jaxcyn he was told to give Kyon time to deal with everything that's happened. He then met with Zayn to discuss a few things. They walked along the beach as the sun started to creep behind the horizon.

"Zayn, is there any news about Qendrin?" Aiden asked. Zayn did not answer right away and for once, Aiden was able to detect that Zayn was hiding something from him. "What is it?"

"I have taught you well," he answered with a faint smile. "I have reason to believe Qendrin is responsible for the murder of his mentor."

"I thought you guys weren't sure?" Aiden asked.

"That's true, and the pattern is consistent with signs of an actual struggle, but I have been unable to sense him anywhere. This is most unusual and the only conclusion I can come to is that he may be a *shadow*."

"A *shadow!?* How's that possible? I thought you could tell if someone was a *shadow* by seeing them with spiritual sight?" asked Aiden.

"I fear the workings of *Shadows* can elude even the best of us..." Zayn responded. Aiden thought about it for a long moment.

"I guess that would explain why he has it in for me," Aiden suggested.

"Not him, They do not act on their own agenda. It would mean that *Aphotician* has a particular interest in you, no doubt your dazzling success in this academy has sent ripples to the distant reaches of the universe - ripples that *Shadows* are sensitive to as well as others like us." Zayn explained.

"So what does that mean?" asked Aiden with concern.

"It means that you must continue to train as hard as you can, and be vigilant of threats that may loom everywhere you go. There is a reason God has granted you so much talent and we must do all we can to allow him to continue to develop that talent. You now bear the scars of a tragic battle, ones that will hopefully make you stronger in the greater battle to come." Said Zayn.

Aiden was unable to fully concentrate over the next few days, his classes were full of students wanting to know more of his thrilling tale and he felt eyes on him wherever he went. So he spent most of his time either studying in his room or practicing spiritual gifts alone in the Practical Applications classroom. He had been trying his best at learning to communicate telepathically through *The Keeper* but most of his practice was limited to his sessions with Zayn and Arthanis. If he could learn this he would be able to speak with Vyleah whenever he wanted. But It was a difficult concept to grasp, he was told to imagine our galaxy spiraling around in space, then he had to let the name of the person resonate, keeping all focus on that person. Then the image of the galaxy should warp in to the point where they are and connect with them, like an intergalactic phone-call. It sounded easy enough, but the slightest shift of focus threw Aiden's brain into disarray, causing him to start all over.

Three weeks went by and Aiden did not see Kyon; he wondered how long it would take himself to recover from the shock of losing one's entire race. One rainy evening a chime came from his door at past midnight, a joyous feeling rushed through Aiden as he rose to meet Kyon. But Zayn stood before him, looking out of breath and drenched.

"Get dressed as quick as you can and come with me," he said darkly.

Aiden did not ask any questions and dressed speedily. A few minutes later they arrived in the Vehicle Housing Facility, and boarded a small circular craft equipped with an advanced cloaking system. Zayn took off and they zoomed away into the heavens.

"As of this moment you are being granted a field promotion to Lieutenant." Zayn said sounding quite serious.

"Umm, thanks?" replied Aiden, unsure what was happening. "Why am I being promoted, what's going on?"

"Lieutenant is the lowest rank available to perform negotiations on behalf of the academy." Zayn answered still looking straight ahead.

"Negotiations, what are you talking about?" Aiden asked, clearly bewildered.

"It's Vyleah...she's been taken." Zayn said shortly.

"WHAT?" Aiden shouted.

"I don't know the details," said Zayn, looking determined. "All I know is I was asleep when I heard her call out a single word: "*Help*". Since then I've been unable to contact her, but when we near Earth I should be able to find where she is."

Almost three hours later they were arriving in Earth's solar system. Aiden wanted this moment to be special when he returned to Earth but under the circumstances he had only one thing on his mind: Find Vyleah and hurt whoever took her. His senses were sharper than they had ever been and all his thoughts were consumed with his determination to get to her. The craft came to a stop in a low orbit and Zayn closed his eyes for a moment then opened them and pulled up a display showing a region not far from Aiden's hometown; Camp Pendleton was a Marine base twenty-five minutes south of his home. Aiden took the controls and flew the craft lower towards the coordinates listed. Zayn continued to meditate on finding the exact building she was being kept in. He pulled up the schematics on a seemingly basic-looking bunker and pointed to the bottom floor.

"Here, she's somewhere on this floor, I wish I could be more specific but I lost contact with her." Zayn said concerned. Aiden landed the ship in a clearing nearly two hundred yards away from the bunker entrance. "I'm afraid I can't go with you, Academy orders, we aren't allowed to take hostile action against a people we aren't in diplomatic relations with." Aiden nodded, he had no intention of using diplomacy here, he'd let his pistol do all the talking. Ten minutes and eight dead guards later, Aiden arrived on the bottom floor of the bunker – which looked like a hybrid version of a prison and a hospital. He passed cell after cell; each one was empty. At last he reached the last cell, the blazing red hair of a girl sitting in a corner. He shot open the lock and rushed to her side. Her face was deathly pale and covered in bruises and cuts.

"Vyleah, Vyleah! Can you hear me! I'm here!" Aiden spoke softly. She stirred slowly and could barely open her eyes.

"A..Aiden...?" she whispered.

"Yeah, it's me. We gotta get you outta here, can you walk?" he said hastily.

"I'm...s..so sorry..." she said a bit softer, her voice fading.

"No...no..don't worry, you'll be fine." He said, his throat now tightening.

"I...Love....You..." she uttered with one last effort, then slumped lifeless into his arms. Aiden's heart shattered as the chilling thought pierced his body - Vyleah, was dead.

Chapter 17 - Aid from Above

Aiden rocketed back to reality as the vision of Vyleah subsided. He was back at the Academy, both worried that Vyleah would soon be the victim of some government kidnapping, and grateful that he has a chance to prevent it. He wouldn't make the same mistake as Phobon.

He rushed out of the classroom where he noted the storm clouds out in the distance, it was today – the vision he just had would happen sometime in the next twelve hours. Ten minutes later Aiden stood with Zayn before the council and relayed the disturbing news. Zayn confirmed that he could not contact his sister and the council broke into discussion about the course of action. Tchyntar quieted them down and spoke,

"Cadet Shepherd, surely you know that our laws forbid us from taking any kind of hostile action against your people..." Aiden prepared to respond but Tchyntar overruled him, "Captain Vyleah was well aware of the risks that accompanied her mission. As we have not yet established formal diplomatic relations with Earth yet it is impossible for us to do anything."

"I don't believe this! You're going to condemn her to death all because…." Aiden began, but was cut off again by Tchyntar's growing impatience.

"I am not condemning her! *Your* people took her."

"So let *me* go talk to them!" Aiden shot back.

"Only a qualified academy graduate has the right to represent this council in these situations. If you choose to act, you will do so on your own behalf and will be expelled from our ranks." Aiden was about to argue again when Zayn stepped forward and spoke instead,

"Councilmen please allow me to speak to my student in private for a moment." He urged Aiden to the outer chamber, but instead of stopping there he continued walking toward the lift. Slightly puzzled, Aiden followed silently as Zayn led him to the Vehicle Housing Facility. Rows of CASE guards had been assigned to guard the ships ever since Aiden and Kyon's daring escapade. Zayn approached the one standing before the ship from Aiden's vision and explained their intention,

"I am on orders to escort Acting-Lieutenant Shepherd to Earth for negotiations regarding the release of one of our Captains." The CASE looked from Zayn to Aiden then back to Zayn and replied,

"I have received no record of this order, sir, nor of Cadet Shepherd's promotion...." Zayn had his excuse ready and lazily spoke as if the situation was boring him,

"Surely you understand the need for such information to be kept classified; we can't worry people that academy officers are being snatched on alien worlds."

"Yes sir! I see your point! We wouldn't want to cause a panic. The ship is all ready, good luck sirs!" said the CASE and stepped aside before snapping a salute.

Almost three hours later Aiden was arriving at Earth in the small, cloaked ship - Zayn by his side. He had been thinking intensely about what course of action to take, but seeing Earth again after being away for so long gave him a moment of freedom from the combined stress of anger and anxiousness.

"So what's the plan?" Aiden asked.

"Well, we need to speak to the person in charge of this whole thing, right?" Zayn suggested. Aiden nodded and Zayn pulled up a list of officers for Camp Pendleton, Sophie commented that there were many classified files but one of the highest people in the chain led back to a man named Robert Williams, the current Secretary of Defense.

"I need you to get me the phone number for the Secretary of Defense" Aiden said, beginning to imagine a possible idea. Zayn gave a nervous look before pulling the number up on the view-screen. Aiden himself wasn't sure if this plan would work, surely someone as high ranked as the S.o.D. would know of military actions concerning the capture of aliens.

"Okay it's ringing..." Zayn said. A moment later a woman answered.

"Hello this is Pam, you've reached the office for the Secretary of Defense, how may I help you?"

"Hi Pam, This is Lieutenant...." Aiden quickly thought of a fake alias, "Lieutenant Johnson, I need to speak with the Secretary right away." Aiden said smacking his own forehead for not coming up with a better surname.

"Is he expecting your call?" Pam asked politely.

"No, he isn't, but you can tell him if he values the well-being of the country he'll stop what he's doing and speak with me." Aiden answered.

"I'm sorry Lieutenant but he's gone home for the night and if you don't have an appointment I'm afraid you'll have to schedule one. Furthermore if you have any concerns I can transfer to you Homeland Security," Pam said. Aiden ended the call abruptly and steered the ship down through the atmosphere towards Washington D.C. - Zayn guiding him to the Secretary's house. They arrived at a beautiful Victorian home on the outskirts of the capitol. A rotating patrol of six secret service agents were keeping watch, every now and then speaking into a microphone clipped to the side of their collars.

Aiden guided the ship to the balcony attached to the master bedroom, taking care to not collide with the railing. Inside he could see the Secretary and his wife lying in bed sporting a matching set of bathrobes, one reading, and one watching television.

"What are you going to do?" Zayn asked, slightly puzzled.

"Umm, not sure yet, I'll improvise" Aiden answered. Zayn looked extremely uncomfortable with this idea but knew that time was against them.

Aiden opened the hatch on the ship and carefully inched along the invisible surface, then hopped over the rail and hid to the left of a set of balcony doors. He withdrew his weapon from its holster set it for stun and counted softly in his head,

"One....Two....THREE!" He whirled about and kicked the door with all his might. Several of the glass panes shattered and the Secretary's wife gave a loud scream as Aiden burst through and produced two well-placed stun bolts at both Secretary and his wife. Shouts from agents sounded all around,

"Code 3, Code 3, we have a break-in!"

The Secretary groaned and fell limply to one side as Aiden rushed over and caught him before he fell out of bed. He hurled him over his shoulder and carried him back toward the balcony rail, where Zayn helped him carry the stunned man inside the craft. The hatch closed just as the bedroom door burst into splinters and four agents scattered through the room, one of them rushing to the stunned woman. Aiden and Zayn plotted a course for California and glided soundlessly away.

"What are you doing!?" Zayn hissed.

"I didn't have a choice, You know those agents would have shot me on sight. I have a hunch that this man can order whoever's holding Vyleah prisoner to let her go," Aiden answered, trying to rouse the Secretary.

"Have you lost your mind!? These kinds of acts aren't easily forgiven!" Zayn continued.

"I don't care, they can't just snatch people like that. Not to mention, Vyleah is going to die if we don't get to her soon," Aiden said, praying this would work. The man groaned to life and Aiden drew his gun once more. The Secretary's eyes bulged as he became aware of the situation.

"What is this? Who are you people? What have you done to my wife?" he said quickly.

"I'm really sorry I had to do this but your office refused to forward my call. As you can see you're aboard my ship," Aiden said confidently. The Secretary was speechless; he looked around and realized they were indeed in a ship.

"Wh…what do you want?" he asked.

"You have a prisoner being held without cause at Camp Pendleton Marine Base in California. She's from another world and she will die in several hours unless you give her to us." Aiden explained.

"H…how do you know that?" uttered the Secretary.

"It's complicated, but you will do as I've requested or else." Aiden suggested coolly.

"Th…This is an act of terrorism…the United States… does not negotiate…" The Secretary breathed.

"And what do you call kidnapping a woman who hasn't done anything…?" Aiden replied, his gun still pointed steadily.

"It's not a woman, it's a thing. An alien creature that has trespassed on *our* world. Just like you two…" the man snarled. Aiden inched his gun a bit closer as his anger began to boil.

"As a matter of fact, I happen to be from Earth. And that *thing*….*is* a woman, and she's the woman I love. So you need to realize I don't care who I have to go through to get her back…" Aiden retorted, his hand now shaking. Zayn was descending the ship to the same clearing Aiden had envisioned in his prophecy. The hatch opened and Aiden followed the Secretary out, still keeping his gun traced. They walked toward the bunker entrance and the two guards drew their rifles in a ready position.

"What's going on here?" One of them shouted.

"You're going to let me inside or you both get to pick up what's left of the Secretary of Defense." Aiden said, staying tucked behind the Secretary. The guards looked at each other, then slowly lowered their rifles. "Thank you," said Aiden politely then shot both with stun bolts. The men fell before either knew what happened.

"You don't know how much trouble you're in for this, son." Said the Secretary as Aiden forced him inside.

"It's nothing compared to what I'll do if she's not alive when we get down there, now move…" Aiden retorted. They passed several more checkpoints, each one requiring the Secretary to submit to a retinal, fingerprint, and voice check to allow clearance. Aiden disposed of another six guards with stuns before they reached the bottom floor. He led the Secretary to the back cell where he found Vyleah, sitting in a corner. Though a bit pale it appeared Aiden had arrived before they had interrogated her. Aiden cranked up the power on his gun and melted the lock. She leapt to her feet in astonishment and wrapped her arms around him, giving him as many kisses as she could before he pried away from her grip. But in his excitement of seeing her, the Secretary had slipped away and was most certainly raising some sort of alarm or calling for back up. They would have to move quickly.

"Let's get you out of here," Aiden said leading her by the hand. He had to blast his way back through the doors since he could no longer get through. They reached the top level and Aiden's fears were confirmed. Several hundred feet away were two trucks full of soldiers roaring toward the bunker.

"Head for the clearing! Go! GO!" Aiden yelled and started firing back toward the trucks that were now unloading soldiers taking aim. Machine gun fire erupted and a wave of tracers flew past them. One bullet ripped itself through Aiden's right shoulder causing him to cry out in agonizing pain as he tumbled to the ground. Vyleah pulled him behind a large group of trees.

"I'm okay! Let's just get.....to.... the ship" Aiden said, his voice trailing as his eyes met one the most peculiar things since arriving at Teros – A circle of two hundred men and women stood shoulder to shoulder around the ship. Each were at least seven feet tall and clothed in black robes. They began to walk toward Aiden and Vyleah and continued past them toward the soldiers; one helped Aiden to his feet and he instantly felt the searing pain subside as his wound was healed. The man's hand felt like what Aiden imagined would have been a cloud wrapped in silk.

"Come on, they're here to help!" breathed Vyleah. Shrieks of horror sounded as soldiers were tossed through the air and bullets bounced off the mysterious guardians. Aiden did not stay long enough to see what happened; they hopped aboard the ship and lifted off. Vyleah hugged her brother in gratitude and gave several more kisses to Aiden as they floated north towards home.

"Not quite the way I would have recommended, but I thank you for your actions, Aiden," Zayn commented. "I think it's time you were reunited with your family." Zayn commented.

"Thanks," said Aiden still shaking with adrenaline, "I don't even know what I'm going to say."

"Just take it slow, and when the time comes you can show them what they need to see." Zayn counseled.

A minute later they silently landed at Vyleah and Zayn's home and cleaned themselves up as best they could.

"Aren't we risking getting caught again by coming back here?" Aiden asked, wiping blood off his hands.

"I don't think so..." Vyleah answered, as she finished drying her hair, "I was at the market when some local police grabbed me, I overheard one of them saying they got an anonymous tip from someone in the parking lot that I was shoplifting or something. Once they checked my file and saw they didn't have any information about me they took me to their station - where two gentlemen in suits were waiting with a few soldiers in camo-uniforms. They brought me to that base and were supposedly going to interrogate me, when my *hero* showed up and saved me."

"Qendrin....It had to be him, no one outside the Academy knew she was on Earth, This proves Zayn was right." Aiden thought. He decided to not bring Qendrin to Vyleah's attention yet. They walked outside and Aiden stood in front of his home – wondering what his family would think of all this.

He walked up his driveway and was met with the friendly barks of his mother's dog, calling from the upstairs window. He gave a wave and climbed the steps to his front door. He took a deep breath and rang the bell. The dog's barks grew more frantic and annoyed as the lock clicked open. The door swung open to reveal the shocked expression of Aiden's mother.

Mrs. Stuart's eyes exploded into tears as she embraced her son, the pain of several months' worry and joy of this moment were too much. Aiden's younger brother Tyler and his stepfather Tristan both joined the hug as they emerged from the downstairs common room. Vyleah and Zayn stood happily at the foot of the steps leading up to the door and admired the scene; Aiden beckoned them in.

"Guys, you know Zayn, and his sister... Vyleah...my *girlfriend*," said Aiden proudly.

"Yes, yes come in, you have to tell us where the heck you've been!" his mother exclaimed.

"Well, you should call the family over cause it's quite a story and I don't want to have to tell it over and over," Aiden requested.

An hour later, what started as a gathering to tell his tale, turned in to a full-blown "Welcome Home" party. Aiden's favorite pizza was delivered and all of his local relatives were invited. Everyone that arrived gave great hugs and strange looks as they saw his uniform and gun holster. Thirty-minutes into the party Aiden's long-time friend, Jeri Spencer, arrived looking shakily; though he had been told by

Aiden's family that he was alright, he too hadn't received much of an explanation of his whereabouts. The last relatives arrived and the twenty of them took their seats in the living room, awaiting what would surely be the most fantastic story they'd ever heard. Aiden cleared his throat,

"Thank you all for everything; this has been a truly incredible day not to mention an interesting last few months. I'll try to keep this brief 'cause truth be told I could talk for weeks."

"As many of you know it has been a passion of mine for these past years to explore the miraculous and mysterious things regarding not only Christianity, but the world around us in general - Tales of UFOs screaming past the Nevada desert, people's encounters with paranormal events, and the like. I tried my hardest to understand these things and I prayed for knowledge of how they affect us in everyday situations. The Bible says we should seek to learn spiritual gifts and bless the church doing the Lord's work, but like many of you I have always had a problem believing that such gifts were possible. Thus my story begins."

"I met Zayn in Yosemite after I had gone on a hike by myself; he told me that he'd been sent by God to answer the many questions I asked in my prayers. So we hiked for a while until we reached a lake at the top of a mountain. At the top of the lake Zayn revealed to me that he was not an Angel, but a foreigner from another world. A world called: Teros." Aiden let the commotion die down before continuing.

"Please, no questions yet. So Zayn gave me the option of leaving my old life behind to pursue a meaningful one doing what God meant for me and I accepted. An enormous spaceship came out of the lake and off we went. When we arrived I was inducted into the Terosian Science Academy: A military organization of sorts that was built to help recruit and train individuals from numerous worlds to rewire their belief system to allow for better access to the Holy Spirit. So it has been since then that I have progressed through their teachings and become, according to them, one of its "most promising students". Now I can see on almost all of your faces that most of you have no idea what I just said and don't believe one word of it." His family nodded in agreement.

"Is this some kind of joke, son?" Mr. Shepherd asked.

"No, dad, it's no joke. You've been patient and heard what I had to say and now we'll show you God's glory so you can see yourselves." Aiden replied. He stretched out his hand and, despite hearing a few giggles, closed his eyes and imagined the hundred or so marbles sitting within the vase on the living room table, rise up and float around the room.

Knowing that this would be more difficult to do with much less spiritual support than he was used to on Teros, Vyleah and Zayn stretched forth their hands as well and offered Aiden reinforcement for his demonstration. Gasps of terror replaced the giggles as the marbles floated up and dispersed, then took on the quality of being weightless as they floated around, bouncing off the walls and family members' heads. Then the marbles flew neatly back into the jar and Aiden waited for his family's response. They were frozen in their seats, unable to move or speak.

Vyleah and Zayn broke the ice with applause and cheers, which the rest of them slowly mimicked when they realized what had happened. It soon became a frenzy of questions. *"What do other aliens look like?" "Will Jesus return soon?" "Can you heal my arthritis?"* Vyleah and Zayn did their best to assist him, at one point Tyler shouted,

"Can we see your space ship?" Zayn gave a nod to Aiden.

"Okay but I have to show you two at a time, we can't have neighbors wondering why everyone's outside huddled around an invisible object." Aiden suggested. So each pair he took outside to Zayn's driveway. The invisible ship opened its hatch and allowed then to climb in, only after Aiden had made sure no one was watching.

"Wow! So can we fly it?" Tyler insisted.

"Haha, not so fast, little bro. Maybe someday but these aren't toys. Trust me, I've already crashed one...we'll actually got shot down. That's another story though."

After several more hours of questions most of his family returned home and Aiden retreated to his backyard to share a drink with Jeri, Vyleah, and Zayn. Tyler joined too since he was acting like a monkey on a sugar high.

"So.." said Aiden, "What a day..."

"Yeah..." agreed Zayn. Vyleah said nothing, she just held him closer and felt like she could live in this moment. Jeri had regained some color in his face and finally spoke,

"So....Aliens huh?"

The five of them broke into laughter and continued to talk as Aiden stared up every now and then, gazing at the stars.

Morning came and they all had a breakfast of pancakes with bacon and eggs. Aiden took a bite and nudged his younger brother,

"Mmmm, these are great, but I gotta get you guys an FPD." When Tyler looked confused Aiden explained how the Food Processing Device worked and how it was used.

"That is by far the coolest invention ever!" said Tyler, a parade of hundreds of foods flashing through his mind.

"This was wonderful Mrs. Stuart, but unfortunately we must be leaving soon," Zayn said looking at Vyleah and Aiden, "The council will want a report on all this."

Mrs. Stuart thanked him and Vyleah and broke into tears again as she kissed Aiden goodbye. He assured her that he would try to visit as often as the Academy would allow, but he still had much training to complete.

"See ya, little bro. Next time I come back I'll take you guys back to Teros for a visit, I promise." Aiden said and gave his brother a hug. His family followed them out and waved their final goodbyes as Aiden boarded the cloaked ship. It slowly rose up and became visible just before it warped away in a flash of gleaming light.

As the three of them left Earth behind Aiden was feeling a great range of emotions for what had happened in the past twenty-four hours; he felt guilty for acting rashly and potentially threatening relations between Teros and Earth, but he also felt great relief for saving Vyleah and finally being able to see his family after all these months. Unfortunately Aiden feared that his stay on Teros would be short-lived since Tchyntar had made it perfectly clear what fate awaited him if he should take action: expulsion from The Academy. The feelings of despair hollowed themselves into the pit of his stomach. He did not want to leave the place he had come to love in such a short time. This place had become his life, his mission. If he were removed from it he couldn't imagine the life he would live; an exiled warrior of God, taking up some dead-end job back on Earth?

Aiden finally decided to get himself prepared for their arrival and sat for a few minutes in silence. He meditated hard on clearing his negative emotions and as the ship soared through the atmosphere Aiden felt an odd sense of comfort.

As they landed in the hanger the first thing they noticed was that there was no reception to meet them this time.

"No guards?" Aiden asked.

"The council knows they don't need them, they know we'll come to them." Zayn explained in a chilling calmness. They took the lift up to the council chambers and for the third time Aiden entered and wondered why fate lie in store for him. Three seats sat before the crescent table and Tchyntar looked absolutely livid. As the three of them sat down he spoke coldly,

"Captain Vyleah, though we are glad for your safe return this meeting is to determine the actions to be taken for Lieutenant Commander Zayn and Cadet Shepherd. You are dismissed." Vyleah wanted desperately to stay by their side but she knew of all times, now was not a good one to challenge the council. She decided to return to her home to be reunited with her parents and sister. Tchyntar eyed Zayn, then Aiden; and spoke after he had gathered his thoughts,

"What am I going to do with you two?" he said almost sadly. "A mentor and his pupil who defy orders and put two worlds in jeopardy. I know what I should do....I should exile the both of you and be done with it; but fortunately for you both this council has more than just one voice and your sentences have been decided upon by all of us." Aiden shuffled uncomfortably at the sound of *"sentences"*. He felt like something horrible awaited them.

"Zayn we are demoting you to the rank of Captain, and you are on suspension until further notice." Tchyntar continued. "Cadet Shepherd...there is no doubt in our mind that you are a unique student. But being a part of this academy requires that its members be in compliance with the wishes of its leadership. You have defied those wishes on several occasions, which leads us to believe one of two things: First, that you are not ready to become a part of our organization and should return to Earth until you mature. Or second, that you believe your talents grant you the right to have special privileges over the rest of its members and your training should be modified to accommodate your unique gifts. What would you like to do, Cadet, we are letting you choose your sentence."

Aiden stared for a moment at the thirteen members of the council. He did not understand his options, either go back to Earth or stay here? The obvious choice blurted out before he could over-analyze it.

"I want to stay here," Aiden said. To his right Aiden could feel an uneasiness emanate from his mentor – which is something he had never felt within Zayn. This is the first time since he entered that he began to feel fear for what was to come.

"Very well, Cadet. Your sentence then, is to begin the traditional *Walk of Trials*."

"I PROTEST!" Zayn shouted, scaring Aiden and surprising the council. "My pupil is not ready for his *walk* and I must urge the council to deliberate further!" Aiden was confused, his whole time here he had never even heard of the *Walk of Trials*. No alumni ever mentioned it and he had never read about it in his handbook.

"Our judgement is final, Zayn." Tchyntar said calmly. "Surely you can agree that Cadet Shepherd has accomplished more than any other cadet in this amount of time. If *The Creator* continues to give him such distinction we feel he is more than ready for this task."

"If you ask this of him then you most certainly condemn him to death!" Zayn continued, still angry but regaining some composure. "Exile me and let him continue his instruction with another so he will be ready."

"It is between Aiden and God now, you will accept this council's decision and you *will* do are you're told. The ceremony to see the Cadet off will begin tomorrow at midnight." Zayn opened his mouth again to voice his objections again but Aiden put a hand on his shoulder and Zayn knew there was nothing more he could do. As the council departed Aiden finally asked the question that now consumed him,

"Zayn, what is the *Walk of Trials?*" Zayn was deep in thought and hesitated for a moment before answering.

"The *Walk of Trials* is the final test one must pass before they may graduate from The Academy."

"Really!" Aiden said excitedly, his concerns now fading. "I don't get it, isn't this a good thing?"

"No, Aiden, This is far worse a punishment than anything else they could have ordered." Zayn replied coldly. "This test is unlike any you have ever experienced, but I do not wish to worry you right now. The ceremony begins tomorrow night and you will need all the rest you can muster this evening." Aiden retreated to his room, still pondering relentlessly about what this *Walk of Trials* would consist of. As he exited the lift in front of his room a snoring

Kyon lay before his door. Kyon was unshaven, disheveled, and in desperate need of a shower. Aiden knelt down beside him and shook him awake.

"Mmmm," groaned Kyon and slowly sat up. "Where you been? I've been here for hours." Aiden helped him to his feet and welcomed him into his room.

"Have a seat," said Aiden. He rubbed his eyes and sighed heavily. "Where do I begin...?" Over the next hour Aiden recounted his rescue and sentence from the council. Kyon sat in silence for most of the tale, asking questions here and there. But Aiden sensed something weighing heavy on his mind and as he wrapped up his story he felt he could no long avoid asking about it.

"So, Kyon, how are you?"

"I'm doing better." He answered, looking down at his feet. " I've just been working a lot of stuff out, you know, between me and God."

"Uh huh," Aiden responded. "And how's that going?"

"I don't know," shrugged Kyon. "I've practically spent the last month saying the most obnoxious things I could think of to Him and a few days ago I finally realized it wasn't

His fault. It was my own people that killed each other. But anyway long story short I have a favor to ask." Aiden had just prepared two cups of coffee in the FPD and walked back over to hand one to Kyon.

"Just name it," said Aiden with a sip from his mug.

"Can you...help me ask God to enter my heart, or whatever it is that people do." Kyon said softly. Aiden was speechless. He never had someone ask for him to help them receive the Lord.

"Of course I will!" he answered when the shock wore off. Aiden put his mug on the desk and place a hand on Kyon's shoulder. "Close your eyes, and be sincere while we pray." Kyon did as he was told and bowed his head. Aiden did the same and began the prayer, letting The Keeper provide the right words,

"Lord we come before You tonight to ask You to welcome another to our ranks. Fill Kyon with Your Spirit and grace. Bring him peace over the great loss he has experienced, and forgive him for the wrong he has done. Let him be reunited with the Holy Spirit and watch over him as I enter into this *Trial*, because I won't be around to keep him from getting into trouble. In Your names we

pray—Amen." Aiden opened his eyes to see his friend with tears running down his face. Kyon rose from the chair and embraced Aiden for the first time as his brother in God.

Chapter 20 - The Walk of Trials

Aiden awoke around midday, and though he still felt unsure about his upcoming task, he was absolutely beaming with joy from his experience with Kyon the night before. He received a text from Zayn, inviting him and Kyon to lunch at his house. He showered, dressed, and met Kyon in the VHF twenty minutes later. Kyon looked like a different person – not just because he had washed and shaved – he now stood much taller than before and he had decided to remove his visor, despite still squinting violently at the bright light from Teros's sun. Aiden weaved in and out of buildings with the shuttle and tried to ignore Kyon's complaints about either flying too reckless or the sun being too bright.

"Kyon if it still bothers you why did you take the visor off?" Aiden asked for the third time.

"I'm sick of wearing that damn thing!" he shot back. "If I'm ever gonna learn to use *Spiritual Sight* I should at least learn to use my eyes first." Aiden could only smile. They arrived and took the lift to Zayn's home. Vyleah greeted them warmly and held Aiden for a long time before Zayn finally urged them to sit.

"Alright," Zayn said heavily. "So Aiden, we are not allowed to speak to you about what is directly involved in the *Walk of Trials*. It is Terosian tradition for each Cadet to be sent on this *walk* when the mentor feels their pupil is ready to join The Academy as a full member. The idea is that you will have to use every ounce of knowledge you have to successfully complete this. You will have to hear *The Keeper* more clearly than ever before because He will be the only thing guiding you as you venture out on your own."

"Okay," Aiden nodded. "So, how long does this *trial* take?"

"That is between you and *The Keeper*." Vyleah answered. "*He* will inform you when it is time to return. It could be a day, it could be a year."

"A *Year!*" Aiden repeated frantically. "What the hell am I doing exactly?!?"

"We cannot say," Zayn said calmly. "But remember your training, Aiden. God will never put any obstacle in your path that you can't take on with His help."

Zayn and Vyleah spent the next ten hours reviewing everything Aiden had learned at The Academy since he would not be allowed to bring Sophie with him. He would only be given enough water to last him four days, and a Terosian blade twenty-two inches in length. As midnight approached Vyleah pulled him aside to the balcony to wish him farewell alone. They kissed, then embraced and stood looking out over the city.

"Here I just get you back and I already have to let you go again." Aiden said with a sniff.

"Yeah," Vyleah agreed and wiped a tear from her face. "Just make sure you come back to me, okay?"

"Okay," he agreed.

"Promise me," she asked, looking up into his eyes.

"I promise," he replied and met her gaze.

The time had come for Aiden and Kyon to return to The Academy. As they parked their shuttle they could see twelve of the thirteen council members waiting for them in the hanger - All but Tchyntar were present. Kyon was told to return to his quarters and Aiden was led to chamber deep within the lower levels of The Academy. Here a circle of thirteen fire pits sat behind thirteen stone slabs. Surrounding the circle of fire were twelve very old pillars and a thirteenth fallen pillar — each one coated in Terosian writing and symbols.

"Kneel here," said one of the council, pointing toward the center of the circle. Aiden did so and the twelve members exited through a door on the opposite side of the room. Aiden waited for several minutes before Tchyntar led the twelve other council members from the room. Each wore a set of white robes and a traditional Terosian sword in the hilts on their waists. They assembled into a single file line and the first councilmen approached Aiden.

"Bow your head," he ordered. Aiden did so, still kneeling uncomfortably in the center of the circle. The councilman drew his sword and rested it on Aiden's right shoulder. He then began to pray in hushed words that Aiden was unable to hear clearly. When he finished he lifted the sword and took his place atop one of the stone slabs. One by one they approached Aiden, drew their swords, and said a prayer before standing upon one of the stone slabs resting before the fires. At last Tchyntar approached and said his prayer, then took a step back and occupied the last space in the circle. Aiden finally opened his eyes and one of the swords was lying before him on the ground.

"Cadet Shepherd," Tchyntar said forcefully. "Arise and place your blade at your waist." Aiden stood up and attached the hilt to his belt. "You are to remain here until called for. You may rest for the next few hours." Aiden stood puzzled as the council departed once more through the doors. He walked over to the fallen pillar and sat down, wondering what bizarre ceremony would come next.

Hours later a CASE robot emerged from the doors carrying a backpack full of water, similar to a "camel-pak" on Earth. Aiden was told to put it on and follow the CASE through a set of very old looking doors on the left side of the room. Aiden was struck with an amazing sight. A grand spiral walkway curved its way up to a speck of light hundreds of feet above.

"Climb," said the CASE, and then it disappeared back through the worn doors. Aiden shifted the sword and pack a bit and began to ascend up the passage.

He climbed for the better part of a half-hour, stopping every so often to look up and check his progress. The sweat dripped gently on the old stone steps and Aiden coughed a few times to clear his throat.

"This isn't so bad..." he thought as he neared the final set of spirals. He reached the top at last and a roar like ten thousand lions exploded all around him. It took Aiden a moment to realize he was standing on the platform at the bottom of the coliseum – the same one that had been used in the welcoming ceremony several months before. Standing in a circle around him were the councilmen, and seated in the audience were the thousands of cadets and alumni of The Academy.

Tchyntar motioned, and the crowd grew silent. "Cadet Shepherd now faces the most challenging test a hopeful cadet will be given. The *Walk of Trials!*" He said loudly and another roar of praise sounded from the crowd. Once they had quieted he turned and addressed Aiden in a whisper. "You are to enter through that door when you are ready." He said and pointed to a door Aiden had never noticed before. It was another very worn door that bore the symbol of The Academy upon it in ornate patterns. Aiden gave a nod and looked back up at the crowd, hoping to spot Vyleah, Zayn, and Kyon - But he couldn't find them. Aiden readjusted his pack and sword and began walking towards the door. Applause and cheers broke out once more and as Aiden passed through the doors the noise drowned out immediately and he found himself in a passageway lit by torches.

Aiden took a deep breath and began to walk. The first hour was spent walking through very narrow passages and did not stray very much from a straight line. He did not know how long the torch lit caves would last but several hours later he assumed he was approaching the end of them when he emerged into a grand cavern filled with the sound of running water. A very old bridge spanned across the water and led to even more tunnels. Soon after this Aiden began to lose track of how long he'd been walking.

After a solid eight hours he emerged at another water filled cavern that was slightly more illuminated. He sat atop a nearby rock and removed his sword and backpack. Exhausted and not knowing how long it would be until he saw daylight, he leaned back against the wall and quickly drifted off to sleep.

As he awoke the next day he continued on through the increasingly twisting tunnels. But up ahead he noticed the first potential problem; the tunnel came to a fork and split into two directions. Aiden gave a sigh and sat for a few minutes, examining the options that lay before him. Both directions looked identical and deciding he wouldn't waste anymore time, he walked towards the path on the right and felt confident that he was heading the correct way.

"I hope I'm going the right way..." Aiden thought, as he once again fell asleep for the second day.

He awoke on the third day and continued on towards his unknown destination. He knew he must have traveled at least ten miles, which meant that he would have passed underneath the nearby mountain range just beyond the edge of the *Stone Forest*.

A sudden strong gust of wind blew through the passage and Aiden's senses sharpen; his adrenaline kicked in and he felt he was close to the end of his underground adventure. He walked for another twenty minutes and finally saw the first natural light near the end of the tunnel. He jogged towards it and as he emerged in the dawn of another day he was met with the grand sight of a mountainous valley stretching out before him. The peaks were covered in fresh snow and a river of clear icy water ran by. His eyes squinted in the morning sunlight and crisp cool air filled his lungs.

Aiden climbed down from the rocky tunnel exit to the shores of the river. He took his backpack off and pushed it beneath the icy water. The water was extremely cold but felt refreshing on his dry skin. He washed his hands and scraped the dirt from beneath his fingernails. He took his boots off to rest his feet, and washed them as well. Then he splashed his face and ran his fingers through his hair to spruce it up.

Aiden rested for about twenty minutes then decided he'd better get a move on. He didn't know where to go but remembered that staying near a source of fresh water was always a good idea. He put his boots back on and looked down the valley into the distance.

"Alright," He said confidently. "Here we go."

Afterword

"Thank you for reading Book One of the Aiden Shepherd Series! As I continue to write these stories I hope there are those out there who are as excited to read about what adventures Aiden still has as I am about writing them. For news and information about the progress of Book 2: *Aiden Shepherd and the Halls of Prophecy,* please feel free to follow me online at **dillonhammon.com** and my blog **dillonhammon.tumblr.com**. May God Bless You!"

-Dillon J. Hammon